THE RANCH: DELAWARE

VOLUME ONE

Ben Tzu

The Ranch: Delaware (Volume One)
Ben Tzu

Published by Synergy Publishing Group, Belmont, NC
Cover illustration by Mikel Gann

Hardcover, November 2025, ISBN 978-1-960892-56-0
Softcover, November 2025, ISBN 978-1-960892-55-3
E-book, November 2025, ISBN 978-1-960892-57-7

For Mom and Dad
Who always said I could

PREFACE

Dear Reader,

This book is for YOU, for the pleasure of *your* reading experience. So, if you don't get a reference, don't know what something looks like, what it is or what it does, please just Google it! Get the most out of the experience that you can. It will be much more fun to read, and the story line will make much more sense. Stay curious about your world.

And besides, it really is true:

Charlie don't surf.

The world is different now than it once was. Frequently, the world changes slowly over time as each new generation, and its relative values, assume the mantle of power and lead the country and its population into the future. But there is another way the world can change:

Quickly and violently.

For example, the world was different before and after the advent and development of the Internet over thirty years versus the events of 9/11. My generation, *Generation X*, has survived both types (to date), and this author would like to share with you, reader, a few observations that may assist in understanding and comprehending the themes and message of this series better.

Government is necessary, but it is inherently flawed as it consists of imperfect humans. For now, anyway.

We will see where this "AI" thing takes us...

My generation began at the end of America's most unpopular war, the Vietnam War. Many lessons were *not* learned from it, including the all but certain victory of our "enemy" virtually from the proverbial door. The Vietnamese had been dominated for a thousand years by the Chinese, then colonized by the French during the Age of Imperialism. By the time poor, unwitting US came along seeking to subdue communism in Southeast Asia, all the Vietnamese people wanted was to be left the hell alone and govern themselves for a change. Despite superior technology, equipment, fuel, and manpower, the US lost that war.

Why?

Because one man defending his home in pursuit of freedom will prevail over ten conscripted and conflicted soldiers fighting for a specific form of government.

In a place they don't even live.

Generation X had the dubious honor of being born into a world where the "back to back World Champions" of the First and Second World Wars had subsequently stumbled in Korea and outright failed in Vietnam.

To be clear, the *government*, and its poor decisions, were to blame.

Not the troops.

Read that again, please.

No really.

We will all wait.

An iconic scene of a movie demonstrating this principle was the US helicopter attack on a Vietnamese village scene of *Apocalypse Now*. You can YouTube a short in five minutes.

Now that you've done that (hint, hint), the opening events of volume one of *The Ranch: Delaware*, the world in which it is set, and the characters will make much more sense.

Sort of.

—Ben Tzu

RANCH HISTORICAL FIGURES

(In Order of Appearance)

Ben McKnight: Former owner of the Ranch, its beef company & Bighouse

Dexter Horn: Ben's best friend & former ranch manager of beef company

Mike Fuse: QRT Actual, Ben's close friend from the Before

Tanner Miller: Butcher & Agriculture Actual, Ben's farmhouse neighbor, married to Ben's second cousin

Sage Horn: Stable Actual, Livestock Asset Manager, Dexter's daughter, former Livestock Coordinator for beef company

Teeter: Palomino mare quarter horse, 15 hands (5'0")

Buckshot: Bay gelding quarter horse, 14 hands (4'8")

Reno: Paint gelding quarter horse, 15.3 hands (5'1")

Jackson Weeks: Ben's neighbor, married to Ben's second cousin Bree

Bliss Weaver: Ward Actual, R.N., Dexter's longtime girlfriend

Rachele Day: R.N., Ben's partner

Major Richard Johnson: Acting Commander of 436th Airlift Wing, Dover Air Force Base

First Lieutenant Christopher Median: Major Johnson's adjutant

Staff Sergeant Marcus Carter: Combat operator assigned to protect Major Johnson

Moonshine: Palomino stallion quarter horse, 14.2 hands (4'10")

Saul McKnight: Construction & Maintenance Actual, Ben's first cousin, Sherrie's husband, Bree's father & Jackson's father-in-law

Sherrie McKnight: Kitchen Actual, Saul's wife, Bree's mother & Jackson's mother-in law

Brutus: Percheron draft horse, 18.1 hands (6'1")

Dr. Bree McKnight: Saul & Sherrie's daughter, Jackson's wife, Westin's mother & Clinical psychologist

Akim Bennett: Ben's close friend from the Before, world class Butcher & Former Agricultural Management Specialist

Gladius: Percheron draft horse, 19 hands (6'4")

Luna: Percheron draft horse, 17.2 hands (5'10")

Jack Simmons: QRT Operator, Ex-Navy SEAL, Nguyen's boyfriend

Kim Nguyen: Pandemic survivor, former Army, Simmons's girlfriend

Neighbor Mike: Greenhouse Actual, former beef company neighbor

Danny Powers: Brig Actual, former Army Military Police, Ben's first cousin

Rita & Annie: Football tribe friends from the Before

Carol Butler: Lifeskills Actual, Ben's father's first cousin, married to Monty

Monty Butler: Carol's husband, Lifeskills Crew

Brett & Steph: Former beef company neighbors, Lifeskills Crew

John Eddington: Fossil Fuel & Solar Power Plant Engineer

Rob Waites: Eddington's son-in-law, Power Plant Maintenance Supervisor

Harper Quigley: Ranch nurse trainee, abuse victim

Neil & Ryan: Abuse victims brought to ranch with Harper

Randy Eastridge: Guitar Hero extraordinaire, Saul's brother-in-law, Ben's cousin by marriage

Harry Nussick: Chicken farmer located a mile beyond the Ranch's SouthGate Checkpoint

RANCH HISTORY 101

CHAPTER 1

"Count Six"

I count six," Ben said.

"That's my count, too," Dex responded, as they stood in the dark staring together at the surveillance camera display in the former master bedroom of the Ranch's Bighouse. Like the rest of the modest ranch style home, it had been converted for maximum occupancy with several cots in addition to the master bed. It also served as the command center for the video camera feeds that were still operational.

The feed came in real time from a solar-powered infrared camera a hundred yards west of the checkpoint known as The "NorthGate" ranch entrance and nearly half a mile to the north from where they stood.

The camera operator was safely snuggled in an old deer stand, camouflaged nearly twenty feet in the air. The high-tech camera had no problem "seeing" its targets in the dark, quarter moon night through the late November leafless trees.

Once, the entire world had enjoyed access to such technology.

But now, the entire world was dead.

Or at least, so it felt to those who had taken refuge and were now living at the Ranch.

The image was a bit pixilated when zoomed in at a distance of nearly sixty yards from the targets, but six figures clearly advanced slowly and cautiously in attempt to flank the Ranch's NorthGate, its first line of defense on Grears Corner Road ("GCR") where the railroad tracks bisected it.

The first and most active checkpoint to date was established in the earliest days of the pandemic, just past where the road crossed a small creek via a bridge. It then made a slight right turn traveling towards the checkpoint before approaching the railroad tracks. Thick woods on either side then gave way to the open grain fields of the Ranch's interior at nearly the same point as the railroad tracks came through perpendicular to the road.

When the Second Pandemic began, the Ranch's original occupants and some friends had dropped large trees across the road to prevent access by the public and thus quarantine themselves from the virus that was quickly killing the entire world.

Those trees had been intentionally laid in a staggered formation to force a vehicle to slow and then carefully negotiate a path through the log maze. The trees were still there, but these days it may as well have been completely sealed off.

No one left the Ranch anymore.

There wasn't anything out there but pain and death.

No law; no order.

Only chaos.

Even the occasional supply runs for non-perishables like clothing and plumbing parts now originated from the south end of the road that ran through the middle of the Ranch. It was, oddly enough, known as "SouthGate." But even those infrequent supply runs were few and far between due to the risk. When they did go, it was in large numbers of heavily armed ranchers in several vehicles and expending precious fuel.

"Standby, QRT," Ben whispered into the radio.

The camera operator simply keyed his mic in response without uttering a word. His earpiece safely allowed him to receive communications without giving away his position.

But speaking would be a different matter.

Ben looked at Dex. They shared a grim acknowledgment: The Ranch was in danger and lives were going to be sacrificed tonight. Without hesitation, Dex dutifully switched channels and raised his radio to his face.

"QRT cleared to engage," he said with conviction.

The decision from the Bighouse had been made.

He waited a beat for an acknowledgment of the order. When none came, he glanced at Ben, who nodded solemnly.

"Do you copy, Mike? You are cleared to engage."

"QRT copies," came the whispered response, although somewhat apprehensively.

A few seconds passed. Then, "You sure?"

"Do it."

CHAPTER 2

"A More Perfect Headshot"

They came out of the darkness like wraiths. Four of the Ranch's best QRT operators, led by Mike, exited their camouflaged foxholes less than ten yards from where their unwitting targets stood. The QRT foxhole placement had been determined from careful analysis concluding this access route was the most likely area for an invading force to exploit. The low-lying creek to the east of the checkpoint would bog down in its muck and trap anyone attempting to sneak past, while the area to the west offered thicker trees and brush for cover as well as higher, denser, dryer ground to traverse. The terrain there had also been intentionally cleared of most leaves, twigs and branches giving the illusion of a game trail, permitting a potentially more silent route for an invader.

In short, it was purposefully created for ambush.

The intruders had first been spotted two nights before by The NorthGate guards doing the 11 p.m. to 7 a.m. shift. Their single infrared "night vision" scope had detected movement that did not register as a deer or other animal.

At least, not unless deer had started carrying assault rifles.

But in this world now... who knew?

The shift change occurred in the early morning light. Over the hour that both shifts slowly exchanged personnel, there was not a single indication any of them had been alerted to intruders' presence. The guards had played it cool overnight. They monitored the intruders' position in the woods a few hundred yards away but continued to play cards by the minimal moonlight and go about their normal routines as they quietly alerted Ben and Dex at the Bighouse. The incoming guard shifts were individually and quietly briefed with a map and written reports of all that had transpired: movements, approximate numbers, and armament. Outwardly, the shift change had consisted only of casual laughter and fake gesturing in the opposite direction from where the intruders had been observed.

Nothing to see here.

The suppressors on the QRT operators' AR15s still pierced the otherwise soundless night as all six intruders dropped in less than a heartbeat. Only properly trained operatives stood a chance at knowing the difference between targets that had gone down due to taking a round and those similarly well-disciplined to drop instantly at the first unexpected sound.

Mike's initial count was four hit, two questionable. But he knew his guys, and he knew their training. He had done most of QRT's training specific to the Ranch himself, and his handpicked guys came from all branches of the US military with a boatload of prior combat experience. As far as he and the rest of QRT were concerned, those targets, hit or not, were still active threats until they turned blue and rigor set in.

And maybe even then.

Never let your guard down.

And certainly not now that there were no emergency services, no hospitals, no police, no 911; no safety or security save what the Ranch provided for itself.

As the QRT operators fanned out and slowly approached the fallen targets, sight pictures professionally swept back and forth, a head suddenly popped up and a rifle quickly followed. Before any of them could react, the boom from the tree line temporarily deafened anyone within a hundred yards.

Mike silently cursed then keyed his microphone.

"Dammit, Tanner, I did not give you that Barrett .50 to deafen the entire Quick Response Team."

"Target down," a neutral, unabashed tone came back in response.

But Tanner was smiling as he said it. He had been sending the video feed to the Bighouse from his perch in the old deer stand overlooking both The NorthGate checkpoint and the ancillary faux game trail and ambush point. His wife and young daughter were only a mere three hundred yards southwest in the family farmhouse, so he considered this intrusion to be a personal threat to his immediate family in addition to his extended family at the Ranch.

Tanner had hunted deer in these woods for decades before even the first pandemic. If so much as a branch had moved or a twig snapped on any given tree over the entire nearly three hundred acres, his mind would automatically register the change. In addition to deer, Tanner also hunted all things winged—geese, duck, quail, and others. Leading a target and anticipating its erratic and unexpected movements were as natural to a redneck hunter as a nipple to a newborn, so he was a perfect fit for The NorthGate checkpoint sniper position.

But his smile was not at taking a human life. Like most combat veterans, that fact barely registered.

At least during waking hours.

Traditionally, when hunting waterfowl or other winged game, one aspired to spare the consumable flesh of shotgun pellets lest one break a tooth during the evening meal.

He was smiling now because never in all those years of hunting could he remember a more perfect headshot than this one.

That motherfucker was definitely never getting up again.

CHAPTER 3

"Resting Bitchface"

Ben and Dex exited the Bighouse through the rear door as the general alarm bell began to ring incessantly at the sound of the powerful Barrett firing. "Bighouse" was a bit of a misnomer as it wasn't a particularly large dwelling; in fact, several of the homes encompassed by the oasis from death all around, known as "The Ranch," were considerably larger in both square footage and number of levels. The Bighouse was so named as it was where the Ranch senior staff most frequently met.

As they descended the back stairs to ground level, Sage rode up on her mare, "Teeter," with two additional mounts tacked and ready in a technique known as "ponying."

Since gasoline, diesel and every other consumable of any value had been extremely scarce since That Day, they now relied primarily on horses for their day-to-day transportation around the Ranch and a host of other tasks. The guys had given her a heads-up to tack their horses in the stable located just behind the Bighouse at dusk and remain on standby ever since the intruders were first spotted.

The Ranch's four QRTs responsible for their cardinal direction sectors of security had also been alerted. The other three QRTs were actively scanning for threats to the south, east and west while closely monitoring ranch radio traffic.

At the sound of the general alert, and the gunfire, the entire camp awoke as if its collective hair was on fire. The population of one hundred and fifteen souls reported to their respective stations as if in the world's most well-choreographed, and deadliest, ballet.

"How many?" Sage asked, voice quivering slightly but hand reflexively touching her pink sidearm.

"Six," Dex responded to his daughter, taking a set of reins from her.

"Zero," Ben quipped, sliding onto Buckshot. "North QRT handled it."

"Let's hope," Dex said, mounting Reno.

Sage just stared at them.

"Ummm," she said disapprovingly. "Really?"

Nobody did resting bitchface better than Sage.

Dex sighed, anticipating an argument that they did not have time for, while Ben smiled in amusement.

"We're not both going up there. Your dad will go to the checkpoint for a visual sitrep. I'm going to Armory up at the Farmhouse and then run checkpoints in case that intrusion was just the tip of the iceberg. There could be a larger coordinated attack, so you're staying here in safety at the Bighouse."

She just stared at them. "Do I need to remind you that I can outride you both?"

"You are *not* going up there," they responded in unison.

"I meant Armory and checkpoints," she said quickly. "I can make sure everyone is where they need to be faster, and you'll get reports faster too." She gestured at her radio.

"You're barely twenty-three," her father, Dex, said sternly.

"Yeah, but she's going to make some poor son of a bitch a great wife one day; he will never have to wonder what he should be doing," Ben chuckled, then said, "Yeah okay, look that's a better plan anyway, Dex." To Sage he said, "Dad and I can't both go up there to see Mike in case there's a second assault, but you and he can go to the Farmhouse, to The Armory to distribute weapons and then you can run the interior defensive perimeter checks faster. Go clockwise to east outposts ("OP") first and then all the way around to north OPs, and radio sitreps back. Then meet us here. Meanwhile, I'll go look at Mike's work and assess if we're still looking at an active threat to the north."

Ben looked over at Dex. "She'll be fine, man, and if it does get hinky, it'll happen in the next few minutes, and she'll still be right next to you *at* The Armory. No safer place on the whole ranch," Ben spun his horse around towards the road leading to the intrusion. "Literally everyone is headed there right now anyway."

Dex thought for a moment and nodded at the logic.

As if on cue, a huge black pickup truck from the home next to the Bighouse roared past with nearly fifteen men crammed into the crew cab and truck bed bristling with rifles.

In emergencies, precious fuel reserves were expended as needed.

"See? Jackson's boys are getting ahead of us already!" Ben pointed out. "You know we can't have that; we'll never hear the end of it."

"Yeah, okay. But watch your back, bro," Dex said as they rode off in their respective directions.

Ben rode up GCR after the truck to the railroad track checkpoint while Dex and his daughter cantered across a field recently harvested of its soybean crop towards the Farmhouse. Ben cantered to the top of the small rise then slowed to a trot and watched the black Chevy 2500 turn an alarmingly hard left onto the Farmhouse driveway, fishtail and straighten, then roar toward the armory, its truck bed occupants holding on for dear life.

Really love that kid, but he seriously needs to slow down, Ben thought as he cued Buckshot back to a canter towards Mike's position at NorthGate.

Jackson was a "cousin-in-law" to Ben, having married into the family before moving next door to the Bighouse with his wife and now their toddler son nearly a decade before That Day. Ben's other cousin's family lived at the Farmhouse towards which Dex and Sage were currently traveling. Tanner lived there with his wife and daughter. Tanner was also technically a "cousin-in-law" too, if there were such a thing in the world.

But there wasn't such a thing at the Ranch.

No forced titles or society-mandated relationships existed there. There never had been, even before the world went to shit.

At the Ranch, whether by blood or by choice, there were only those who were family.

And those who were not.

CHAPTER 4

· 2018–2026 ·

"The Before"

The world had not always been like this, of course. Once, it had been much safer and much, much easier. That time period was commonly referred to at the Ranch as "the Before."

Before the pandemic, Ben, an attorney, and his friend and former client Dex, a millwright and gunsmith, spent their days exchanging dirty memes on the internet and playing cowboy at "The Ranch."

Unmarried with no children, the aging of Ben's parents, and indeed himself, had motivated him to consider what was next when he retired from the practice of law. He decided to embrace his ten-year-old self's fantasy and be...

A cowboy?

His legal career had not been the particularly grueling one a person typically imagines. Sure, there were occasions of hundred-hour work weeks and little sleep, but mostly the practice consisted of criminal defense on relatively minor charges and state funded civil commitments. Ben used to say he represented "good people that had a bad day."

Civil commitments were court proceedings for those with mental illnesses who did not wish to be medicated. After a hearing, the court would typically inform his client that they were required to be medicated under penalty of law, even sanctioning incarceration and forced injections. Ben represented the mentally ill and was compensated by the state.

He was, however, not a state employee but rather merely a vendor. Bureaucracy was the antithesis of efficiency and having been raised as a third-generation grain farmer, Ben had about as much patience for mindless chatter and bureaucratic inefficiency as he had for a grain drill that wouldn't plant seed. In his opinion, to function properly both merely required a "redneck tune up" with a four-pound ball peen hammer.

The criminal defense practice was, of course, funded privately by the client. It had been a somewhat short career at only seventeen years prior to the Second Pandemic, but satisfying and lucrative enough to fund Ben's new passions: steak, horses, and whiskey. He began building a cattle company from scratch, first raising a barn then converting the five hundred square foot chicken coop into a home for his first cow, a Dexter he named "Beth."

Dexters were a small breed of dual-purpose cow originally from the same area of Ireland as Ben's family and were about half the size of a typical cow. They ate half of what a larger bovine consumed but still provided two-thirds of the beef. The lesser amount of pasture required to sustain them, the Irish connection and dual-purpose nature, as they can be milked *and* provided scrumptious beef, proved they were the perfect choice for his ranch.

But the real selling points were the *quality* of the beef and milk, extremely rare calving problems, heartiness, and gentle temperament.

Ben's other job growing up, and even well into middle age, was farming. Together he and his father had tilled four hundred acres a few miles from the Ranch until the first pandemic in 2019, called "Covid," had taken his ninety-year-old father. Both the ranch farm and Ben's father's farm were approximately the same size and engaged in grain production: field corn, soybean, and wheat—the cash crops for this area.

When the Second Pandemic had come in early spring 2027, farming had proven to be a most fortunate situation in which to be born. Although if he were telling the truth: teenage Ben never could understand growing up why they had to do *all* that work. Growing grain and endless, *endless* vegetable gardens. Planting, weeding, harvesting, canning… it *never* ended! *Good Lord people, just go to the grocery store like normal folks,* Teenage Ben had thought.

Teenage Ben had sworn when he grew up, he would never, ever by choice be engaged in an occupation like farming that required *so* much back-breaking work. This was a fact that had amused him in his early fifties just after the First Pandemic while using Dad's big Massey 2675 tractor to till another eight acres for pasture grass to feed his ever-growing array of livestock. The Ranch already had a sizable cattle herd by then and had taken the leap into horses.

By this point, Ben and Dex had long ago become good friends and the former proved himself worth his weight in gold. Or maybe even platinum. A genius at all things electric, mechanical, and constructive coupled with a servant's heart, and a work ethic Ben frequently wished he could turn off somewhere around four a.m. so he himself could get some damn sleep.

The two worked tirelessly after their full-time jobs building a beef company. The fact that Dex had been a former firearms instructor and gunsmith didn't hurt the Ranch's reliance on him either.

Ben had the vision, financial resources, land, and equipment, as well as experience with the agricultural side. While Dex brought the practical, detailed construction and trades knowledge, experience with farm animals, and machining skills. He frequently had fabricated things from scratch the company needed to ensure its success, or sometimes just for their convenience. Ben often joked that Dex could launch a satellite into orbit with only a safety pin and a gum wrapper.

Dex corrected him: he would also require a thumb tack.

With Dex came his daughter Sage, and his girlfriend Bliss, to the Ranch. Sage, a natural animal whisperer, had a passion for horses and had grown up showing cattle at the state fair. Just prior to the Second Pandemic, she was training all the Ranch's horses and assisting with general ranch chore and cattle care, such as palpating pregnant heifers and doctoring injuries between her college classes on her way to veterinary school.

Bliss was a Registered Nurse working at a local hospital, an occupation the Ranch would eventually need in great supply. Other R.N.s included several of Ben's female cousins and Rachele. Ben and Rachele had only been seeing one another for less than a year when Covid-27 hit. She had already essentially been living at the Ranch anyway, but when news of a new pandemic hit the airwaves, Ben had driven her the half hour south to Dover to pillage her home of all necessaries before abandoning it to its fate. Bliss and Rachele were about as different as two women could be but managed to remain civil to one another for the sake of the men they loved.

Despite that, some family political differences and, *much* more vocally contentiously, their football rivalries, their tribe integrated well especially during holiday and football parties before and after the First Pandemic in 2020. By 2025, the world believed it had "recovered" from the pandemic, but the country was more divided than ever politically, with many believing Covid had been blown out of proportion, used to mentally subjugate the population, and was merely a "test run" intentionally released by enemies of America.

Others believed everything the government fed them and blamed the prior US President for his poor and ineffective handling of the naturally occurring pandemic that had taken so many lives. In early 2025, the generally accepted mortality rate for Covid had been 3 percent worldwide. In the United States, it had been a mere 2 percent. Two percent of those who contracted the virus had died. But by that summer this estimate was inexplicably and suddenly upgraded, claiming a whopping 15 percent mortality rate overall.

Wonder what that was about?

Well, it was definitely *not* because the governments of the entire world had overreacted and bowed down to a virus that caused death in only *3 percent* of those who contracted it.

That fact would make them look incompetent.

Because by that logic, the government should ban emo music, late night talk shows and... forks.

By contrast, bubonic plague of the Middle Ages had an estimated 30 percent mortality rate, one in three had died. By the time the Second Pandemic began, with its laboratory enhanced 75–80 percent mortality rate, the Ranch, under the guise of a startup cattle company, had already created or built almost everything they would need to survive the plague and wait it out for recovery.

Almost.

CHAPTER 5

"The Collapse"

The cattle ranch was oriented northwest to southeast across approximately 220 acres.

Of that land, all but forty-four acres of woods were open, tillable fields. Grears Corner Road transected the Ranch along the same northwest to southeast route but a railroad easement, via eminent domain, had been constructed perpendicular to GCR running northeast to southwest connecting the nearby Townsend granary for farmers to transport their harvest.

On the opposite side of GCR from the Ranch was another spacious farm owned by a family named Kintis. Before the Second Pandemic, it was rented to a local farmer to till. After the Collapse, the Ranch folks never saw that farmer or the family again and assumed he had succumbed to the pandemic virus and the Kintis matriarch had taken her household to another state to be with family. But the tenant farmer had left approximately sixty acres of field corn and Kintis a fifty-acre functioning solar farm. After several months of no activity or signs of life from the family or the farmer, the Ranch folks had harvested the corn that fall in addition to their own but had yet to figure out how to tie into the solar array.

The NorthGate checkpoint, first to be constructed by ranch personnel, was logically situated where the railroad tracks crossed GCR, just past a blind turn in the road after it transversed Barlow Branch creek via a small bridge. But establishing the checkpoint was not their first time interfering with traffic flow on "their" road.

Early into the Second Pandemic, Ben saw the writing on the wall. Collapse was coming. He, Jackson, and Dex had already been practicing manufacturing thermite out in the barn in their spare time after their respective full-time job and collective daily ranch chores.

And sometimes after knocking back a few.

Thermite was made from mixing finely powdered aluminum oxide and iron oxide, the latter more commonly known as *rust*. They had tested several techniques to purify and refine the ingredients, even purchasing a small laboratory-grade centrifuge online, until test samples burned at nearly four thousand degrees Fahrenheit. They experimented with it on the hood of an old car and observed through welder's helmets as it burned hot enough to melt steel straight down through the engine block to the ground.

Once perfected, they manufactured enough to burn out the small bridge connecting Grears Corner Road to the town of Townsend and larger Middletown, thus reducing passing traffic on "their" road to zero.

No people, no chance for pandemic contamination.

The State Police had investigated to no avail and Tanner, a heavy equipment operator with the Delaware Department of Transportation, had given the Ranch a heads up when he heard it would be rebuilt. Sure enough, a few days later a crew had come out and repaired the damage.

Ironically enough with Tanner as foreman.

The calculus was simple: If the bridge was rebuilt, then the government still had ample resources and retained some control over a society rapidly crumbling under the weight of the worsening pandemic and its own irresponsible governing.

If it was not rebuilt, then the government had lost control.

Therefore, by destroying the bridge, they were not only preventing desperate and potentially violent people from easily accessing their resources in overwhelming numbers, but also calculating how far society and government control had actually decayed. Might not be very Christian, but they couldn't just allow anyone to come and take what they had worked so hard to build to secure a future for their own.

In those last days with fuel and food outrageously expensive, if could even be procured, road traffic near the end of the Second Pandemic was already very scarce. Occasionally a car would pass by, its occupants gawking at the vegetable gardens and cattle in the pastures. Sometimes, they would knock on Ben, Tanner, or Jackson's door and launch into a heartbreaking sob story of how their starving children hadn't eaten in days.

In his twenties, Ben had traveled extensively around the world and knew one thing for certain: There was no poverty in the United States. At least, not before the Second Pandemic hit.

True poverty existed in *favelas* in Brazil or India's *Dharavi* district. Sure, there were poor people in the United States prior to the Second Pandemic, but no *poverty*. Not like other places in the world had.

Not even close.

At least not until a few months into the Second Pandemic when stores had not been stocked for weeks, and no one even tried going anymore. Covid-27, as it was known on the news, was rampant. The entire United States had become infected virtually the same day. The following day, every State in the Union had confirmed cases.

The day after that, the infamous "Death Count" ticker returned to the lower right-hand corner of all news broadcasts, keeping a running tally of the lives lost to the new pandemic. The Death Count Ticker was criticized heavily during Covid-19 as a scare tactic of the left or the right, depending on which side of the aisle the speaker was on and whether Fox News or CNN was being discussed.

Either way, the countdown was on.

But three days later, when the death toll of Covid-27 had topped 23 million, it mysteriously disappeared from every network.

The following month, the power had gone out in some major cities.

The month after that, it went out across the entire county.

People just huddled helplessly in their homes without heat or electricity in the still, soundless night, eating whatever was lurking in the rear of the pantry: cold canned beets and even dog food. With no news. No communication with the outside.

Finally, they resigned themselves to the fact the government was not coming to save them. Then, quite predictably, they loaded up the family car with worthless junk, all their gas mileage-killing expensive electronic treasures weighing them down and set out "to find some place better" they told their neighbors, before bugging out. Ill-prepared, they catapulted themselves and their loved ones into the unknown with no clear destination.

No plan.

And no protection.

Delaware was a very blue state.

Many never made it out of the state or even out of their own neighborhoods before being descended upon by roving gangs and thugs preying on the innocent for supplies to survive. For a while, when the power was still on and the broadcast "news" was quite clearly anything but the product of freedom of the press, there were nightly news reports about people being victimized by criminals. These reports became so common that by the time they stopped completely, many folks just assumed that meant that travel was now safe and that the looting and victimized epidemic was over.

They were wrong.

What had, in fact, happened was that what remained of the government just shut down free broadcasting in favor of their own, "Report to your nearest government sponsored refugee camp" messages complete with a helpful color-coded local map. The message replayed on an endless loop. Thank God, the sheep believed, the government was in control again!

Except it wasn't.

In fact, it barely even existed at all.

And it had its own immediate problems with unending competing succession claims stemming from entire cabinet senior staff members either dead or missing. Having so many top people just disappear was not a contingency the government had ever contemplated. When the top five senior officers of any given federal or state cabinet department were nowhere to be found, and no clear succession plan for such an event even available... who was in charge?

Chaos was!

And she took those reins gleefully.

Some gangs used abandoned police cars and uniforms to coerce their victim into submission under color of authority. Others just murdered and raped at will before helping themselves to their victims' bounties.

It was truly a jungle out there.

But even before all that madness, still in the early days when "civilized" people still depended on "civilization" to maintain order as, within their lifetime of experiences, it always had, Ranch personnel never answered the door for these unexpected visitors. Instead, they would coordinate an approach from unexpected angles: one from the woods across the street from the house with uninvited visitors, another on horseback from around the side of that house or popping out of the neighbor's house; and always armed to the teeth.

The unwitting, uninvited visitors, usually just desperate, innocent families, were caught completely off guard and overwhelmed. They instantly knew they were no match for the numbers and firepower that abruptly descended upon them from all different directions.

This was done intentionally to discourage any attempts by the uninvited to resort to violence. The Ranch would normally provide such visitors a meal, maybe a jar of canned beans and a loaf of homemade wheat or rye bread, a few gallons of water and then send them on their way after gleaning any useful intelligence. When these visits started occurring several times a week, they knew it was time to start dropping trees at both the north and south ends of GCR.

When they fouled the road a few months later, and this second time more certain collapse was imminent, Tanner, Jackson, Ben, and Dex had taken chainsaws at 3 a.m. and dropped predetermined trees into predetermined positions from both sides of their road. This created a maze that could be traversed by a vehicle, but only at extremely low speeds and requiring multiple "K" turns to navigate through the obstacles.

When no one came to investigate or clear the trees for over a week, they set up their first armed checkpoint to the north and repeated the procedure at a second point at the southernmost end of GCR where it met a crossroad. A week later, they added multiple listening/observation posts in the wooded areas to the east and west and sniper nests to the checkpoints.

It was just in time.

By the end of the next month, nearly eight out of every ten infected people on the planet were dead.

CHAPTER 6

"Kill for a Steak"

Major Richard "Dick" Johnson was pissed. He sat in the rear compartment of the Blackhawk helicopter as it lifted off from the Dover Air Force base fuming at the loss of his six operators thirty miles north in some Podunk backwoods town. His operators had checked in and confirmed reaching the target and initiating surveillance. But there had been no contact ever since.

A bunch of rednecks had evidently barricaded themselves into some farm and had defied the Department of Homeland Security's mandate under martial law to relocate to a refugee camp and surrender their supplies to the greater good. If these backwoods hillbillies thought they were going to get away with killing six of his men without repercussions, well, they were about to be rudely awakened to reality.

Johnson was already livid at the AWOL rate of his Air Force base and indeed his entire beloved Air Force. Absent Without Official Leave was more than a military crime; it was a plague upon his command, as well as all of the other branches of the US military. Even the base commanding officer, the Colonial, had just disappeared.

Whereabouts unknown.

But with all the death from the pandemic, no one knew for sure if he had gone AWOL or was dead. They had nowhere near the resources to track down even one, let alone thousands of people. When the population started dying by the tens of millions, month after month, the whole system had just fallen apart within a couple weeks. And his soldiers just forgot their oaths and ran home to be with their families and children. Fucking pussies.

On top of it, his now immediate supervisor, some thirty-something year old snot nosed kid out of West Point, newly commissioned after the world went to shit, had chewed him out via video link from what was left of the Pentagon for sending his recon operators up there without authorization.

Authorization?

They were a military unit for Christ's sake and those hillbillies were defying DHS orders! Wasn't that *authorization* enough to do the right thing? Civilians had been ordered under martial law to leave their homes, report to the closest relocation center to be processed and sent to a refugee camp for their own damn good. State and federal government had the power in times of chaos to suspend civilian constitutional rights. What did they think they were doing riding horses and growing their own food? Didn't they know martial law had been imposed? What was he supposed to do? Send them an engraved invitation to follow the law? Maybe give each one a personal hand job while he begged them to follow orders...

He hadn't wanted to go up there to that *farm* or whatever at all, let alone on some peace and welfare mission. Peace and welfare? No, sir! He had instead requested permission from his commanders to send an Apache attack helicopter to show those rednecks what the term "firepower" meant but was denied. Fucking bureaucrats. Why couldn't they see what a threat to order and decency those people were? They *murdered* his men, dammit. Peace and welfare?

Fuck that.

The helo thumped its way northwest with two others behind it as Johnson brooded angrily. The other two helos in formation with his were also Blackhawks but in a "gunship" configuration, just bristling with firepower that Johnson was dying to unleash. It had been just a coincidence that the cursed farm had even been spotted at all. A supply plane serving one of the East Coast's largest freight hubs, his Air Force base, had experienced a navigational malfunction and had dropped altitude to navigate by landmarks, a piloting practice known as *dead reckoning.*

Those pilots had spotted this ranch or farm or whatever and its bustling activity of cattle and *beef* and reported the same to Johnson upon landing. Johnson was livid. Beef? Fresh fucking beef? His loyal but skeleton crew that had remained at the base was practically starving, having to survive on those bullshit MREs. He would *kill* for a steak right now.

Absolutely kill.

CHAPTER 7

· FALL 2027 ·

"The Big Dick"

Johnson's helo approached the ranch, and he barked orders into his headset. His Blackhawk made an altitude climb to observe as his gunships dropped low and thundered over the open fields of that stupid hillbilly haven.

He barked more orders into his headset for the other pilots in the gunships to make sure the people below could see the show of force on display.

"Let's see if these backwoods mother fuckers want to play with this," Johnson thought as he watched his gunships below cut through the air as they made a second pass.

He watched as the people below dropped what they were doing and started running. Animals scattered in all directions. Johnson smiled in satisfaction. He was scaring the shit out of them.

Good.

They moved... well, wait. Jesus... were they moving in a coordinated, organized way? It almost looked like they were... reporting to stations? What the hell was this? Intelligent rednecks? Jesus, what next? A politician with balls? *Oh right, that orange guy,* Johnson thought bitterly.

Johnson retained just enough professionalism to recognize military order and formations when he saw them. Suddenly, he was not so certain of his tactic. His plan, formed in anger, had been to come up here and scare them into submission. But they didn't look scared, they looked... well, they looked like they were going to be a fucking problem is what they looked like.

Okay, then, good, he thought with an evil smile, reassuring himself. Perhaps he'd get to unleash some fiery hell after all.

Then another, much darker thought hit him: These idiots wouldn't have surface to air missiles, would they? Lord knows rednecks loved firepower and SAMs were about as bad ass as any redneck could imagine. And you could get anything these days. *Anything at all.* All you had to do was find it and take it. There was no one to stop you. Perhaps some of his own people that had gone AWOL were down there, or other former military personnel with the expertise necessary to operate heavy weapons...

Doesn't matter, Johnson decided, pushing the thought from his mind. Even if they did, they'd just shoot at the gunships below him because they were the immediate threat. His helo was much higher, and besides, it presented no immediate threat nor viable target at altitude.

He waited for several minutes hovering in a slow circle, and when it became clear there would be no tell-tale trail of smoke of a SAM heading toward his birds from below, he ordered his pilot to descend and land.

He considered briefly ordering the pilot to touch down in the middle of a huge vegetable patch and thus destroying it just to show them who was boss. *What the hell was growing here in November, anyway?* But he decided that could invite an unwarranted response when the helo *he* was in was most vulnerable to small arms fire. After all, even though he had enough firepower on scene to turn the entire place into one giant smoking crater, chances are he himself would be killed in a gunfight on the ground or his chopper incapacitated. That couldn't happen. His men depended on him. What would they do without him? No, he had to be smarter than that. This was going to have to be played just right.

His bird touched down, and he jumped out with what he imagined was an imposing and terrifying show of authority. His adjutant exited the helo behind him and joined Major Johnson at his side. They were then joined by two armed operators on either side. The operators hefting their M4 fully automatic rifles were constantly swiveling their heads side to side.

Convinced no immediate danger presented itself, the six of them then moved forward out from under the prop wash generated by the slowing blades. The pilot kept the throttle down, but the transmission engaged for a quick extraction if necessary.

The helo's blades turned lazily in the cool autumn air as the gunships maintained well-spaced but low altitude slow circles around him. The gunship pilots vigilantly searched for any potential threats to their commanding officer on the ground. All they saw were some farmers digging along a tree line southwest of an old farmhouse. But it wasn't frantic digging like for a gun emplacement. More like some mundane farm chore. Maybe an irrigation pipe was broken?

Johnson smiled smugly as he took in the scene around him, relishing the way he imagined this would go. The hillbillies would be contrite and compliant and immediately submit to his authority, as they should.

He looked around surveying the wary individuals hiding behind their pathetic cover. An old tractor, some random, confusing piece of farm equipment. Well, it *was* all metal though. Thick metal. In fact, it may even afford those crouched behind it decent temporary defilade from small arms. No match for his gunships though. The uncertainty flared again briefly.

He spotted an attractive female with large breasts casually holding an AR15 next to a tractor. Her rifle wasn't exactly pointed at them, but it wasn't exactly *not* pointed at them either. Johnson barely noticed the weapon though. *It appears they have some women here,* he thought lustily. It had been a while. In fact, it had been so long that he began to wonder if he could take her... perhaps they would offer her to him as a gift. A sort of "goodwill" gesture to gain his favor.

Here we go, he thought as he broke himself away from his carnal fantasy. Two riders on horseback were coming his way.

Horses?

Jesus, these people knew no shame. *Probably wipe their asses with leaves too,* he mused.

Then Johnson smiled and stepped forward a couple paces, waiting for them to come to him.

It was time for these ignorant hillbillies to meet the Big Dick.

CHAPTER 8

· FALL 2027 ·

"Spook"

First Lieutenant Christopher Median was nervous. Very nervous. He stood beside his boss, Major Johnson, completely exposed in a field belonging to the "enemy."

Except Chris didn't think of them as the enemy. As far as he knew they hadn't done anything except remain in place.

And this *place*... he looked around in sheer amazement. This place reminded him of his Idaho family's farm that had still grown potatoes for McDonald's french fries right up to the Second Pandemic. He had not had contact with them in nearly a year and presumed now that they were all deceased.

But he remembered the lifestyle of growing up around a farm. Chris was well aware that the Major had no such knowledge. The Major was from Chicago and considered grease and dirt to be unseemly. The man had once held up a meeting with a general because a bird had dropped its load on his Jeep en route. The Jeep had to be washed first, Johnson had insisted. Chris smiled when he remembered how the "Big Dick" had been chewed out unforgivingly by his superior when they had finally arrived at the meeting fifteen minutes late and the superior had learned why.

Chris watched as the riders approached and smiled again observing the palomino stallion the short guy was riding. He hadn't seen his horses since enlisting years ago but recognized them both as ranch bred quarter horses.

The bigger guy was on a paint gelding, but Chris could see already that he wasn't the one in charge. More likely, he was security for the shorter guy on the smaller stallion, he surmised. Chris smiled again.

Just like with horses, it's always the smaller ones that you really gotta watch out for.

Then the smile vanished as the riders stopped. Chris braced himself for an eruption of violence and felt their armed escorts tense as well. The riders had stopped fifty yards from them and had made no gestures for them to approach nor indicated that they intended to proceed. One of them briefly spoke into a radio.

"What the fuck do they think they're doing?" He heard Johnson mutter beside him. "I'm not walking all the way over there. *They* need to come to *me*. Why did they stop?" The reason hit Chris immediately.

It was obvious.

"Sir," he began carefully. Speaking to his boss about anything was always a gamble. The man was so hot headed and unpredictable that what had seemed like a cushy assignment in the beginning made a lot more sense when he had learned the Major had fired six prior assistants in as many months before Chris's assignment to him.

No one else had wanted the job.

The Major turned towards him expectantly. He was now committed to finishing the thought.

"It's the horses, sir. Any closer, and they might spook."

"Might *what*, Lieutenant? The Sergeant didn't hear you," Johnson growled, glancing at the black guard next to him then turning towards his subordinate and straightening himself to his complete six-foot five height. He was facing his adjutant full on now, towering over him, an intimidation tactic he had employed ever since middle school to get his way. The black sergeant locked his gaze with Chris and subtly rolled his eyes behind their boss's back. Chris didn't know much about Sergeant Carter, only that he hailed from Georgia, but he now knew that the man knew something about horses.

Something the Major quite obviously did not.

Fuck, Chris thought. What a dumb thing to say to his city-slicker boss. The virtue signaling that had consumed the military had gotten out of control. One look at the Sergeant would tell any sane person that he was not one to be easily offended, least of all unintentionally.

"Sir, my apologies, sir. It's a term that horse people use when a horse reacts unexpectedly and violently to a perceived threat, such as the sound and sight of this helicopter, sir. I think they want us to approach them, so the horses remain calm." His suspicion was confirmed as the larger rider waved them towards him.

"The First Lieutenant is correct, sir." The Sergeant bravely offered. Inviting disagreement with the Major was a well-known no-no among his staff, and Chris silently thanked the Sergeant for his moxy in speaking up. The Major either ignored the comment or did not hear it.

"I am *not* going to them," Johnson responded with conviction, speaking mostly to himself. That wasn't how this worked.

Then he had sudden inspiration. This situation was as unpredictable as they came. Why should he take the risk? He was way too important to the recovery from the pandemic and to the staff at his airbase. Lord knows he had the firepower advantage, but he was on *their* turf.

He turned to his inferior officer Adjutant First Lieutenant Median and smiled, "You go."

"Sir?"

"You deaf now, Lieutenant? *You* will go. You and Sergeant Carter here, since you two both know so much about horses. You go tell them who I am and demand that they meet with me." Chris hesitated only a moment, then glanced at Carter. No expression whatsoever.

"Yes, sir. Do I mention the loss of our men?"

"You are not authorized to negotiate, idiot," Johnson grumbled harshly. "Just get us an invitation to talk somewhere without horses and cow shit and let's find out what we can about their supplies, numbers, and capabilities. The other guards will remain with me."

"Yes, sir."

CHAPTER 9

· FALL 2027 ·

"Definitely a GenXer"

Jackson and Ben sat on their horses well away from the Blackhawk's slowing blades. They rode to the end of Pasture 3 next to one of the Ranch's huge vegetable and herb gardens, currently only producing the cool weather crop of turnips. They couldn't go any further toward the helicopter without risking Moonshine and Reno spooking.

After all, they had never seen a helicopter.

Let alone Hellfire missiles, Ben thought appreciatively, glancing up as a gunship thundered above him overhead. He reached down absently and rubbed Moonshine's neck reassuringly.

Ben was unsuccessfully attempting to tamp down his Irish temper at this unwelcome and highly concerning intrusion. He already suspected a connection to what they had discovered after neutralizing their stealthy, incognito intruders nearly a week before: that they were actually military operators attempting to infiltrate the Ranch.

Now this gaudy display of force by the circling gunships confirmed it was no "meet and greet" type visit.

Although to be fair, if he had to go anywhere beyond the safety of the Ranch these days and had access to a gunship, Ben knew damn well that he would do the same thing. Well, except he'd be blasting Wagner's "Flight of the Valkyries" in true *Apocalypse Now* style.

After all, Charlie don't surf.

"Wave them over."

"Here they come," Jackson said.

"Game faces," Ben reminded him. "No matter what, don't say anything."

A single man hesitantly approached slowly followed by another with an M4 assault rifle. The lead man held his hands out to his sides well away from his body. He appeared to be unarmed.

The second man trailing let his M4 dangle at a low ready position. Not an immediate threat, not aggressive, but somehow broadcasting an air of such competence that it suggested he'd take out both riders with single kill shots before they could so much as draw their sidearms.

Jackson and Ben exchanged a silent glance agreeing to leave their sidearms holstered. The last thing they wanted was a gunfight on the Ranch; especially one they couldn't hope to win on firepower alone.

The man was young, perhaps mid 20s and Ben noticed the single silver bar on his lapel.

When he was within earshot about 10 yards away, Ben said, "Good morning, Lieutenant," as nicely as he could muster.

"Good morning," Chris responded carefully. "My name is Lieutenant Chris Median, adjutant to Major Richard Johnson, acting commander of the 436th Airlift Wing out of Dover Air Force Base. Behind me is Staff Sergeant Carter for my protection. I hope you understand."

The riders nodded but said nothing. An uncomfortable silence ensued. A few moments passed then Chris said, "Is there somewhere the Major may speak with whoever is in charge here?"

"About *what?*" Ben barked. Chris was momentarily thrown off kilter. Lt. Median had expected the more deferential and accommodating disposition his boss had talked about in their pre-flight mission briefing. He glanced back at Carter. The Sergeant remained impassive, giving away nothing on his face.

No help there.

For some reason, Chris had an overwhelming momentary flashback to his grandfather and their potato farm back in Idaho. Then he understood. His mind was telling him to speak to this guy the way one would need to speak to his grandfather.

That man had taken no shit from anyone.

Well, sort of.

Except from his cattle and horses, of course.

Grandpap had a dairy farm and several horses but got involved with growing potatoes on their one-thousand-acre tract. At one point, when Chris was still in grade school, he had witnessed Grandpap throwing the McDonald's representative off his property at gunpoint for merely threatening to kick Grandpap's dog. Chris smiled warmly at the memory. The McDonald's man had literally shit himself while scrambling to his car.

"My apologies, sir, I am not exactly sure. They don't tell us young bucks a whole lot."

No reaction.

Not even a smile.

"If I might say, sir," Chris pressed on. "That is an absolutely gorgeous stallion. Was he foaled here?"

"North Dakota," Ben answered, intensely cognizant of the information he was relaying. No harm in that though. No military or strategic value lay in where Moonshine was born, and he did not want this thing going south. At least not yet, not until he knew what these intruders wanted.

"How old?"

"Just about four now. Is there something non-horse-related that we can do for you and your *helicopters*, Lieutenant?"

Sarcasm, Chris thought. *Definitely a GenXer.*

Chris tried again. "Yes, sir. The Major respectfully requests an audience with you. May I have your name, sir?"

Oops. He'd just given away that he had identified the short one as being in charge.

"I don't think so," Shorty said.

"Sir?" Chris stammered. This wasn't going well at all. The other rider now looked pissed. The short one looked pissed too. Chris glanced backwards. Sergeant Carter remained impassive and... *was that a hint of a smile on his face?*

Carter *never* smiled!

"Look asshole," Ben spoke loudly and clearly. "You guys drop in here out of the sky scaring the shit out of all our animals and all these people who are *already* terrified for their lives every fucking day. And you do it while waving around enough firepower to level a city and you expect us to just jump for you? *Not* going to happen! Now get the fuck off my ranch!" He turned his horse, and the other rider followed suit.

CHAPTER 10

"Pocket Full of Shells"

Chris watched them for a moment thinking how displeased his boss was going to be.

He took a deep breath and turned back towards the helo to face Johnson's rage.

He stopped as he saw Carter hadn't moved, had not even turned to walk back. Carter just stared at him then cocked his head like he was waiting for Chris to figure something out.

Chris suddenly realized his mistake.

He should have addressed this the way Grandpap would have responded to three freaking helicopters arriving uninvited on his farm and its occupants then making demands. Grandpap would have met them on the wraparound porch with a 100-year-old shotgun, a pocket full of shells and gone out with a smile in a blaze of glory defending his home.

Jesus Christ, we're lucky they didn't just start shooting as soon as we landed.

The way to address that situation was obvious.

Don't create it.

But since it was a bit late for *that* revelation, and thus not an option at the moment, he had to find another way.

This mission was FUBAR from conception.

Having sudden inspiration, Chris turned around and called out to the riders.

"Sir! Sir? Please wait a moment."

Both riders immediately turned their horses back, but now Chris noticed they had placed their hands on their still holstered sidearms. A glance back at the Sergeant told Chris that he was keenly aware but did not so much as flinch. He didn't adjust his stance or raise his rifle. He didn't even do an unconscious press check.

He is one cool operator, Chris thought and faced the riders again.

"Sir, may we please schedule an appointment to discuss some critical matters? I apologize for the disruption and intrusion, but it is urgent that the Major be heard."

Ben paused. He started to tell the kid to fuck off again, but glancing at the Sergeant behind him told him that would be a giant mistake for the Ranch. He stared past the kid at the Sergeant. Ben wasn't sure but thought he saw him nod subtlety. With absolutely no reason to trust this perfect stranger, and yet an even stranger feeling that he *could* trust him, Ben went with his gut. He swallowed his pride and...

Well, *most* of his anger.

Sort of.

That Sergeant knew something. Something important. Perhaps something that was even vital to the Ranch's survival.

Ben needed to know what that was.

"Come back Tuesday, just you, the Sergeant there, and your Major Whatever... in *one* unarmed Blackhawk. Noon."

"May I ask why, sir?"

"Because I fucking said so."

Ben had sworn later when recounting the conversation to the Ranch's immediate emergency senior staff meeting, that just as he spun Moonshine around, he had caught out of the corner of his eye the Sergeant unsuccessfully attempting to suppress a grin.

"Don't look back," Ben said as they walked their horses towards the Bighouse.

"You think that was the right way to do that?" Jackson asked, as the Blackhawk spooled up its rotors and lifted into the sky.

"Right up until the moment we get a bullet in the back, I will continue to believe it could have gone worse," Ben responded philosophically.

"You made them make an appointment," Jackson laughed. "I thought that dude was going to shit himself!"

"Just because the world is dead doesn't mean manners have to be. Did you notice the Sergeant?" Ben asked Jackson.

"Yeah, not sure what to make of him. Almost like he..." Jackson trailed off as their radios squawked.

"Everything okay?" Dex's concerned voice came over the airwaves. Ben grabbed his radio.

"Well, the bad news is we evidently have some new admirers. But the good news is we have a luncheon to plan for next week. I'm thinking we have steak."

CHAPTER 11

"Plastic"

Saul and Sherrie McKnight had grown up a very few doors down from one another in a small Delaware country town. They dated in high school, got married at age twenty and bought a house one town over from where their respective mothers and fathers lived in their own homes. Their daughters, Bree and her sister Brynn, followed suit, marrying in their early twenties hardworking young men in the trades and buying homes along GCR where their parents had grown up and met.

Saul was raised in what was now his daughter Bree, her husband Jackson and their son Westin's, home. Saul's father had built it himself, with family help. Sherrie's family home was down the same road after a cross street. Ben and Saul were first cousins, as their respective fathers were brothers. Though Ben's parents lived in Wilmington, Saul and his folks lived next door to their grandfather, Pop. Every Sunday, Ben's parents would visit Pop and Mom at the retirement home their daughter's husband's construction company had built for them.

That home was now the Ranch's "Bighouse."

Childhood Ben and Saul spent glorious summers and every Sunday together on Pop's farm, by then tilled by the next generation of family. They were inseparable when they got together building forts in the seemingly never-ending woods, fishing, and swimming in Pop's pond, picking up arrowheads in the freshly plowed fields... and earning legitimate ass whippings just by basically being the complete asshole McKnight children that they were.

When That Day came, Saul and Sherrie lived about eight minutes from the Ranch in the home where they had raised their daughters,

Bree and Brynn. They were ginormous believers in family and the sanctity of the family unit long before anyone knew the phrase "Covid-19" or either of their girls could say "mama." So, Saul and Sherrie were two of the very first to arrive at the Ranch; although technically they had merely loaded up their necessaries and moved in with Jackson and Bree "until this thing blows over."

By that time, the beef company was located next door to Jackson and Bree at Ben and Saul's former grandparents' residence. Both Ben's and Saul's ancestral homes had once been part of the same farm purchased during the Second World War by their grandfather, Pop, on which now the Ranch was now centered.

Seems the government in Pop's time felt that even in time of war, farmers needed to stay right where they were. That's where men of that skill set belonged. Anyone could hold a rifle, but who would feed the brave men heading into battle and the rest of the country? The government felt so strongly about this that historically any time gasoline and diesel fuel was rationed to the general public, farmers and ranchers still got all they needed to produce food. And they were last to be drafted.

But when the war was over, everyone came home and made babies, creating the Baby Boomer generation. That generation grew up in the mid 1940s to the mid 1960s, when America's economy was roaring, communism was bad, companies built products to last and with pride.

But by the mid 1960s, all of that had changed.

Companies began making cheaper, crappier products that failed and broke, and then didn't stand by them. It wasn't until after ten years of this, when young Ben was five years old, that Congress had passed the Magnuson-Moss Warranty Act in 1975. It required at the federal level that manufacturers and sellers who offer written warranties to provide consumers with detailed information about the warranty coverage. This had not been necessary before or controlled at the State level.

This was true because the historically accepted business creed was that the customer's business was to be *earned* through manufacturing a *better* product or providing a *better* service than the competition. The "snake oil salesman" was an anomaly.

But doing things the right way was time consuming and expensive; so, companies got greedy, state governments got corrupted, products got more cheaply constructed.

And consumers got screwed.

Decades later, Ben, by then a forty-something, childless, confirmed bachelor with a love of fine whiskey and deep thought, had a theory:

Plastic was to blame.

Yep, the development and use of a new manufacturing material in the 1960s.

Plastic.

You see, the theory went, in his father's and grandfather's day, men fixed things. Women fixed things. Children grew up helping their parents fix things. So, everyone learned how to fix things. But by Ben's generation, *GenX*, so named for having no defining event such as "Baby Boomers" and the "Greatest Generation" that won the Second World War before them, that had changed.

Because of plastic.

Plastic was cheap. So cheap it became the preferred construction material for *everything* from toys to even moving machine parts; any moving part of course being the first to wear out in any given machine. As a result, goods were mass produced more cheaply and thus more affordable, which manufacturers and consumers initially both loved. However, the unintended (or perhaps intended) consequence was for the average consumer it became more economically viable to throw out whatever had broken and buy a new one.

After all, plastic made everything much cheaper.

It was terrifying to the older generations to witness the rocketing decline of the general public's collective IQ and peoples' ability to do *anything at all* for themselves.

But whatever, Boomer.

Why bother?

Plastic had the answer.

Your washer broke? Throw it out and get a new one. TV on the fritz? Throw it out and get a new one. Computer doesn't work? Throw it out and get a new one. iPhone busted? Throw it out and get a new one.

So, what happened when your relationship broke?

What had you already been pre-programmed to do in every other area of your life?

Throw it out and get a new one.

So when That Day came, when the chickens came home to roost, the shit hit the fan, whatever phrases people used to describe the inevitable Reckoning with their greed and insatiable self-pleasure—when *That* Day came, Saul and Sherrie had been together over forty years, living in a home they had paid off twenty years before. They were an anachronism to the modern world, the last of their kind:

They knew how to fix things.

Saul fixed things around the house and at work, saving money and teaching his skills to younger helpers. Sherrie fixed their children's discipline problems, the family's clothing, and dinner... and all the other unspoken things women fix out of public view to make a marriage and a family work.

Their daughters even learned how to fix *people*: growing up to be a clinical psychologist and an intensive care unit nurse. And *their* husbands worked in the trades: fixing things like their father had.

One of the very few benefits of the end of the world, of the mass death caused by Covid-27, was the return of people learning how to fix things.

They had no choice.

There was no new industrial level manufacturing then, no stores, no transportation infrastructure to move goods across the country and across continents. Anything that was built, was built locally, homemade, by someone you looked in the eye as you bought it directly from the man or woman who had crafted it with his or her own hands... with *pride*.

And that pride was the only warranty anyone ever needed.

But that wasn't even the best part.

The best part was that their wares could always be purchased with a bartering of food or in conjunction with a homemade item of the buyer's own.

A *quality* item.

Because no one built anything out of plastic anymore.

CHAPTER 12

· FALL 2027 ·

"Notorious D.I.C.s"

The days following the helos' unexpected visit were a flurry of activity. In addition to all of the usual daily tasks and chores to provide food, water, security and some semblance of life at the Ranch, there were multiple meetings with Mike, the four QRT squad leaders, Kitchen staff and other senior staff departments to plan and prepare for their military guests' return.

In addition to all of the normal details to be attended when having guests for dinner in the Before, these days one had to consider things like personal security, operational security and intelligence gathering. The Ranch wanted to maximize the info gained while minimizing the risks and selecting what information was given away.

A certain amount of information trading was necessary, of course. That was the very essence of a "meeting." But the Ranch wasn't ready for anyone on the Outside to know the totality of their resources and defensive capabilities. Several discussions were held, formally and informally, among senior staff as to how this should be accomplished. A "tour" of some sort would only be polite, but it was determined this would be premature. Much debate had occurred over what should or should not be involved or included in a tour.

The consensus was to skip the tour altogether and just hold a reception at the Bighouse with the guests and Ben, Dex, Jackson, and Saul. Keep things abstract, for the first meeting. No need for the Major to know what was done where, why and by whom all at once.

Bighouse settled on a game plan and called a meeting of the necessary individuals to fill them in.

"Makes sense to me," Saul said of the plan for their guests. Ben's cousin was still fixing things, these days running the Ranch's

Construction and Maintenance department and overseeing those operations.

"We want to seem open and friendly, but we limit what they actually see to just the Bighouse."

"And who they know," Ben added. "They've already met me and Jackson. We'll add Dex and you, Saul, to the meeting with them."

"Copy that," Saul acknowledged.

"Kitchen would be happy to cater," Sherrie added. Saul's wife ran the six-thousand-square-foot food preparation, storage, and dining for the Ranch, known as "Kitchen." They typically served a morning and an evening meal to the entire Ranch—no small feat even by Before standards.

"Stable will transport," Sage followed up.

"We've got a comprehensive security plan too," Mike said. "I won't bore you with all the details here, but there is a map that explains it pretty well," he pointed to a table by one of the picture windows. "Suffice to say, QRT will be out in force, and we'll have extra spotters and bodies placed. But we won't look like security or any type of threat. We'll just look like other ranchers doing ranch stuff."

"That'll be a first for QRT guys, won't it?" Ben joked. "Sure you know which end of the hoe to hold?"

"Not our job," Mike responded frankly. "Our job is to keep people from shooting at you while you're doing your job." He smiled.

"I'm just saying grabbing a hoe by the wrong end is a guaranteed give-away that you don't know what you're doing."

"Said your ex," Dex quipped to a couple laughs.

"In all fairness, that only described..." He pretended to count off fingers, listing imaginary names in his mind. When he needed a second hand, he stopped and just dead panned, "Never mind."

"Good choice," Rachele commented, casting Ben a stern look and running her hands over her slightly swollen belly. Their child would be here before summer began, and she had only so much time left to whip his adolescent-minded ass into shape for fatherhood.

No. Small. Task.

"I know you want to fill the Bighouse with QRT operators," Dex said when the laughter died down. "But Ben and I think that sends the wrong message, Mike. We appreciate the concern, but more of our guys means they're going to want more of their guys... next thing you know we'll have to rent the fire hall in town for this event. Besides, if it's a fight they wanted, they wouldn't even need to get out of their helicopters."

"Our plan calls for every rancher appearing to be out working on chores, but to have access to a rifle within three seconds," Mike confirmed. "They can hide them next to them wherever they are, in a hay bale, under a tractor or mixed in with other tools... wherever. Even if spotted at these distances, is it so unreasonable we'd be armed? But that's a lot different than meeting the helo with the entire complement of QRT combat operators."

"We're also going to need everyone to have a radio. And Saul, let's make some effort to camo the OPs from overhead view. Not something we'd thought to do before. All previous threats were ground based," Ben added.

"Already on it. Jackson's riding around making sure the OP guards know to spend part of their shifts making sure they can't be spotted from above," Saul said.

"How would you feel about constructing a heli-pad for our guests' arrival?" Ben inquired.

"You serious? You know how much concrete that would take?"

"Nah, you're missing my point. QRT has already dialed in, as best they can, the last place they landed. Let's make that their permanent spot," he said with a wink.

"How?"

"Got any spray paint?" Ben asked, then explained what to do.

"Ward is ready to receive casualties," Dex's girlfriend Nurse Bliss said. She ran the Ranch's hospital known as The Ward. "All staff is on call for the duration of the time our guests are here, and we're running a skeleton crew overnight the night before to ensure everyone else is as rested as possible."

"The more pressing issue is what to do about the intruders we killed," Dex pointed out.

"Yeah, that's another reason to keep this meeting small, and play our cards close to the vest, at least at first," Ben agreed. "But if they were his, we're going to have to tell him. No matter how he reacts, we tell him the truth. If he's any measure of a man, that will mean something. Otherwise, the uncertainty will breed distrust, and we can kiss any long-term positive relationship goodbye."

"All of our ex-military QRT guys think those intruders were definitely soldiers," Mike confirmed heavily.

"Right, and Ben and I don't think a Blackhawk dropping in on us less than a week later is a coincidence," Dex said in agreement.

"That might have been what that sergeant was trying to convey to me," Ben said thoughtfully. "That the Major is on the warpath about his missing men."

"Well, if they are familiar with the complete breakdown of society and rampant lawlessness, they can't be too surprised we reacted as we did to six armed assholes trying to sneak in here in the middle of the night," Rachele commented, receiving several nods in agreement.

"Either that or they're pissed we ignored the relocation order," Saul suggested.

"They've got to have bigger problems to deal with than us," Sherrie pointed out.

"Yeah, we're just taking care of ourselves, not bothering anybody, and minding our own business. Who could have a problem with that?" Young Sage asked.

"The government," Ben, Dex, Mike, and Saul responded in unison.

"But I agree it's not a large enough issue alone for them to warrant a Major in a Blackhawk," Ben continued. "No, I think he's looking for something. And I think it's personal for him."

"His missing men," Bliss said. "Which reminds me, what are you planning to do on observing infection protocols?"

Jackson knocked and entered. He looked around in confusion, "Where's everyone else?"

"We didn't see the need to involve the other Actuals and Asset Managers for this," Dex responded. "They'll be informed, of course. But Ag, Lifeskills and the rest won't be part of the first meeting. We're going to keep it simple."

"To answer your question, Bliss," Ben said, returning to the conversation at hand, "I'm thinking we take our cues from them. It's highly unlikely at this stage that they are infected, and we know that we aren't. After six or seven months, Covid-27 has probably burned itself out. If a concern arises, the four of us can self-quarantine for two weeks here in the Bighouse. Another reason to keep it small. But if we keep our distance, ensure positive flow ventilation in this room, and don't share utensils or needles, we should be okay."

"Aww man, not even one hit?" Jackson asked, rubbing the vein at his elbow with one hand and feigning disappointment.

"And just because that disease is gone, doesn't mean there isn't a new or different one. Ward will send up buckets and bleach water for hand sanitation," Bliss offered, making a note.

"What color does that get?" Ben teased her. Bliss had a penchant for color coding every single thing she touched.

"Black, to match your eye if you keep it up," she shot back with a smile.

"Okay, are there any more items?" Dex asked.

"Well, you and I have one," Ben reminded him.

"You lovers need us to leave?" Saul mocked.

Bighouse also thought Market should be shut down for the day. Technically, the government could see those wares having been obtained by looting.

Which of course, technically, they had been.

And the good Major just might take issue with that.

Market was held every other Tuesday from dawn until dusk to give everyone on and off duty a chance to swing by. It was kind of like a flea market and carnival rolled into one.

With guns.

Guns being bought, sold, traded, and repaired.

Lots and lots of guns.

It was set up on the driveway behind Jackson's house on the gravel drive leading from GCR past the sheep pens, Lifeskills, and finally terminating at Kitchen and Ward, a quarter mile of non-stop, busting private enterprise. But there was concern about the appropriateness of holding Market on the same day as the return of their military guests.

"I don't think we should shut it down totally; people count on that for a sense of normalcy. It's like when kids used to go to the mall. There's food, stuff to do, games and all," Sage pointed out. "Why don't we hold it the day before, just this time? Keep everyone positive going into our guests' return?"

"You need more nail polish?" Her father, Dex, teased her. She dropped straight into RBF in what had to be a new record time.

"Yes, but it was going to be a surprise birthday gift for *you*," Rachele teased him.

"That makes sense to me," Mike offered about Sage's suggestion, ignoring the playful banter. "But definitely no QRT in sight when our guests arrive. Obviously, it will be an 'all hands on deck' for us with everyone on duty for the duration and they won't see us, as we discussed. But if it were me in their shoes, I'd run a recon in advance to see what we're up to preparation wise, so maybe the day after is better."

"Smart crew," Ben commented. "But let's hold it the day before they arrive this time. If they see it from a distance doing recon, so what? It'll look like any other block wide yard sale in the Before. And keeping morale up is definitely a priority."

As the meeting broke up and everyone was departing to attend to their respective tasks, Jackson paused by the rear Bighouse door. Ben and Dex had a map of the Ranch spread over the lower of the split-level bar next to the door reviewing Mike's security strategy.

"How did you guys ever come up with the 'Bighouse' name, anyway"? Jackson inquired,standing by the door.

"Because when we let everyone refer to us as 'Those Two Assholes,' not as much got done," Dex quipped.

"It *was* fitting, though," Sage commented with a smirk, taking a seat at the bar.

"It was used in one of the first books I ever read of a situation in the world like we find ourselves in now. It was called *Satan's Mallet* or something like that. Plus, it's traditionally how ranches refer to the boss's place. 'Bighouse' is descriptive, indicative of hierarchy, chain of command. Everyone knows what it means," Ben said. "But at the same time, it has more of a 'Mission Control' cooperation-like feel to it. Like Dex and I are directing the bigger picture, coordinating the launching of a Space Shuttle or something. It's just less authoritarian than..."

"The Man?" Saul said, walking by Jackson with a smile as he went through the door on his way out.

"King Assholes?" Sherrie added, following her husband.

"Head hoes?" Mike laughed as he slid by.

"Douchebags-In-Charge?" added Bliss, taking her turn passing through the door. Saul overheard her and stopped at the top of the deck landing where he was putting on his boots.

"Hey, I like that one!"

"Yeah, the 'Notorious 'D.I.C.'s.'" Jackson laughed.

Saul grabbed his radio and put it to his lips.

"Don't you fucking dare, Saul!" Ben barked.

Without pushing the transmit button, Saul imitated Ben, "D.I.C. to Jackson, please come give me and my boyfriend hand jobs, stat!"

They all broke out in laughter except Ben who only smirked, "Very funny, cuz. Look, any time you want all the responsibility here, you say the word. I'll hand you the reins and head off to Aruba."

"Aruba doesn't exist anymore," Dex reminded him. "And you don't have any way..."

"Jesus, I know. I'm making a point."

"Not me, cuz," Saul said. "I got enough headaches just managing the construction and maintenance crews. Some of these younger guys don't know their ass from a hammer. But as far as running this place, how hard could it be? All you two ever do is give orders and sip Margaritas," he said, knowing damn well that wasn't true.

The Bighouse cowboys drank whiskey.

Not to mention Ben and Dex had spent more total hours in operations individually than any other five ranchers combined.

And *everyone* knew it.

Ben and Dex were always seen volunteering for some of the most difficult jobs no one else wanted to do. They made a point of doing it.

No one on the Ranch outworked them.

And that was saying something because work was nearly all that any of the hundred plus survivors of Covid-27 even did anymore.

"Probably got some chick in a bikini hidden around here somewhere to dance for you, too," Jackson commented.

Dex nodded and gestured playfully towards Bliss who immediately batted her eyes and shook her hips.

"Next show's at 7 boys," she cooed.

"Y'all just get out of my house," Ben laughed and went back to the map.

CHAPTER 13

"Caveat Emptor"

Even by the relatively well-to-do standards of the ranch, at least compared to the rest of the world, Market went all "extra" that week. Free enterprise showed up in full force, and new gun owners hit a record high. The Armory was always available for the community's general defense and secured to keep an inventory of weapon systems and ammunition supplies at a known certainty. But private ownership was encouraged as well.

Very encouraged.

Firearms, and all other sorts of scavenged manufactured items from the Before, as well as post-collapse homemade wares, were out for display and available for barter or purchase with Market credits. Most attractive and popular were homemade baked goods prepared by various Ranchers.

When it came to free market enterprise, the Ranch didn't fuck around.

Market credits were just pieces of gold weighing one ounce. In the Before, they could be worth several thousand US dollars. Dex smelted the simple coins himself using salvaged gold, a clay crucible, and borax as a flux. Flux lowered the melting point, prevented oxidation, and removed impurities.

They used gold because everyone remembered when it was a thing of value.

Dex then used a small branding iron featuring the 𝕋 in a circle logo from the beef company as a "brand" for Market use. Although this particular small brand had never been used on actual cattle, Dex had machined several different size branding irons with the company logo for different uses.

This particular one was used to brand children.

Sort of.

Kids loved being "branded" in colorful paint at the beef company's annual public event known as MOO-A-PalOOza, a word play on the once famous music festival Lollapalooza.

Dex always worked alone on smelting the coins not even allowing Ben to help. The clay crucible was kept in a place known only to Dex and Ben. Uncirculated solid gold Market credits were kept…

Well, never you mind where they are kept.

Ben strolled down the central walkway with vendor shops set up on either side. It was a crisp November morning, so vendors and buyers alike were bundled up against the cold. A light, but cold wind blew in from the northwest, as it always did this time of year. Ben flipped up the collar of his fleece pullover nestled underneath his plate carrier against the wind. He shifted the strap of his custom AR he'd built himself, from his right shoulder to his left, freeing his right hand.

He stopped and pointed at a section of a vendor's table in front of him laid with various baked goods.

"Good morning! This is… ?" he inquired of the stall's proprietor.

"Coconut creme, sir."

Ben made a show of swinging around and observing the surrounding trees.

"Don't see any date palms around here, where'd you get the coconut?"

The proprietor smiled at his disingenuous confusion and reached under the table. She produced several cans of pie filling and showed him the expiration date.

"From our last supply run. My husband was a volunteer and brought a lot of baking ingredients back for me. See? Expiration 2/2029."

"You got me," Ben threw up his hands in submission. "Just doing my job, ma'am," he said, tipping his Australian bush hat at her.

She laughed. "We all know the rules, sir. No *caveat emptor* here. The buyer does not need to beware. We are responsible for what we sell. Strict liability, I believe you lawyers call it."

"Yes ma'am, you are correct. So, I can safely eat this without getting the runs or *E.coli?*"

"Yes, sir, you certainly can," she responded with a bright smile. "All the other ingredients—the cream, milk, butter, flour—all came from Ranch's public stock hold."

"Hmmm. Well, you had better just give me two then. Wouldn't want to ruin my figure," he said, patting his slightly bulging belly. "Though to be honest, I don't have quite the 'dad bod' that I did in the Before."

"None of us have much of that excess anymore, probably from not having so much excess!" She laughed pleasantly, and he handed her two credits.

She wrapped the pies in a swath of brown paper and handed them over with an admonishment, "Now sir, these must be either consumed this evening or kept below forty degrees." She glanced up, taking in the weather, "That won't be a problem tonight, but don't leave them in the sun or anywhere warm... Oh, what am I thinking? The Bighouse has electricity, right? You'll just need to refrigerate them," she said lightly, but with a direct gaze.

Ben gazed back.

"Is this the part where I apologize for thinking ahead and building all of this?"

She dropped her eyes, momentarily ashamed of her insolence.

"No sir. I'm sorry, I..."

"Ma'am?"

She returned her gaze like a chastened child, and Ben held it.

"We are all adjusting as best we can. And just looking at this pie, I can tell you've adjusted better than most. I can't wait to try it."

She smiled weakly, "Thank you."

"But I seriously doubt you want to hear about all the sacrifices in the Before that allowed us to have this previously comfortable moment here today. Do you?" He stared at her more sternly now.

"No, sir. I'm sorry."

"Don't be sorry, ma'am. Be *better*. It is all any of us can do, be better than we were last year, yesterday or ten seconds ago. We are all struggling to adapt to this new world; and the moment we can make ranch-wide power happen for everyone, we will. But right now, what we have is stretched out as far as it can go, ma'am. Just in keeping us all alive. I know you're nervous about our visitors tomorrow, but I'm not. You know why?"

"No, sir?"

"Because I'm going to serve them this pie, and after that they're going to be falling all over themselves to please us," he winked at her.

She smiled genuinely and Ben bid her good day. He continued on past stalls of games, clothing, toys, and various homemade wares to one of several booths hawking firearms. Some kids at the booth on the other side of the drive from the firearms stall were playing a carnival-like game where the contestant tried to toss a golf ball in a wide mouth glass from ten feet away. Various prizes hung up for display enticing passersby to try their luck. Three throws for a credit. Ben eyed the stall proprietor warily.

"You running a clean game over there, Tom?" He called across the way, with a wave and a smile.

"Yes sir, even have a scale here if you want to check."

Good, because I really wouldn't want to have to come over there and weigh your balls, Ben thought to himself, but didn't say it out loud in front of the kids. Weighted balls would throw off the kids' throw, unfairly balancing the game in the house's favor and earning more credits than fairness allowed. He made a note to have Dex stop by later and do it anyway, as he waved the gaming stall off with a laugh and turned back towards the firearms stall.

"Good morning, sir!" The proprietor called merrily. "Whatcha in the market for today?"

"Got any Apache attack helicopters back there?" Ben joked, leaning over to look around behind the proprietor.

"Fresh out, sir. Mr. Dex bought the last one," he laughed back. Dex's love for all things that went boom was well known among the Ranchers. "Name is Henry," the proprietor said, extending his hand.

Ben shook it and said, "Pleasure to meet you, sir. Been here long?"

"A couple months. Me and the wife lived in Clayton. I think the same neighborhood as C&M Actual McKnight. We knew each other casually back then, and sometimes he would bring over his deer gun for a modification or a repair he didn't want to do himself."

"*My* cousin farmed out a firearms job?" Ben asked with surprise. "Oh, just wait 'til I see him next! Speaking of which, I've got this for you today," he pointed to his AR.

Now, Dex was a gunsmith. Mike was a gunsmith. Ben's cousin Randy was a gunsmith. But Ben liked doing business with the folks at Market, not because he didn't know any gunsmiths, but because it was good for people to see him and Dex interacting with the community. It was why he bought the homemade pies instead of requesting them from Kitchen, even though Sherrie's food was damn near impossible to beat.

"Like you to take a look at one of my ARs," Ben said, setting his package down at an empty place on the table displaying firearms for sale in front of him. He slid the weapon's strap off his shoulder and popped out the magazine. He cleared the chamber and locked the bolt open, then handed it to the proprietor.

"What's the issue?" Henry asked, accepting the rifle and immediately performing his own check clearing the weapon for safety.

"The bolt doesn't stick often, but when it does it causes a misfire, and the ejected casing gets stuck in the breach."

"Hmm, that will just not do at all," Henry agreed, nodding his understanding. "Mind if I take a look?"

"That's why I'm here."

Henry popped the takedown pin and swiveled the rifle apart on the pivot pin. His brow creased as his face took on a look of concentration.

"You, uh, mill this lower receiver yourself?" he asked cautiously.

"I'll take the Fifth on that, Henry," Ben smirked.

CHAPTER 14

· FALL 2027 ·

"Rabid Chupacabra"

The Blackhawk thumped its way through the late Tuesday morning sky after lifting off from Dover Air Force Base at twenty of noon. It was a half hour drive by car in the Before but an even shorter trip of ten minutes in the air by Blackhawk.

By 11:30 a.m., all was ready for their guests' arrival at the Ranch. Four tacked horses stood ready. QRT Reserve operators and spotters with radios were everywhere disguised as training yearling horses, tending cattle, working on a "broken down" tractor and other innocuous tasks.

All coincidently, and conveniently, located very close to available cover.

And of course, all four QRTs were secretly pre-positioned at full strength. OP guards were told to be on high alert from *exterior* threats; they were not to be turned towards the interior watching the "show" that was the visitation.

Especially if they heard gunfire.

Saul had his crew use several cans of spray paint to mark a giant "H" in a circle, the universal sign for a helicopter landing pad, in the area the Blackhawk had previously landed. Sixty-millimeter shells for the M224 mortars were severely limited, so they did not bother wasting them on dialing in the range. They set the mortars' elevation using the sight units, similar to a surveyor's transom, and aiming stakes. They were confident the rounds would land close enough to compromise the helo's airworthiness. Whether or not they could ground it wasn't the problem.

The problem would come with what happened next.

The Ranch would never survive an aerial assault from military aircraft, so they considered this to be a last resort.

The helo arrived and gracefully touched down in the same, now designated, spot. Jackson and Dex were waiting at the edge of Pasture 3.

On foot.

The men had elected to walk the two hundred yards this time, reasoning at the last moment that there was no need to risk the horses spooking or some other misfeasance for such a short walk.

Johnson jumped out of the passenger compartment behind the pilots as they shut their bird down. Median and Carter followed. Major Johnson and Lieutenant Median came forward while Sergeant Carter lingered, clearly unhappily, by the helo. They shook hands with Dex and Jackson, who were unarmed.

At least to the casual observer.

The Ranchers' security was being provided by the entire complement of Ranch QRT, although neither Johnson nor Median was aware.

Glassing the entourage from the Bighouse with high powered binoculars, Saul muttered to Ben, "He looks like an asshole."

"Dex always looks like that, it's where Sage got her RBF. Or did you mean Jackson?"

"I meant the asshole with the helicopter, cuz," Saul said, lowering his binoculars to look over at Ben. He shook his head and resumed viewing the approach when he saw Ben smiling.

"The LT looks like he's got a portable radio," Ben commented. "But I don't see any weapons other than the Major's sidearm."

"Sergeant's staying with the helo, too," Saul observed. "Must not see us as a threat?"

"That's my read."

"Let's back up some," Saul suggested.

"Good idea."

They were standing by the south facing picture window in the Bighouse's Greatroom. Although hidden by the blinds and the glare of the midday sun bouncing off the window, as the delegation came closer it was possible they would be spotted observing. Not a big deal in itself, but at this point the Ranch preferred to keep what secrets they still had.

Dex was speaking animatedly to Johnson, who was clearly ignoring him. Median and Jackson both looked uncomfortable and kept exchanging looks.

"I think the Major is being rude to his hosts," Ben observed.

"Maybe we should have sent a more appropriate welcome wagon?" Saul responded.

"We talked about it, doing a tour, rolling out the proverbial red carpet. Cuz, we don't *know* what they want... seems to me the less they know the better for us."

"Agreed."

The delegation arrived at the Bighouse and climbed the stairs on the hot tub deck by the rear entrance. Dex and Jackson removed their boots while standing at the top of the landing, gesturing for the Major and his adjutant to sit in the two available deck chairs to do the same. Chris sat and began unlacing his boots.

Grandpap would approve.

His boss did not.

Johnson shot him a violent look and shook his head. Neither Jackson nor Dex commented. Dex walked to the door and opened it, allowing the door to swing inside while remaining on the landing by the stairs.

"Gentlemen, if you will? We have prepared a lunch in anticipation of your arrival. I hope you like steak, mashed potatoes, and green beans?" he said, inviting them inside where a fire could be seen from the doorway crackling with warmth and invitation.

This meeting is not going well, Median thought to himself, seated next to his boss in the Bighouse's Greatroom.

Johnson had begun by putting himself in the spotlight and launching into a lengthy lecture.

About himself.

His droning diatribe led off with him identifying himself "for the record" and then proceeding to basically bore his audience to death with his life story, seemingly unendingly detailing his long list of promotions, achievements, medals, commendations, and combat ribbons. The entire twenty minute presentation could be summarized in four easy steps and in less than nine seconds, as follows:

1. I was born into a military family.

2. At the age of majority, I joined the military.

3. I spent my life in the military doing military stuff.

4. For our purposes here, I *am* the military.

There also was an unspoken part: You all are *not* military.

Johnson emphasized this point directly at the conclusion of his walk down Self-Congratulatory Lane by stating snarkily, "I assume you all are *aware* that martial law has been declared?" The smug look on his face confirmed he knew the answer regardless of any forthcoming response.

It turned out, however, that he did not know this particular family of Ranchers.

By then, the staff present had heard way more than enough to see what was coming: an unconditional demand for them to submit to his authority. Yeah...

Good luck with that.

So, they reacted accordingly at Johnson's attempt to patronize them.

Major Johnson wasn't prepared for the collective gasps of surprise and the incredulous faces that owned the room.

"Really?" Saul asked.

"When?" Ben gasped.

"Holy shit!" Jackson blurted.

"No way!" Dex shouted.

Johnson was momentarily thrown off kilter. "How could you *morons* possibly not know?" He demanded angrily.

"Well, for one, we don't get out much, because we don't need to," Ben answered. "Plus, as you say, we're '*morons.*'"

The way he said that last word was just dripping with venom.

"And *with* that," Dex added innocently. "Our cable TV is out, and we don't have a radio."

"No Wi-Fi, either," Jackson concluded, shrugging.

Johnson looked incredulous.

His adjutant just looked scared.

"So what does that mean? 'Martial...' what did you call it?" The former attorney asked innocuously, doing his best puppy-dog eyes. In reality, all he actually managed to accomplish was a pretty convincing imitation of a rabid chupacabra.

Johnson hesitated. Were these assholes mocking him? Him? He'd had enough of their redneck bullshit.

"Where the fuck are my men?" He yelled suddenly.

"Sir, you have to understand, this is... " Saul started.

"We shot them," Ben said bluntly, straight faced and solemnly. "Of course, at the time all we knew was that six armed individuals were attempting to sneak in here at night intentionally avoiding a legitimate daytime, peaceful calling on our gate guards. We didn't know them to be soldiers under orders, but even so... We have children here, Major. Women too. Everyone here has had their lives torn apart, lost nearly everyone they have *ever* known. And you send in armed men with no warning surreptitiously under the cover of night to... what? Sell us Girl Scout cookies? What did you think would happen? What the fuck were you even thinking?" Ben raised his voice slightly with the last statement.

"I don't think you idiots get it," Johnson roared, jumping out of his chair and knocking the coffee tray over. "You don't get to..."

His tirade was cut short by a clicking sound and the feel of cold steel.

Jackson stood directly behind him with his sidearm pressed at arm's length against the back of Johnson's head.

CHAPTER 15

"Cave-Hookers"

Dex stood and slowly walked towards the Major staring him in the eye as he relieved him of his sidearm. Jackson maintained contact of the business end of his Kimber .45 against the Major's suddenly very still *cabeza*.

"No, sir. I don't think *you* do," Ben said flatly, as Dex returned to his seat.

Dex sat down and began unloading and disassembling Johnson's weapon, while never once breaking eye contact with the Major. In seconds, the experienced gunsmith had reduced Johnson's firearm to its most basic parts which Dex then casually tossed between him and Johnson. As the harmless shapes scattered and rolled across the floor sliding to a stop directly in front of the Major, Dex sat back and crossed his legs while holding Johnson's death stare.

No one spoke for a long time.

Finally, Johnson broke eye contact with Dex and stared at Ben with undisguised hatred. Ben spoke softly and gestured to the chair.

"Sit down please, Major."

The Major continued standing defiantly.

In a flash, Jackson holstered his sidearm with one hand and with the other he grabbed the collar of Johnson's uniform and yanked him backwards. Johnson collapsed ungracefully into his chair.

"The man said 'sit,' bitch." Jackson loomed over the now seated Major, who made no attempt to stand again. "You are in *our* house, and you *will* show some respect."

Ben again spoke calmly, "Continue, Saul."

"You have to understand, sir, this is our home," Saul started slowly, leaning forward and attempting to keep his rage in check.

"But *you* come *in here*, sneaking around like cowards, then showing up in your helicopters and threatening our home, our *family… my children?*" His voice got louder with each final syllable.

"Saul," Ben said gently. "In check, brother," Saul exhaled loudly in disgust and sat heavily back in his seat, collecting himself.

Turning back to the Major, Ben continued for him, although his Irish temper, too, was currently only a half a degree below his cousin Saul's.

"You have to understand, Major, we don't need you," Ben continued slowly, with an eerie calmness belying the tension in the room. "We don't want your help, and we don't need your protection. Governments everywhere have always needed people like us to produce the food to feed the country and provide all of the necessary goods. To pay taxes so the government could still spend its way into bankruptcy. Always taking for granted that the *entire* food chain begins, and as it turns out now, *ends* with the production of food. No other occupation or specialty, including yours, Major, is possible without food production; for without it every single person would spend the entirety of their waking hours in pursuit of sustenance for themselves and their family.

"People still alive today all understand that now in a way they never did before. Food production is the *original* occupation, and specialization by a group dedicated to producing food for the family, tribe, community, or city is a cornerstone of *society itself.* For literal millennia now, farms and ranches do this *for* you, so your time is free for "other" pursuits. Prostitution is not the oldest profession, Major. *Food production* is. Which is to say 'hunting and gathering,' replaced with agriculture and animal husbandry in *homo erectus's* earliest days. And we know this is fact because for the very concept of prostitution to exist, the cave-men had to *have* something to pay their cave-hookers *with*, right?"

"Now what would they have used for that? The concept of money wouldn't come about for several thousands of years later. So, what *would* have actually been valuable enough in those days to persuade hot little Betty Rubble to give that dumb dingus Barney a roll in the hay and make Pebbles?" Ben asked rhetorically, slapping back the placation tenfold over.

"Food," Dex said nonchalantly, as if he were describing the sky as being blue.

"Pimps up, hoes down," Jackson confirmed, shrugging again. The inference being, of course, that Johnson himself was the "ho" of their analogy.

Johnson just stared.

Ben let the words hang in the air for a few beats of his heart, then continued.

"So, you see Major, you need us a hell of a lot more than we need you, or the 'government' you represent. And that is only more true now."

"We have historically always provided both for ourselves, food, and protection; farms and ranches by definition being far away from the nearest towns and your concept of 'civilization.' Granted we provided protection with varying degrees of success and true justice."

"But we have nothing against the military here; in fact, before the pandemic a lot of us were supporters and had friends and family that served."

Ben intentionally omitted the number and existence of former and even current military servicemen and women who had made the Ranch their home after the Second Pandemic hit.

"The point is," Ben continued, more harshly now. "Of course, we regret the loss of your men, but it was completely avoidable. There was entirely too much death as it is before your dumb ass sent them up here to die. Your actions left us little choice. All we want is to be free and left the hell alone. Not be harassed as you most definitely have been doing; and the way you went about this was nothing short in itself an act of war… *against us.*" He let the words hang in the tension filled air.

The Major just glared unswayed.

He's not even listening, let alone comprehending, Ben thought.

The Ranch personnel in the room all realized in that moment that the meeting had been a complete failure. There was no way this bureaucratic bully could accept anything other than the giving and unquestioning execution of his immaculate orders.

But Ben was aware of something else. He had noted throughout the meeting that the adjutant was listening intently. He even thought he observed a hint of an unconscious nod of agreement at certain points.

That gave him an idea.

"I think that is all we have for you, Major, but we appreciate you stopping by. We would like to gift some beef for your men, if that would be okay?"

He waited a couple moments for a response and when none was forthcoming, Ben glanced at Saul then spoke to Jackson.

"Would you two kindly see the Major out? I'd like to speak with his adjutant alone for a moment."

Dex stood while Ben was speaking and briefly left the room whispering into his radio.

"Now wait just a goddamned minute, I am the one in charge here…" Johnson began, practically screaming.

He started to stand and say something else, but without warning Saul leapt up with a quickness and grace uncommon for his size and laid a powerful right cross on Johnson's jaw that sent him to the floor, instantly unconscious.

"Sweet dreams, bitch," Saul muttered, shaking out his wrist.

Neither Ben nor Jackson reacted at the sudden violence. Chris stiffened and looked around uncertainly. Dex poked his head around the corner, smiled, and vanished again.

"Now that it's finally quiet," Ben said to the adjutant. "I don't believe I caught your name? Chris was it?"

"Yes, sir."

"Would you care for a whiskey?"

Chris hesitated for a moment, looked at Saul, then wisely decided that accepting a drink trumped receiving a punch from the big guy every damned time. As Jackson moved towards the bar and Dex returned, Chris looked down at his unconscious, humiliated boss and then smiled weakly.

"Yes, sir, I would. Very much," he paused, looked directly at Dex and then over to Ben. "In fact, sirs, as the Major appears currently indisposed, if it isn't any trouble, I'll have the Major's too."

CHAPTER 16

· FALL 2027 ·

"Without Whiskey"

They all shared a tentative laugh at the unconscious Major's expense as Jackson poured out three double ryes and handed them around. Then he helped Saul pick the still unconscious Major up and dump him unceremoniously in a nearby recliner. Saul and Jackson excused themselves out the back door to keep an eye on the helo and its guards, glancing at Dex who nodded confirming the QRTs had all been alerted for potential action.

"Where are you from?" Ben asked.

"Dickshooter, Idaho, sir," Chris responded. "A couple hours from Boise." Ben and Dex eyed him suspiciously.

"You making that up?"

"If you don't want to tell us, just say so!" Ben laughed.

"No, sirs, it's an actual place. Look it up... oh right."

"Yeah, not sure how we'd do that today," Ben pointed out.

"Well anyway, I was sincere in what I said before about your stallion, sir. He is gorgeous."

"His name is 'Moonshine,'" Dex told him. "We figured you for a farm boy when Ben and Jackson were debriefing us on your first meeting."

"Well, I'm not really, sir" Chris began modestly, recognizing the intent of a compliment but feeling the need to be honest and transparent.

Grandpap would have told him to do so.

"Not truly, sir. I mean, not like this," He gestured towards a six-foot-wide picture window overlooking the gardens, cattle, and pastures to the southwest; and beyond where the helo waited in a fallow field. "I only visited Grandpap on weekends and holidays as a kid. Didn't really 'grow up' with it, as you say."

"I would disagree," Ben said, leaning forward and cupping his whiskey glass in both hands. The effect was one of authenticity.

"Maybe you didn't *live* there, but being there every weekend, and then some, for the duration of your formative years means you definitely *did* 'grow up' with it, by definition. I came up the same way. This house was built by my grandparents, my father's parents, when they retired from farming. I was only three or so then but even though we lived forty minutes away in Wilmington, we were here every Sunday after church for the day and stayed through dinner. I was forty years old before I moved here full time. Well, 'full time' on *my* terms, anyway. Seems whenever the heavy, backbreaking work needed to be done, it always coincided nicely with when the younger generation was visiting," Ben smiled.

Chris nodded genuinely and shared a grin. "Funny how that always happened, wasn't it? Those older generations had amazing organizational skills to always coordinate that so perfectly." They both chuckled, then sipped in silence for a few moments.

Ben was keenly aware their time was running short. The Major could recover and wake at any moment.

"You don't seem the Major's type," Ben offered, seeing if the adjutant wanted to explain.

"I was assigned to him just before the pandemic hit," Chris said. "By the time I realized what a jackass he is, we were in a full blown national and worldwide crisis. No one would have looked at my transfer request even if I had the time to file one. Plus... honestly, it was a safe place to be. The whole world was falling apart right before our eyes, and every day..." He trailed off, a haunted look cast upon his face.

"Why are you guys really here, Chris," Dex coaxed softly. When he didn't immediately respond, Dex added, "What are you after? Revenge?"

Chris shook his head vigorously. "No, sir. Well, not me, sir. That's Big... um, that's the Major's department. It was his idea to send operators up here to check you guys out, but they were only supposed to observe, not engage."

Ben and Dex exchanged a brief look, then Ben said sternly, "Well that certainly got fucked up, didn't it?"

"Yes, sir. I suppose it did. To be honest, I don't really know what the Major was after, other than answers about his missing men and information about your resources."

"What did you start to call him?" Dex inquired. "Big what?"

Chris got a sheepish look on his face and nearly whispered, "He calls himself 'Big Dick Johnson'... The 'Big Dick.'"

This admission was followed by absolute silence. Then Ben and Dex burst out laughing and Chris joined in, but this time without reservation.

"Perhaps we can help each other," Ben said, getting back to the business at hand. He nodded at Dex and handed him his empty tumbler. "I believe we could all use a refill. Chris?" Median nodded and handed over his empty glass.

Dex collected them and crossed to the bar to refresh their drinks.

Now the meeting was down to just Ben and Chris.

It was a hell of a gamble, but Ben had a good feeling about the adjutant. He seemed like a good kid and certainly knew what a douchebag Johnson was.

"Chris, would you like to discuss a trade? A bartering relationship? For example, the beef we had for lunch, there's more of it. A lot more. In the freezers, canned in jars and out there still on the hoof." He waved one hand towards the picture window overlooking Pasture 2 where dozens of Dexter cattle munched contentedly on the sweet pasture grass. "Could probably spare some fresh vegetables too, come spring. Now, I am very aware that you could come back and try to take it by force, and you might even succeed. But we both know whatever you left with would be all you would ever get. What I'm offering is a better alternative: an ongoing, mutually beneficial trade relationship."

Dex returned and handed out the whiskey. They sipped in silence for a while, savoring the amber liquid so rare these days.

Instead of answering, Chris said, "I have to say this whiskey is about the best I've ever had."

"Basil-Hayden," Dex told him. "We have quite a few bottles, might be convinced to part with one if we can make a deal."

"How is it you guys have so much of... of everything?"

Ben and Dex both laughed. "Well, it wasn't by accident. This whole pandemic thing, the writing was on the wall even before the first one.

It was bound to happen sooner or later and as it turned out, it was sooner. We were already in pretty good shape here just by doing what country people do, growing food, hunting, canning. So, by the time Townsend and then larger nearby Middletown became ghost towns—either by death or migration—we started supply runs. One of the first runs just so happened to pass by the local liquor store." Ben said with a wink and a grin. "Totally Dex's idea, though."

"Uh, actually, I think your exact words were 'Don't come back without whiskey,'" Dex shot back, laughing.

"You guys realize you just admitted to looting, right?" Chris said sternly, then relaxed and smiled, obviously playing.

"Yeah, guess we did," Ben confessed. "Want us to put it back on the shelves for no one to enjoy?"

"Hmm, don't see much to be gained by that." Chris conceded, helping himself to another sip.

A radio crackled. The helo team was getting nervous and was checking in. Chris was suddenly returned to reality and was instantly terrified.

"Oh shit, they're asking for a sitrep from the Major! What do I tell them?"

CHAPTER 17

"Sounds Like a Steal"

Ben's eyes traveled to the whiskey glass in Chris' hand. He quickly stood and walked over to the bar while saying, "Tell him the Major had too much to drink and has passed out. You got any friends there? Anyone you trust in his entourage?"

"I barely know any of them," Chris responded, clearly panicking. "Wait the Sergeant, um Carter. He seems okay."

Since only the Bighouse had stable electric power, many Ranch tasks for livestock, Ward, laundry, and construction that required power were transported, if possible, to the convenience and efficiency of being done by electrical work there. Ben collected used syringes from Stable once a week and sterilized them at the bar's small bar-ware dishwasher. He grabbed one of the recently sterilized cattle syringes and filled it from his own whiskey glass, then added more from the opened bottle, filling the large 200cc syringe to capacity. He walked over to the unconscious Major and sprayed Johnson's hair and clothes with a bit, so he virtually reeked of whiskey. Then he gently opened his mouth with the syringe. He placed it at the back of the Major's throat, pushing down his tongue while carefully tilting back Johnson's head.

Ben slowly but firmly depressed the plunger, effectively force-feeding six shots of 80-proof alcohol down Johnson's throat. Johnson reflexively swallowed and began coughing violently and returning to consciousness.

The voice on the helo's end of the radio was now losing his mind, demanding to speak with his C.O. Chris pacified him as best he could while stifling his own outbursts of laughter at the absurdity of the situation. Here they were at the end of civilization behaving like a bunch of frat boys playing pranks with alcohol.

And their lives.

"Can you get Carter on our side?" Dex asked Median quietly but urgently. The military side of Adjutant First Lieutenant Christopher Median instantly recognized the simple brilliance of the plan. Once the pilot and crew of the Blackhawk saw the beef and the Major's intoxicated condition, ol' Big Dick would have no choice but to go along with Chris's version of events, whether he remembered them or not, especially if Sergeant Carter was willing to bear witness.

Even if Johnson did recall what actually happened, his reputation would suffer even more at his incompetence at being outmaneuvered by his self-described "stupid redneck" adversaries, and his men would be dangerously demoralized even more so at finding out there would be no repeat of the fresh beef meal.

"I think so. The Sergeant doesn't have much use for Major Johnson," Median whispered back. "In fact, on the way back from our first encounter he was smiling at me the entire way. Carter *never* smiles. After we offloaded back at base, I took him aside privately at chow and asked him why. Know what he said? He told me, 'Those ranchers aren't the problem, and you know it too. In fact, they have a better chance of making it through this than we do.'"

"Okay, good. I had a feeling about both of you from our first encounter," Ben said as he pulled an ice pack from the bar medical kit and cracked it to begin the chemical cooling process. "So, you'll just have to tell the good Sergeant how his C.O. got so excited at brokering our trade agreement, he jumped up to shake hands on it and lost his balance from all the whiskey he'd greedily sucked down, fell and smacked his jaw on the coffee table, knocking himself out."

Chris nodded in agreement, then smiled and said, "I cannot tell you how hard the enlisted will laugh at that."

"We don't have a coffee table," Dex reminded him, forever the practical voice of reason.

"They don't know that. Besides, of course we don't. Big Dick fell on it and broke it, remember? Here, Dex, give this to Chris to put on Little Pecker's jaw."

"I've got to get him back," Chris said. He spoke a few words into the radio that they would be returning momentarily then used the compression roll Dex handed him next to secure the ice pack to the

Major's jaw by wrapping it several times around his head. He was barely conscious and moaned softly.

Chris stood and faced Ben and Dex. He held out his hand to Ben. "Sir, it's been a pleasure."

Ben took his hand and shook it but didn't let go.

"You didn't answer my question, Chris."

The adjutant paused, then hesitantly said, "I don't have the authority," Chris admitted. "Sure, I would do it, but..."

"What would you trade with?" Dex challenged immediately.

Good man, Ben thought, hearing the question and appreciating the timing of it. *Go for the kill. Median knows time is short, too.*

Chris thought briefly and said, "Well, I know we have a ton of extra ammunition..."

Dex and Ben exchanged a knowing look. Ben nodded and shook Median's hand again then released his grip as Dex raised his radio.

"Kitchen, Bighouse."

"Go for Kitchen," came the immediate response from one of Sherrie's staff. They had been expecting, and indeed hoping, for this message to come.

"Please immediately pack 200 pounds of ground beef as a gift for our departing guests."

"Kitchen copies." It had already been done.

"Stable, Bighouse."

"Go for Stable Actual," Sage responded.

"Prep Brutus for cart transport. Kitchen to helo in Pasture Three."

"Stable copies. ETA five." Brutus, one of the Percheron draft horses, had been tacked and hitched to a wagon nearly an hour ago in anticipation.

Ben turned back to Chris, "Tell them we're coming out now, the cart with the coolers will join us in five minutes."

Chris relayed the information to the helo crew and the relief was evident in their reply. They watched out the picture window as the Blackhawk's blades began their initial slow, lazy rotation. Then Ben turned to face Chris.

"Now listen, Chris, this is *very* important: Make sure your superior officer, when he sobers up, and *especially* all of his men, know it was the Big Dick's brilliant negotiating that provided them this meal. And that there is plenty more to come, thanks to their commanding officer.”

“And, of course, his competent adjutant.” Dex added diplomatically.

Chris nodded with a conspiratorial smile.

“So, Chris,” Ben continued nonchalantly. “One hundred rounds of .556 per pound sound about right?” Chris smiled and glanced back at his empty plate.

20,000 rounds.

They had over twenty million rounds in shipment inventory as the East Coast’s largest military supply hub, plus two million rounds in their own armory that could now be parlayed into a hell of a lot of food.

“Hell yes, sir. The Major should be very proud of his negotiation. Sounds like a steal to me.”

CHAPTER 18

"Can't Hold His Liquor"

Staff Sergeant Carter watched through binoculars with growing concern as the delegation returned to the helo across an expanse of pasture. He had heard the radio transmissions between Median and the pilots, but something just felt wrong. The Major, sitting on the buckboard sandwiched between the driver of the wagon and Median, did not look himself. His head was lolling to one side and appeared to be bandaged. Lt. Median next to him did not appear to be under duress. Shorty and his younger bodyguard were behind on horseback.

But something was wrong. Carter could just feel it but was far too professional to so much as press check his weapon, thus giving away his concerns or signaling intent. Instead, he remained extremely vigilant in his observations.

The delegation stopped about 100 yards away from the helo. A homemade wagon crafted from what looked like the bed of a Ford pickup and drawn by a single draft horse slowly made its way perpendicularly across a pasture to rendezvous with the delegation. They met up and proceeded together even more slowly towards the helo.

Carter didn't like it.

"Flight, not sure what this is, but be prepared for a hasty exfil," he whispered into the headset connected to his combat helmet.

"Feeling the same way, Sergeant," came the pilot's reply.

Carter had pleaded with the Big Dick to remain on comms during his meeting with the ranch people, but the Major had refused, his arrogance at handling "those hillbillies" having taken priority over common sense as well as military protocol. And the way he said "those hillbillies" reminded Carter of the way some of his white Georgian acquaintances had spat out another, much uglier word in reference to himself.

He had no love for Johnson personally and considered the man a buffoon with more self-love and career ambition than concern for the troops under his command. But Staff Sergeant Carter was a professional soldier, and protecting his C.O. was his express order on this mission. He had convinced the LT to take a handheld radio with him to the meeting in case of trouble.

The party approached and Carter could see several large Styrofoam coolers in the bed of the homemade wagon. His senses went on high alert, and he stepped forward for a better view. As the helo spooled up its blades, the horse-drawn procession stopped. The Ranch folks looked confused, but Lt. Median jumped out and walked back to the bed of the pickup-wagon. As he did, Johnson fell over on the wagon's bench seat and then vomited repeatedly. No one from the delegation seemed to notice.

The LT and Shorty each grabbed one end of a huge cooler and began walking the last fifty yards to the helo. The driver of the wagon cart, a big guy obviously of considerable strength, grabbed another cooler easily by himself and followed. Carter's combat mindset automatically registered that although Shorty's security man had stayed with the horses, meaning he was not anticipating a security threat, the ones approaching all wore sidearms and were coming towards his bird with who knows what concealed inside those coolers. And his C.O. appeared compromised and marginally unconscious.

Oh, hell no! thought Carter as he jogged towards them waving his arms for them to stop. His M4 rifle slapped against his chest as he moved quickly to intercept before reaching the Blackhawk. The Lieutenant and Shorty stopped and set the cooler down. The one behind followed suit. Carter noticed with some confusion that Median had a big smile on his face. As Carter slowed and approached the last ten yards at a brisk walk, his hands unconsciously returned to the rifle slung loosely across his chest. He cautiously walked up to the smiling group where the coolers sat on the ground just as the LT bent over and slid the top off the one in front.

"Hey Sergeant, how do you Georgia boys feel about hamburgers?" Chris asked with a giant shit-eating grin. "The Major is a goddamned genius! Can't hold his liquor though."

CHAPTER 19

· FALL 2027 ·

"A Horse or Your Dinner"

So, you're just trusting them to keep their word?" Saul asked incredulously. He and Jackson had returned to the Bighouse to meet with the rest of the senior staff after supervising the loading of the beef and the groggy Johnson onto the helo. It had lifted off and disappeared into the afternoon sun without further incident.

"Look, what were our options?" Ben explained patiently. "They've got enough firepower on just one of those helos we saw to level this place five times over. If they come back with the ammo, then we have established a mutually beneficial barter agreement. If they come back blazing, we have bought at least a bit of time to be as prepared as we can for it. More so than if it had happened today, at least. Because really, that could have happened either of the other times they have come here. And besides, you're the one that hit him," he added with a smile.

"He's the one that deserved it!" Saul retorted.

"No argument there, cuz. But again, what were our options?"

Silence ensued. After a moment, Ben continued. "We've got one, maybe two of them on our side. Dex and I agree the Major has a serious morale and/or personnel problem on his hands, judging by Chris's statements. If we play our cards right, this barter could be an ongoing thing. Not only do we keep the peace, and maybe even gain an ally, there's also the possibility we can get some fuel and machine parts out of it. Maybe even some bigger firepower."

"Fuck, yeah!" said Mike and high fived the East QRT operator next to him. The QRT guys in the room were now all grinning ear to ear. Ben rolled his eyes theatrically and turned to his second in-command.

"Dex, what do you want to bet they've mentally checked out of the rest of this convo already and are making Christmas lists in their heads instead?" Ben asked.

Dex appeared not to hear him but then muttered softly, seemingly to himself, "... and definitely some undermounted 40mm grenade launchers for the ARs... wait, what?" His head jerked up suddenly, and he looked at Ben questioningly.

"Man, fuck you guys," Ben laughed.

After the staff meeting, Ben spent the rest of the afternoon on his lists. If it was needed, working, not working, created to do one thing but identifying as capable of substituting as a part or system for something else, it was on one of Ben's lists.

Lists for parts needed and what they were needed for, daily lists of OP schedules, weekly & monthly task lists completed, QRT rotations, herd statistics, horse data, Armory inventory. Lists of Kitchen's equipment problems, C&Ms completed and to do projects in order of priority, maintenance schemes, planting schedules, canned food inventories, firewood cut per day and in reserve, fuel on hand... he had lists for almost everything.

But there was one list that Ben did not have.

"I need a damn list of my lists," he muttered to himself, alone in the Bighouse. Searching through legal pads, binders and assorted chaos that reigned over the Bighouse desk. "I really need to borrow Bliss for a week."

He gave up after chuckling at a list he hadn't expected to find. Reviewing it briefly, he ascertained the information contained within was still accurate and up to date. He decided to head off to Kitchen for the evening meal. He left the unexpected find on top of the Bighouse desk for Dex to review and comment. It was his favorite list of all, captioned:

"Evidence That Dex Is Gay."

The Ranch's Kitchen was housed in a six-thousand-square-foot converted pole barn next to Ward. "Neighbor Mike," as he was known to distinguish him from the QRT Actual Mike, had a spacious home and gigantic 60 x 100-foot barn adjacent to Ben's farm. Well...

Sort of.

"Used to have" would be more accurate.

If sacrificing his pole barn to the greater good of the Ranch to establish its Kitchen wasn't generous enough, poor Neighbor Mike also donated his giant two story home too, all 3,000 square feet having been converted into Ward adjacent to Kitchen.

Neighbor Mike was a hell of a team player.

He and his wife and their six zillion kids were crammed into a guesthouse overlooking his greenhouses, where Neighbor Mike served as Greenhouse Actual. "Greenhouse" was actually several one-hundred-foot-long and forty-foot-wide glass structures with tilting windows for temperature regulation in the warmer months. Irrigation was provided by a rugged solar driven pump and drip system to an assortment of cold and warm weather crops depending on the particular building and time of year.

In the six-thousand-square-foot pole-barn-turned-Kitchen was housed one of the most eclectic collections of cooking apparatus outside of a museum. In fact, several of their 1910s era wood burning kitchen stoves and ovens *had* actually come from a local agricultural museum. There were also natural gas burners, stainless steel food prep tables and trays liberated from some of the local restaurants. And of course, a wood fired brick pizza oven.

Ben had a thing for pizza.

Two thousand square feet of Kitchen were devoted to food preparation and cooking facilities. There was also a complete set of commercial dish washing and sanitizing equipment that was unfortunately going to have to wait for reliable and plentiful AC power. At present, all dish washing, utensils, baking pans, pots... *all of it* was done by hand.

Twice a day.

Kitchen employed thirty full time staff in two shifts of fifteen persons each, and had first dibs on available volunteers, absent an emergency elsewhere. It served two meals per day, morning and evening, available to everyone.

Another three thousand square feet was devoted to canned and preserved food storage, sacks of grain brought in as needed from the Farmhouse's grain tanks, dry goods, and a few DC powered refrigerators for Ranch-produced raw products such as chicken, milk, eggs, butter and of course...

That delicious Dexter beef!

There were also aging pantries for products requiring that, such as cheese. A smoker was connected to an outdoor wood-burning furnace for smoking and preserving meats, especially in the winter months.

The final thousand square feet were an open space at the front of the building near the sliding fifteen-foot doors. When separated, a thirty-foot-wide opening with a view of the sheep pens as well as the more distant horse and cattle Pasture 4 was created along the sixty-foot-long wall that had been designated for dining. Twenty plastic and wooden picnic tables sat in four rows of five. Most were usually full.

It was generally unusual at Kitchen to see anyone eating alone. A table holding six people would completely fill up with folks, even ones that rarely saw one another, before anyone would start a new table. This was not a rule, it's just how the Ranch was.

Social and very insular.

People talked about what their jobs were, what they had done that day, projects and challenges attempted, completed, or stalled. They'd talk about the weather or their kids. The kids, for their part, socialized with other kids while the grownups talked about boring grownup things. Sometimes they did coloring books, crossword puzzles or played games like "I Spy" or "Tic Tac Toe." There was an entire wall of board games and books for children and adults for long dinner meetings over business or relationships. That was one of the few times Ranchers *didn't* join a partially full table, and everyone knew what it meant when a couple of folks sat off by themselves.

Private enterprise was beginning to be discussed. People loved to talk about all that they would do *later*. "Later, when we get the power on, we can..." and, "Later, when everything calms down, we can start a business, because people will want to..."

When recovery began, when they could branch out beyond the Ranch...

Later.

Ben already knew the Ranch would look to Bighouse to create a more official currency when the time came. They couldn't just use dollars or even gold. Anyone could just run to the Outside and fill a dump truck with either. It was too common, and too easy to get, to have any real value. They would have to come up with something new, like how the Romans minted their own coins, but less prone to counterfeiting.

But it was okay; Ben had a list for that... somewhere.

He just needed to find it.

Neighbor Mike's home had been converted to the Ranch infirmary known as Ward largely because of the outdoor wood burning stove that heated it. Because of its circulator, now powered by DC batteries charged by the Bighouse's solar system, there was also a constant supply of hot water. That hot water heated Ward, Greenhouse and, just recently, now Kitchen too. It also provided hot water to Ward and Kitchen. Of course, getting hot water wasn't *that* easy these days.

There was a catch.

The circulator had to maintain its volume, so whatever one took out in hot, one had to put back in cold to be heated as it flowed through the system. Two 275-gallon Intermediate Bulk Container ("IBC") totes sat nearby to handle the refill task automatically. They were square plastic containers within a metal frame used to transport liquids around the world. IBC totes had become very popular with homesteaders and had nearly endless applications. Four of them were on a small trailer for easy transport to the Bighouse well pump for refilling.

Even better, the giant wood furnace provided heat for the even larger steam distiller that had been liberated from a local distillery. It sat in a lean-to constructed by, who else, Saul and his C&M crew. The distiller wasn't making booze anymore though.

Much to Ben and Dex's disappointment, these days it only distilled water.

A thousand gallons at a time.

That water was used for drinking and cooking. The massive amount of dead bodies left behind by the wrath of Covid-27 had passed their health risk stage to the living by now. Decomposition of the unburied was largely completed after a hot summer plus several more months, and no shortage of scavenging animals and insects.

But water contamination took many forms such as overflowing septic systems and sewers, released or overflowing wastewater treatment plants, and of course...

All of those dead bodies.

And all of that rain and contaminated water did the exact same thing. It all ran downhill to the nearest watershed and filled it. That placed the contaminated water in proximity to the underground streams and aquifers that fed the wells. And the wells were where the well pumps drew water from the... Well, you get it.

So much for clean drinking water.

Even though Ben knew their well water at the Ranch came from three confined aquifers, meaning they were protected from surface contamination by overlying layers of rock and clay, he also knew that there was no shortage of illnesses one could contract drinking unpurified water at the end of the world.

The question was, how to purify it?

Boiling it would solve some problems such as bacterial contamination. Large filters helped remove suspended particles like dirt or debris, but depending on the quality of the filter, they could even remove contaminants as tiny as 0.035 microns, cleansing the water of extremely small particles including some viruses, bacteria, and sediment.

But heavy metals, pesticides, herbicides, industrial waste, and a host of other contaminants couldn't be removed for certain by either of these methods.

So, the Ranch got creative.

Bighouse sent a special expedition to a well-known local distillery, a half hour from the Ranch, with instructions to disassemble and return with their steam distiller. The distiller had its own firebox built underneath of it to heat the water, but it just took too much time to convert 1,000 gallons of water to steam with a single heat source. So, they augmented it with the heating power of the massive outdoor furnace by adding circulator pipes from it running through the interior of the distiller, and to Kitchen and Greenhouse while they were at it.

This allowed a secondary internal heat source to cut the production time nearly in half. They could do smaller batches, but since the furnace ran as hot as it was anyway, they elected to make as much hay as possible while the sun was shining, to borrow an old farm proverb.

So once every ten days, the Bighouse's solar powered well pump transferred a thousand gallons of water to a trailer loaded with four of the same type of IBC totes. That well water was then filtered through a complete series of... weird science geek stuff. It was all "micron" this and "charcoal" that engineered by Steph's husband Brett and constructed by C&M with parts scavenged from the beef company's inventory and on supply runs.

All told, the well water ran through seventeen different filtration systems, each targeting a particular potential pathogen, before collecting in yet another array of 275-gallon totes. From there, it was pumped into the distiller with electric DC powered pumps.

Steam distilling was an old but reliable technology. The principle was simple: When water turned to steam it left almost all impurities behind it in the evaporating vessel, in this case, in the distiller. It was a closed system, so the steam had only one available direction of travel. It went through a tube mounted in the top of the distiller and traveled down into a condenser. They had settled on an old outdoor pool for the condenser's massive stainless-steel coil of tubing to run through. 'Round and 'round in the coils the steam traveled while being cooled by the surrounding cold water. As the condenser cooled the steam, turning it back into water, it then travelled outside the system to...

You guessed it.

More 275-gallon IBC totes.

This process was repeated once every ten days, on average, under the purview of Kitchen. Kitchen staff did it all, relying only on Stable's draft horses to pull the trailers. They obtained the well water, conducted the filtration process, and followed all the way through to loading the final product in the last totes and ensuring delivery to Kitchen, Greenhouse, and Ward as well as to make available for public use. Others from Custodial assisted with the cleaning processes.

It took nearly a week to distill then scrub out and sanitize the tank. The totes were cleaned with bleach water every other cycle. They averaged nearly three thousand gallons per month of distilled drinking and cooking water. A thousand gallons of well water only yielded about 950 gallons of distilled water. A person used about ten gallons of water a month on average, and sometimes it was rationed when there was an issue with the system. So, multiplied times 115 ranchers, they needed roughly 1,500 gallons per month for drinking, including tea, coffee, powdered flavor drinks, hydration for the OP and QRT guys, teeth brushing and every other internally consumable use.

The remainder of the distilled water was used by Kitchen for cooking, with a reserve set for three days. When they were down to only enough distilled water for six more meals, it was time to fire up the distiller again. But these days they had it down to a science and a ten-day schedule.

C&M, Butcher, and Ag spent an awful lot of time splitting wood to fire the distiller.

They would drop trees to season and then come back and cut them up and use one of seven wood splitters to make sure the fuel was properly seasoned to burn when needed. Wood cutting was virtually a full-time job. Danny and his Brig guards would routinely pitch in when there were no incarcerated to watch.

Everything else like washing clothes, dishes, bathing, and the like was done with untreated well or rainwater.

The cattle and horses alone consumed over 500 gallons *per day,* not to mention the chickens, ducks, geese, sheep, pigs. In summer, or when nursing, those numbers could go higher. They simply could not distill, or even merely boil, enough to meet that demand. The decision was made to collect as much rainwater as possible for them and substitute the odd pasture with well water with only a few animals, to see how they fared. So far, they had luckily not experienced any outbreaks of illness among the livestock.

Of course, cases of bottled water were a high priority on every supply run.

Add that to the appropriate list, Ben thought as he grabbed a tray at Kitchen's buffet style service and said hello to a couple Ward nurses in line ahead of him.

"Good evening, sir."

Ben broke from his mental calisthenics to see a Kitchen staffer smiling at him with a ladle of... something?

"Good evening, I'll have some of the... uh, that."

"One bowl of Cream of the That, coming up," he smiled.

"What else is on today?"

"Main course is chicken. Sherrie fried most of it, but there's also a baked option."

Who the fuck had fresh, healthy food options at the end of the world?

The Ranch did.

"Sounds good, I'll do the fried. What else?"

"New selection of cheeses just out of the aging pantry, a sharp and an American cheese. And of course, Farmhouse cheese is always here," he responded. "Oh, and we just got a new batch of bagels from Steph. She and Carol evidently had "culinary day" with Lifeskills. The class came into Kitchen and made 500 bagels and..."

"Oh! Gimme two Steph bagels! Now, now!" Ben cried excitedly.

Kitchen forked them over with a big grin and added a serving of farmhouse cheese as a topping.

"Veggies?"

"Hey..." Ben said, staring at the bagels. "What are the odds you guys could make little pizzas with these?"

"Odds are good, for tomorrow."

"Sold! Okay, let's see, some green beans, carrots, and fresh turnips."

"You got it."

Ben filled his Yeti travel mug with water from the distilled water dispenser and looked around for a table. A couple was sitting at the far side, deep in convo.

That was definitely out.

Six other tables were occupied but all full.

He sat down at the empty table next to the last full one.

"Guess this is what happens when you're late to dinner," he said to a family of six at the next table. He didn't know their names but vaguely remembered they had come in through NorthGate several months ago. Vetting by staffers had revealed that he was a machinist, now working at, unsurprisingly, Machining. She was a trained seamstress offering services privately at Market, but currently worked on Kitchen staff, probably night shift, judging by her exhausted expression.

The kids were young, maybe the oldest two were ten or twelve. The parents had the look of brisk efficiency of old hat parents but not quite able to cover up an irritable tiredness that no amount of sleep would cure. She smiled politely, he just grunted and went back to attacking his plate.

"Oh sure, 'Bighouse' is too good to eat with us," he heard Carol calling. He looked the other way and found her and Monty were finishing up and about to leave. Rita and Annie waved from their table, empty plates in front of them and engaged in conversation with another couple.

Ben waved back but stayed seated. They were leaving anyway and he was starving.

"Just the guy I wanted to see," he heard over his shoulder before the fork made it to his mouth with the first bite. He set the fork down and turned around.

"Name's Todd Jenkins," said a man of about seventy with an enormous grey beard. He stuck out his hand.

"Nice to meet you," Ben said, standing briefly to shake it. "Tell me sir, where are you from?"

"Well originally, my family came over…"

"I only ask, Mr. Jenkins, because I'm wondering if the people there like being interrupted when they are about to eat?"

"I tried making an appointment," he said defensively. "But you guys are always too busy to see me."

Ben sighed. Now it made sense.

He was *that* Jenkins.

"That" Jenkins always had a problem he needed someone to solve for him, because "you wouldn't like the way" *he* would solve it, he would say.

"Well, in all fairness, we are pretty busy with all this," Ben said, gesturing around him. "But what can I do for you?"

"I'd like to know how I can have a new criminal law added."

Ben put his fork down a second time, still unsuccessful in having it actually reach his mouth. He grabbed his tray.

"Let's you and me find a table, Mr. Jenkins."

They moved to a relatively empty area and found an open table two away from the couple talking privately. None of it would stay private for long, as Kitchen was kicking into high gear for the evening meal and a long line was forming at the serving area.

Ben didn't care, he finally got some food in his mouth.

"Oh God, that's good," he said around a mouthful of Steph bagel. "Now what's the issue, sir?"

"I bought a table from the black fella at Market last week, know who I mean?" Jenkins said, scowling.

Ben stared at him, chewing silently. Then a few moments later, after swallowing his food and most of the more combative parts of his Irish temper, he said "You do know the 'black fellas' have names now, right?"

"Well, I don't know it," he said testily, revealing much. "I bought this kitchen table from him, and the damn thing collapsed the very first day."

"Did he offer to fix it?"

"Well, yeah, but that's not the point. He owes me for what got broke when it fell apart."

"Which is…" Ben was still cramming food down his throat as fast as the conversation would allow.

"What difference does that make?" Jenkins demanded.

Ben didn't respond and focused on finishing his meal. After a few moments, Jenkins got more irritable.

"Well?"

"The difference, Mr. Jenkins, is whether you put a horse or your dinner on it."

"So, you taking his side?"

"Mr. Jenkins, how did you come to be here?"

"I was looking for you, I told you. I couldn't…"

"Not what I mean," Ben interrupted rudely. He was losing patience with this conversation rapidly.

A new criminal charge?

Really?

"I mean, how did you come to be at this Ranch?"

"What does..." Jenkins stopped himself. He stared at Ben as if that alone could alter the direction of the conversation, but Ben just ignored him and continued cleaning his plate.

The message was pretty clear.

After finally having a few moments of uninterrupted actual peace and quiet, Ben said, "Mr. Jenkins, I will expect the craftsman to replace your table, this time. But it is only warranted for the purpose for which it was crafted. In other words, if you bought a 'kitchen' table, you can expect to put dinner on it without it collapsing. Not anything heavier because it was not built for that purpose."

"What about what broke?"

"What about it?

"You're not going to make him pay me for it?"

"I am not, for two reasons. One, I don't make anyone do anything. Everyone is here by choice. If anyone doesn't like it here, they are free to leave. And two, you don't strike me as someone who has difficulty doing things, fixing things. Fairly handy, are you?"

Jenkins just stared at him.

"That's what I thought. So, you likely *knew* whatever you put on that table was too heavy for it. If it was a five-thousand-dollar table your wife bought in the Before, you wouldn't dream of treating it that way. So, tell me, Mr. Jenkins, is there some other problem you have with the person you bought the table from?"

More silent glaring.

"A man asked you a straight question, Mr. Jenkins."

"No," he grunted as he stood up.

"Good. But I *am* going to grant your request for a new criminal charge," Ben smiled amicably, then looked to make sure his plate was completely devoid of any remaining morsels that may have tried hiding. "How does 'Making A Fraudulent Accusation' sound?"

But when he looked up again, Jenkins was already gone.

CHAPTER 20

"A Little Early in the Date"

W e're returning now," Ben said into his radio. "Brutus is bringing Mike some gifts back to Stable with him." Brutus the draft horse was drawing a modified hay wagon with a driver's bench at the front and 40,000 rounds of ammunition for their AR15 and M4 rifles on the bed.

Along with a few other goodies.

Johnson had evidently elected to play ball and honor their trade "agreement" having sent Median back with another 20,000 rounds to procure another 200 pounds of that delicious Dexter beef. That was in addition to the 20,000 rounds owed from the original beef gifting. There were also some "sweeteners" included to deal with if Median could talk the rednecks into parting with some actual *steaks*.

Ben glanced at the crates of military grade C-4 plastic explosives and detonators, four crates of 60mm shells for the two M224 included mortars (they now actually had five mortars total!), six crates various of grenades, two M240 light machine guns with 1,000 rounds each and even two freaking M136 AT4 single-use, shoulder-fired anti-tank weapons! Ten brand new, still-in-the-packaging ballistic vests, also known as plate carriers, sat against the crates. Ben smiled to himself. QRT were going to absolutely piss themselves.

So was Dex.

Johnson hadn't exactly "agreed" to part with most of that. Well, technically he hadn't even been asked. He had his hands full from his

bosses trying to support the last vestiges of the federal government in an attempt to quell gigantic riots in both New York City and Philadelphia where one and a half million and several hundred thousand survivors, respectively, of the millions that had lived in each city before fought each other now over the scraps of their burned out and decaying cities. They didn't have to worry about Washington D.C., though.

D.C. was a ghost town.

One of the other few blessings of Covid-27.

Philly, in particular, was good for burning shit. Philly always burned shit. In the Before, Philly really burned shit when their teams lost. But they burned even more shit when their teams won. And by now, they were burning everything in sight.

The whole city was on fire.

But the Quartermaster back at Dover AFB was a big fan of Chris and fresh food, and an even bigger fan of the 750ml bottle of Basil-Hayden Chris had gifted to him from his last Ranch encounter.

Somehow, Chris didn't think Major Johnson would want it.

Or even needed to know about it.

So when Johnson had ordered Median to "find a few things we don't need and won't miss" to sweeten the deal for steak, it hadn't taken much convincing from Chris for the Quartermaster to lose some paperwork and change a few numbers on bills of lading and supply manifests when Chris visited the him in one of Dover AFB's giant supply depot with *his* idea for what "a few extras" for their next trade run with the ranchers meant.

When they arrived at the Ranch, Chris found that the Ranchers met him in their usual place, fifty yards off from where the Blackhawk had touched down upon a giant "H" in a circle spray painted in the field. But this time, the Ranchers came with two tacked horses in addition to those being ridden.

Median was riding Buckshot with a big smile next to Ben on Moonshine to his left. Jackson and Reno were on his right. Turned out that Carter knew horses, Chris explained, but wasn't a fan so he'd elected to ride shotgun on the wagon's bench seat alongside the cart's driver.

Ben suspected it was more of an operational security ("Opsec") decision than a genuine aversion to horses. He noticed how Carter kept looking back wistfully at Sage's mare tied to the rear of the cart as part of his constant scanning of his surroundings. Carter would know that his combat effectiveness, if needed, would be seriously compromised if he were upon an unknown horse, and a mare at that, if trouble broke out.

"You guys former military?" Median inquired casually.

This was exactly the sort of sensitive Opsec information the Ranch specifically sought to avoid disseminating. Fortunately, Ben had a plan. Even though he had thought he would be having this conversation with Johnson himself, Ben put his plan into action.

He just locked eyes with Chris as they rode and didn't say a word.

The message was clear.

"I'm just asking because of your radio lingo. It's… interesting," Median explained, backpedaling quickly.

"It works for us, and frankly the less you know about it, the better I feel. You and me, we're good, Chris. We have nothing but respect for you and the good Sergeant there, so please don't misunderstand. I appreciate the faith and trust you've demonstrated so far. In fact, your decision not to insist at our first… um, 'meeting' is exactly why you were invited back. But I am, quite understandably I think, a bit less sure about your boss, and his intentions. So put yourself in my position, responsible for the welfare of this place and all of these people. It's a little early in the date to be putting your hand on my leg."

Chris nodded his understanding and smiled but was obviously uncomfortable with the analogy.

Ben noticed that.

Perfect. Mission accomplished, Ben thought. *He won't be asking us anything else any time soon.*

"Oh, I almost forgot," Chris said, reaching into his vest.

Ben barely paid attention to him, as they passed a 1,200 square foot vegetable garden where Ranchers from Agriculture, or "Ag" as it was known, were spreading manure in preparation for next spring's planting season. Two draft horses were doing the bulk of the work. Gladius was pulling a modified moldboard three bottom plow in front, turning over huge chunks of soil. Luna was yoked to the ground driven manure spreader that used the friction of the wheels' rotation of the against the earth to drive the spreader action. The Ag ranchers smiled and waved, and Ben waived back, diverting his attention from Chris momentarily. He knew Chris was no threat at this point.

And he wanted Chris to know that he knew that.

Median pulled out two boxes of ammo from one side of his body armor, set them on the saddle between his legs, then reached into the other side and pulled out two more. He handed the boxes individually to Ben, who stuffed them in his saddlebags.

"For your Glock. And, of course, to apologize for, uh, 'breaking your coffee table,'" Median smiled. "Johnson's idea, said to tell you he was sorry he couldn't make it, but he was…"

"Way too embarrassed?"

"Way too 'busy,'" Chris said, with a wink. "But he asked me what caliber your sidearm was and I told him. The Major actually had us go on the hunt for it."

"So, does he remember what actually happened? And hey, these aren't going to blow up in my face, are they?" Ben looked at the boxes doubtfully.

"No idea, but I can tell you he respects the hell out of you guys now. You got done what you wanted and did it without humiliating him. Well, not as much as you *could* have. Hell, you even made sure *he* got the credit for making the deal he slept through! Not surprisingly, he hasn't talked about it since. Or looked me or the Staff Sergeant there in the eye either, huh, Carter?"

Carter looked over and grinned.

"That's two smiles in one week, Sergeant. One more and I'm going to stop being afraid of you," Chris said. Carter instantly dropped into a resting bitchface to rival Sage's. Then smiled again.

"Never mind him, Sergeant. Just tell the LT to put a sock in it," Ben called over to him.

Carter grinned again as he lowered and shook his head. Then it snapped back up in surprise.

"Sorry, there isn't more, but .357 SIG isn't a common round for us," Median continued, not noticing Carter's reaction.

"Or anyone else," Ben said. "That's why I got it. If the shit hits the fan, which obviously it did, 9mm, .223/556- and 12-gauge shotgun shells would be the first to go, purchased in the Before and looted after collapse. What would be left?"

"Nothing, because stores that sell ammo usually also sell guns. Looters are going to take *everything* there."

"Yeah, well as it turned out you're mostly right. But among the boxes of ammo we *did* find on our supply runs, .357 SIG was always there. Boxes of common rounds? Zero. Sometimes, you can only carry so much, so oddball rounds get left behind. But thanks!"

"Can't have too much ammo."

"Or food," Ben agreed.

"Food spoils, but ammo keeps forever," Dex pointed out, overhearing them from the top of the deck by the rear door as they arrived at the Bighouse. They dismounted and tied the horses off at the hitching post.

"Just for that, I'm not sharing our new toys," Ben told him.

"Only 'steers and queers' shoot odd-caliber ammo, and I don't see a red numbered tag hanging from your earlobe," Dex shot back. "And *with* that..." Dex's eyes traveled to the rear of the wagon, and he suddenly stopped speaking. "Wait, is that..."

"Yup, too bad I'm not sharing now..."

"Fuck THAT!" Dex shouted with excitement, bolting down the stairs to the wagon. "Are you freaking kidding me? That's... that's... holy shit!"

"Use your words," Ben coaxed helpfully. "You can do it."

Dex turned and looked at him grinning ear to ear, then his face suddenly dropped. "Wait, what did all this cost us?" He asked suspiciously.

"Well, let's just say you might want to go brush your teeth before Chris tells you," Ben said, howling with laughter at Dex's reaction to their windfall.

"Shit, I'll gargle with mouthwash too if..."

"Jesus, don't involve *me* in this! You two are just fucked in the head," Median said smiling, shaking his head in wonder. "Are you guys ever serious?"

Ben and Dex immediately and simultaneously stopped laughing, turned to face Median and stared at him coldly.

Sergeant Carter, who had climbed down from the wagon and slung his rifle casually over his shoulder, immediately froze in position, watching warily, but not moving.

Not even a twitch.

"Fuck with our Ranch family and I promise you; you *will* find out."

When they entered the Bighouse's rear door and entered the Greatroom, Dex's valid question was answered by Ben on his radio.

"Butcher, Bighouse."

"Go for Butcher Actual," Tanner said.

"Are you and Akim busy?"

"No sir, just sitting here twiddling our thumbs," came the response with a heavy sigh. Ben looked at Dex and they both smirked.

They seriously doubted *that*.

"What do y'all have on the butcher block today?" Ben inquired.

"Well, 73 is next up for freezer camp," Tanner said. "But if it were me, to eat today, I'd go with 65. He's still a little on the young side at only twenty-seven months, but he's a big boy; and he'll be extra tender."

Ben couldn't help but notice Median and Carter practically drooling at this news.

"How long to prep 65, seal him up, pack him on ice and send him home with our guests?"

"You don't need to seal him," Median and Carter said simultaneously, then exchanged glances self-consciously. Then Median explained, "Believe me, they probably already have the barbeque grills going back at base."

"About three hours, with me and Akim on it steady," Tanner replied.

"65 it is!"

"Copy that, how much to go?"

"All of him. And throw 73 in too."

Median and Carter just stared at each other, mouths dropped open. *That's got to be over 700 pounds of beef.* Chris rapidly calculated in his head. Even given Dexter's smaller size, they'd be an easy 400 pounds hanging weight. *Fifteen roasts, over a hundred cuts of various mouth-watering steaks, not to mention prime ribs, briskets... and Christ! Nearly 300 pounds of ground beef!*

"That's going to take longer."

"Estimate?"

"Well, shit, most of the day, chief."

Dex looked over at Median. "Y'all got that kind of clock? Or are you expected back?"

Chris shrugged. "I'll leave it up to the Sergeant, here; I'm good to wait. Hell, for that delicious Dexter beef, I'll shoot the turbine off the Blackhawk myself if that's what it takes to stay."

"Better get started then, we'll send you some hands," Ben said into his radio and nodded to Dex to secure a detail of assistants, known as "Ables," to help Tanner and Akim. Dex got on his radio and called for volunteers from Lifeskills and Kitchen, priority.

"Bighouse out," Ben signed off.

"What do you think, Staff Sergeant?" Median asked.

Carter looked back at him like he'd just sprouted wings. Then, with great showmanship, leaned over and set his rifle down by his chair and stretched back comfortably in the recliner. He crossed his legs, tilted his combat helmet down over his eyes and folded his hands across his chest.

"I think you should wake me when it's time for chow, LT."

CHAPTER 21

"A Sock for Larry"

Sergeant Carter smiled and sat back up as Chris informed Flight to radio back to base with the good news that they would be awhile.

"Mr. McKnight, sir, you and I have met before, sir."

"Call me 'sir' one more time, and I'm going to shove that rifle up your dickhole, Sergeant," Ben said. "And I'm guessing it'd probably fit nicely."

The senior staff had begun filing into the Bighouse when they had seen the helo arrive for the meeting and everyone tensed, except Ben. And the Sergeant.

Both were smiling.

"You and I actually have met before..." Carter started to say "sir" out of habit but caught himself and grinned widely. "You were my lawyer."

Ben stared at Carter, but recognition eluded him. Carter saw the struggle on his face and offered a hint.

"Oh, put a sock in it, Larry!" Carter fairly mimicked Ben's "court" voice. "It didn't hit me until our ride up when you said to tell the LT to put a sock in it. I knew when I saw you at our first meeting, when the LT was making an ass of himself, that I'd met you before, just couldn't place it. You look different without a suit and tie."

Recognition hit Ben and the floodgates burst open with memories like water from a punctured outdoor pool. A bullshit traffic stop downstate. A Fourth Amendment violation? Unreasonable detention, was it? As the Bighouse door opened again and several more senior staff began streaming in, Ben tried to remember.

No, that's right, there were about five Constitutional violations to at least three Amendments! Search and Seizure, Right to Counsel, Confrontation Clause.

"Oh, put a sock in it, Larry," Ben had said to the rookie prosecutor before a stunned judge in open court when the newbie lawyer had tried to justify the arrest. "What you know about this case couldn't fill a thimble."

A drug dog had "hit" on the trunk of a car driven by a black man without headlights on an hour *before* dusk. A backwoods police unit, looking for a reason, pulled him over. Then the gung-ho municipal cops attempted to coerce and threaten a confession out of an innocent and honorable man whose only true offense was unknowingly renting a car that had been used to transport a few keys of Columbian bam-bam by the previous user.

A search of the trunk had eliminated the obvious, but even after the cops had torn the rental apart and found absolutely *nothing*, to cover their embarrassment, the pissed off officers had still charged him with felony drug possession. With absolutely zero physical evidence, they just assumed he'd plead out to a lesser offense.

After all, they reasoned, he *was* black.

The charge alone had destroyed any chance for advancement in Carter's otherwise spotless military career.

According to the extremely biased police report, Carter had, even by the officers' own account, remained respectful and polite throughout his ordeal. Ben had joked with him that his only actual offense was known as "BBISC."

"BBISC? What's that, sir?" his then-client Carter had asked, confused.

"Being Black in Sussex County," Ben had responded with a smile. "They don't formally charge you with it, of course, Civil Rights Act, Equal Protection clause and all that. But trust me, for some old timers, it's definitely a discretionary sentence enhancer, and shit like that just pisses me off. That's why I said the thing about a sock for Larry. Kid didn't know shit about that, but the judge did. And I wanted the judge to know that *I* knew and was prepared to go off the rails about it if it wasn't dismissed outright. This was right after the Delaware Medical Examiner's office was in the news for weeks when it came out in a trial, to everyone's surprise, that some of the people charged with safekeeping evidence, for storing the drugs, locking up the drugs had, in reality, actually been *doing* the drugs. So, the last thing the judge wanted was another black eye for the state. Though in all fairness, I know the kid thought he was doing 'justice' by prosecuting you."

In the Before, Ben had dealt with every other client screaming racism, profiling, planting of evidence and other assorted nonsense that were the traditional staple claims of the guilty. But the facts of this particular case had been shocking to the conscious. Because of that, and the Sergeant's exemplary military service, Ben had refunded the entire fee to him after successfully having the case dismissed pre-trial, with the Court's uncompromising apology to Carter. The bear hug Ben received outside the courtroom from the genuinely appreciative Sergeant had nearly crushed the life out of him.

"Listen up," Ben said loudly, and everyone stopped talking to focus their attention. "I want you all to meet the only truly innocent man I ever represented."

"Hey!" came several playful objections from senior staff.

"You've represented nearly everyone in the room!" Jackson pointed out.

"I stand by my statement," Ben laughed. "Just look at the lot of you, criminals all!"

CHAPTER 22

"Point of Order"

A knock at the Bighouse's rear door about twenty minutes later was answered by Kitchen Actual Sherrie McKnight, who had been in close radio contact with her Kitchen staff via private channel. Brutus had been unloaded, and Median's gifts were being inventoried at the Bighouse's Barn by a group of off duty QRT who reacted to the delivery with all the poise and self-control of coked up six-year-olds on Christmas morning. Brutus had then been sent to Kitchen and returned to the Bighouse with lunch for the senior staff meeting and their guests.

Sage's second at Stable, a sweet teen girl by the name of Dee who was a former beef company intern, entered with a big Dee smile and a few of the kitchen staff, all of whom were bearing trays upon trays of steaming deliciousness. They set up a buffet style service on the bar and everyone grabbed a plate and utensils.

There were sides of mac and cheese made from wheat flour grown at the Ranch, milk and butter and cheese from the cattle; green bean casserole from ingredients grown on the Ranch, pickled beets from last spring, fresh turnips, mashed potatoes from the subterranean root cellar's thirty cubic foot potato bin.

Lt. Chris Median approved, and asked Sherrie if she could arrange for plates to be taken out to the helo's flight crew.

It was a gloriously extravagant meal for the times.

But the real treat was the fresh *beef!* Dexter beef burgers, Dexter beef steaks, Dexter beef tacos, Dexter beef and barley soup.

Chris could guess where the barley came from, as Ben explained each of the menu items, focusing on the Dexter entrees.

Christ, it's like the guy thinks he's still running a beef company and trying to sell us beef! Median smiled to himself, as Ben rattled off the benefits of Dexter cattle.

After they had eaten, the meeting came to order. As usual, hyper-organized Bliss was tapped to take the minutes. They had several matters to discuss and were already running late as everyone had remained in animated discussions and laughing with their guests after their bellies were full.

"Let's identify ourselves for the record. Ben McKnight, Bighouse command."

"Dex Horn, Bighouse command second, Machining Asset Manager."

"Mike Fuse, Quick Response Team Actual."

"Danny Powers, Brig Actual, Armory & Quarantine Asset Manager."

"Bliss Weaver, Ward Actual."

"Christy Powers, R.N, co-Asset Manager Quarantine, Ward second."

"Sage Horn, Stable Actual, Livestock Asset Manager."

"Saul McKnight, Construction & Maintenance Actual.

"Neighbor Mike, Greenhouse Actual."

"Don't you have a last name, Mike?" Ben asked.

Mike just shrugged. "Can't remember it, but I think it was something Italian?"

"Carol Butler, Lifeskills Actual."

"Sherrie McKnight, Kitchen Actual."

"Craig Jones, Kennel Asset Manager."

"Matt Simms, Custodial Actual."

"Thank you," Ben said. "And for the record, Tanner Miller, Butcher & Agricultural Actual and his second Akim Bennett are tied up preparing a couple steer for our esteemed special guests, First Lieutenant Christopher Median, US Air Force, and Staff Sergeant Marcus Carter, US Army. Gentlemen, welcome."

"Custodial?" Median inquired curiously. "Like custody? Adoptions and such?"

"No, as in "custodian," caretaking. They handle the laundry, sanitizing Ward, power washing the distiller, buildings and machines, latrine cleanliness, things of that nature. One thing all this covid BS taught us was how important proper sanitation is. Now, we have a rather immediate agenda item involving you guys," Ben gestured to the guests. "So, I expect it most prudent to begin there. First, we'd like to thank you for the unexpected new 'toys' you delivered to us. I trust you found our trade satisfactory?"

"Yes, sir," Median said. Ben noticed he seemed a bit distracted and followed his gaze to...

Sage.

It figures, Ben smiled to himself.

"Do you ride?" Sage asked him with a smile, returning his gaze.

"Let's put a sock on the flirting 'til the meeting is over, shall we?" Ben said humorously, winking at Chris but then casting her a stern look.

Remember your job here, Sage.

They both turned bright red and everyone else pretended, very poorly, not to notice.

Except Sergeant Carter.

No one could help but notice Carter's wide grin.

He loved seeing his LT embarrassed.

"I didn't mean any disrespect, sir." Chris apologized, looking guilty. He wouldn't look at Carter.

No doubt the flight home was going to be brutal for poor Chris.

"No disrespect taken, sir. Hell, no one even blames you; but let's stay on topic," a grinning Ben told him.

"Yes, sir. And yes, we are definitely satisfied with the trade, sir. The Major will be thrilled."

"And how is the good Major?"

"Well, he's been preoccupied with the riots to the north in Philly and New York. As far as I can tell he has pretty much delegated to me keeping our bartering relationship ongoing."

This was news to the Ranch. They had no information on anything happening in the rest of the country.

Or even if there still *was a* country.

"That's about the smartest move he could have made, assigning you point man on our trade relationship," Ben noted with satisfaction. "So, Chris, I have to ask, because it affects everyone here at the Ranch. Now that we know our midnight intruders were yours, how is it that the Major is just going to let that go? Not that I'm complaining, mind you."

"With 90 percent of the base MIA or AWOL, they may just as well have succumbed to the illness or disappeared like everyone else. I honestly don't know how he did the paperwork on it. I do know that Major Johnson did not have clearance to send those operators up here, and I highly doubt they disobeyed a direct order like he says by attempting to infiltrate instead of just observing. That means they were either supposed to engage, which I doubt, or complete some type of reconnaissance operation within the Ranch boundaries. Who knows? But my feeling is the Major just wants it to go away now too. He definitely overstepped his authority. And, well, frankly, you bested him with your whiskey and trade stunts. For him to come after you now would mean exposing to an already pissed off Brass all of his dirty laundry."

"What about the martial law mandate to report to relocation centers?"

"Look guys, I can't tell you what to do, but I've seen those places. You're better off here."

"We know that, Chris. I'm not asking you for advice. I'm trying to ascertain if the Big Dick is going to try to make us?"

"Again, I don't think so. We do that, we lose the food. We do something about the six operators, we lose the food. You have more bargaining power here than you realize, sir."

Ben just smiled.

No, Chris. We have more than YOU realized.

"We would like to pick your brain about the state of our great nation in a bit, if that would be okay?"

"Yes, sir. That would be fine. Do you have any special requests for our next meeting?" Median inquired, nodding, having recovered from his embarrassment.

"Mike? What do you have?"

Mike pulled out a sheet of paper. "Top of the list would be ammo for the M240 machine guns. We blew through most of it just getting QRT re-familiarized with them."

"Uh huh, and all the giggling you and your girls were doing during this 'training' didn't happen to result in any unnecessary ammo expenditures, did it?" Ben asked with a smile.

Mike looked sheepish. "Well, we might have…"

"Just take the Fifth, sir!" Carter called with a laugh from the sidelines.

"Yeah, what the Sergeant said!" Mike agreed quickly with a smile.

"Tanner asked me to mention fuel," Danny offered.

"Definitely, what do we need?"

"Tanner says we're down to less than fifty gallons diesel, twice that in gasoline as far as the tanks go. Plus, whatever is in the machinery and vehicles now."

"QRT has a security protocol for a 'fuel only' supply run, a quick in-and-out to raid the nearest gas station and syphon a couple hundred gallons from their underground tanks with the DC powered pumps on the trailered transfer tanks," Mike said.

"Well, since Tanner and Akim are absent, I feel I can speak competently for the Ag Actual and his second," Ben began. "That's damn low fuel in reserve, it will get us through winter clearing the roads, paths and then tilling and prepping for spring, or maybe it may be enough to begin planting season. But, it definitely will *not* do both. Most of the tractors and trucks are diesel, but gas is important, too, for things like chainsaws and the field pumps to drain heavy spring rain runoff. Not to mention running the generators for power to the well pump and other essentials if solar goes offline. So, Chris, we'd like a few hundred gallons of diesel and gasoline, if possible, for agricultural operations. Also, kerosene and home heating oil, if possible."

"Right," Saul said. "That was on my list too. We were able to get a couple homes heated this year running the circulators off of DC batteries with inverters. For example, at Lifeskills," Saul looked to Carol.

"Kids tend to learn better when they aren't shivering, okay?" Carol confirmed with a smile. "We had also talked about installing a wood stove in the classroom, but it takes up a lot of space and time to keep burning. And it would be distracting to the students. Oil heat is definitely better."

Median looked over at Carter, who nodded that he was making a notation on the notepad in his lap.

"We have the draft horses for Ag," Sage pointed out.

"The tractors are more efficient," Ben stated. "Brutus, Gladius and Luna are definitely valuable and an excellent backup. But they can't be everywhere doing everything at once. Nor can they operate the hydraulics required for the planters and grain drills. They also are needed to draw the wagons for anything Stable transports, such as meal deliveries, unless we make multiple and less efficient runs via bicycles. But more importantly, when spring comes, we are going to need all hands on deck and a hell of a lot of luck to produce enough food just for ourselves, let alone to trade with. No, Danny and Tanner are right. Fuel is essential. How about it, Chris?"

Median and Carter exchanged glances. Carter shrugged.

"To be honest, sir, it's not up to me," Median explained. "But I have a feeling the Major is going to say no on that one. We're spread thin as it is, and it's only because of this beef that he is trading with you at all. I don't think he would have done it for chicken or pork or string beans. I've never had beef that good. On the other hand, we have enough fuel to run a war, but we're *supposed* to. The military doesn't think of it as 'extra' or 'surplus.' Honestly, until this riot thing dropped in on us, almost no operations were taking place locally, and we hardly have any pilots or ground crew now. So, it also could be that he sees it that we can spare what we normally would have used in, say, a week, because we barely used anything at all until recently. I just don't know."

"Well, work on it, Lieutenant. You may consider reminding him that it's going to be hard to feed cattle if we don't have the fuel to plant new forage seed for the pastures that need it, harvest the grain to feed the animals and spread manure to fertilize the grass to feed the cattle. Copy?"

"Yes, sir, I do. But I'll put that into 'city-boy' lingo for him so he'll understand," Chris said with a grin. "I don't think he knows the term 'manure' or its purpose as fertilizer."

"Hard to believe, given how full of..." Saul started.

"Cuz... no," Ben warned.

"Not wrong, though," Saul shrugged.

"Um, point of order?" from Dex.

"You have the floor, sir."

"I have taken the liberty of preparing a short list of items as well." Dex smiled and looked at Bliss. She reached to her left on the sectional couch and handed Dex a three-ring binder.

Two inches thick.

Color-coded.

The following morning, the entire Ranch stopped what they were doing at 7:30 a.m. to watch the unexpected sight of an Air Force C-130 "Hercules" cargo transport plane descend overhead in a gentle corkscrew rotation. Its speed continued to slow as it straightened out over the Ranch's "heliport" designation until it appeared to actually hover like a helicopter. In reality, it had turned into the wind, extended its flaps, and maintained a slight descent, keeping its airspeed just a knot or two over stall speed. Any slower and it would literally drop to the earth like a stone.

The rear cargo door had already been lowered, and a Blackhawk thumped a wide rotation around it several hundred feet overhead, supervising the operation. Six large cylinder-shaped rolls eight feet in diameter dropped from the inside of the massive plane out the opened cargo door and into the sky about 2,000 feet above the fallow field aside Pasture 3. Static ripcords attached to the cylinders immediately pulled enormous parachutes from their rigging, and the parachutes filled with air to slow the rate of descent.

The Ranchers stared at the amazing sight.

The cylinders touched down in the fallow field with a gentle bounce or two and came to rest. The parachutes fluttered down harmlessly beside them. The C-130 powered up its throttle and the rear door slowly slid closed as the massive aircraft spooled up its turboprops and rapidly picked up speed, soon disappearing south over the horizon on its way back to Dover.

The Blackhawk hovered above for a few moments, then touched down on the circle H designated landing site. Jackson and Dex rode horses out to meet them while Sage followed in a cart drawn by Gladius. Ben watched from the Bighouse picture window with binoculars as Chris handed off several smaller items to Jackson and Dex, pointing out various specifics about them, then engaged in conversation with Sage.

"Status?" Ben called over the radio.

"Complete. We even got stabilizer, plus the couplings and connectors for attachment to our tanks."

"How'd we do?"

"Let's just say I hope Sonny, Rip and Redbull are out there doing their jobs," Dex responded, sounding stunned.

"They're the only ones you never have to remind," Ben said of the herd sires. He was as amazed at the landing of the fuel bladders as the rest of the Ranchers.

"Better hope so, we're going to need a hell of a lot of steers to pay for this," Dex responded. "We've got... let's see... Jesus, Ben! Ten thousand rounds of M240 ammo! Eleven *thousand* gallons of diesel, seven *thousand* gallons of gasoline, and thirty-five hundred gallons of kerosene! Where are we going to put it all?"

"We're going to leave it out there, away from people and buildings. But tell Sage, when she's done gawking at the LT, to have Dee start tacking up the other two draft horses and hitch to wagons with transfer tanks. We need to immediately start siphoning out and moving enough to fill the Ranch's fuel holding tanks. And have Ag fill every single machine we have to capacity, even the non-working vehicles. See if Jackson can grab a couple of his boys to assist."

"Copy the fuck out of that, bro!"

But the meeting had not resulted in all good news. After a laugh at Bliss's color-coding of Dex's itemized and ridiculously detailed Christmas list, some very important and very previously overlooked items were requested of Median. He said he would do his best, but understood fuel was the priority.

Mission accomplished on that one, for sure.

But the news of the Outside had been darker.

Much, much darker.

Scuttlebutt at Dover AFB was that the United States of America was no more. A constitutionally questionable claim of succession to the Presidency had been made by the governor of California, as well as two senators and some guy in Chicago claiming to be Obama's half-brother.

NORAD largely remained intact and operational, but supplies had to be running low, so it was just a matter of time before they had to cease operations. Most of the country's naval assets, carriers, submarines, and any craft on extended duty had come home to try to find someone in charge. Only one of the Joint Chiefs of Staff could be located. He was making noise about the prior imposition of martial law, the military control of the country, giving him the lawful right to succession of the presidency.

Just "temporarily," of course.

For its part, the rank and file of the United States' military, or what was left of it, appeared to be taking orders from anyone who could produce a reasonable authentication code, even if those orders conflicted with previous orders. National Guard operations, Air Force bases, Army bases, Fort Bragg, Marine Camp Pendleton, and the like had four different idiot bosses with four different idiotic plans.

The widely held belief was that the real danger, Median had confessed to the Ranchers at the Bighouse meeting, wasn't lack of leadership, or even bad leadership. A leader could be found to fill the void of no leadership. A bad leader could be replaced.

The real danger was *conflicting* leadership.

While succession claims were bitterly disputed among those asserting the right to lead what was left of the country, anyone could see where it was going. With no federal judiciary, and surely no Supreme Court, to resolve the dispute constitutionally, sooner or later, it was going to come down to who had the power to *enforce* their claim.

So that was what was happening now.

Chess pieces were being positioned by each prospective "legitimate interim President" to woo the military commanders onto "their" side before the final showdown.

Survival of the fittest.

National edition.

Overseas was even less certain. Riots were going on in every continent except Antarctica.

Hell, maybe the penguins were rioting there, too.

No one knew.

McMurdo had been transmitting until a month after the pandemic started, then it went silent. The last message from the only permanent US Antarctic research station was that of a resupply flight, but the pilot had had a bad cold, and they were worried.

Then silence ever since.

Europe was a mess. The density of population was now causing wave after wave of cholera, tuberculosis, and other outbreaks of disease from the literal hundreds of millions of corpses rotting away into the air and water supply. Mass cremations were underway to dispose of the dead, but that was only contributing to the illness problem and creating a new one:

As the survivors desperately attempted to solve one problem by cremating the cadavers, they got sick themselves from what diseases they were trying to combat.

Thus, the cremation fires burned out of control and spread to everything consumable around them, with no organized effort to put them out. The manpower and infrastructure to extinguish or at least control the fires didn't exist now, so tragedy bred even greater tragedy and those who could fled from the uncontrolled burns. But everywhere they went, same problem.

More cadavers. More disease. More fires.

Repeat.

Australia was dark, Africa was darker, having less original infrastructure than its neighbor Europe to the north. However, as a continent, Africa had survived *in toto* more violent wars, brutal dictators, and ethnic cleansings than anywhere else on the planet. It would take a while to bounce back, but they had this. And they knew it.

Africa was where survival had been invented.

India was also a disaster, with ethnic rivalries taking center stage according to broadcasts. New Delhi was still broadcasting radio and television, though all internet and digital services countrywide were down.

The irony of *that* was lost on no one that heard it.

And Israel… poor Israel was in the middle of an all-out, long-awaited *jihad*, and losing badly. Calls to the White House for assistance were met with the all too familiar *"the number you have reached is not in service"* message.

Asia seemed to be faring well, there were still pockets of government and towns where life was fairly normal. Mask wearing was largely second nature to the Asian cultures, so they were far ahead of the game before Covid-27 had even hit. Additionally, given all the wars and conflicts Asia had historically endured, it really was not that surprising to Ben that they fared better than relatively fat, lazy Western Civilization.

But the biggest worry was... well, a couple of anomalies. Russia had been silent. Orbiting satellites viewed by what was left of the national intelligence services showed a situation similar to Europe in most of the Russian Federation. But Moscow looked quite active and controlled, given the circumstances. Vehicles could even be seen driving around the still powered city.

And China...

China was all about business.

CHAPTER 23

"Ivan & His Wife"

Standard protocol at the Ranch from nearly the inception of the first checkpoint at NorthGate was to alert security reinforcements whenever anyone approached from the Outside. If a threat was determined, a radio call went out to sound the Ranch call-to-stations alarm bell.

The bell itself had been relocated from the corral outside of Stable to the second floor of the Farmhouse Barn so it could be heard up to a mile away. It was just an old bronze ship's bell Ben had purchased on eBay to train the horses and cattle to gather in the corral for feeding.

Whenever it rang these days to warn the Ranch of a potential threat, the livestock still got all excited, though.

Once Mike arrived at the Ranch, he and a few guys he had with him were tapped by Ben and Dex to be the Ranch's security force, known as its "Quick Response Team." In addition to firearms instruction, Mike also taught basic life support classes in the Before and did so now at the Ranch. Ben had sponsored an emergency medical class for his staff at the beef company through Mike years before, reasoning it made sense for his staff to be able to help one another. The beef company staff was thus trained in handling both small, common medical matters as well as serious, emergent ones, such as breaking bones from falling off a horse to even being gored by a bull.

It was, unfortunately, training they would all eventually need after the Collapse.

Mike was QRT Actual, meaning he was responsible for the combat effectiveness and readiness of South, East and West QRTs in addition to leading the North QRT operators. North QRT responded to NorthGate and were by far the most often mobilized, so it was composed of ten full time operators. The other squads had their own unit leaders but were comprised of only half a dozen operators each. The QRT Reserve was just a collection of Ranchers willing to substitute manpower needs on occasion or wanting to learn more about and assist with protecting themselves and their Ranch.

QRTs comprised nearly a quarter of the Ranch's total population totaling twenty-eight full time operators. That left eighty-seven people, excluding the quarantined who had not yet been officially admitted, to manage all of the tasks required for the Ranch to sustain itself. Everything from nursing, cooking, and education to food production and preservation to laundry.

QRT wasn't a bad job most days, at least not as post-Armageddon careers went. They never had to travel to Kitchen for meals, never did guard duty in an OP unless no one else could, and they definitely couldn't tell a weed from a corn stalk. Their meals were delivered by Stable folks twice a day in horse drawn cart or via bicycle with a homemade trailer, and they had meager canned, preserved or seasonally fresh provisions for cooking meals in each of their four bunk-style QRT quarters.

When peace allowed, they spent time on weapons cleaning and maintenance, routine OP spot checks, maintaining and reviewing NorthGate, SouthGate and OP reports on suspicious or acute activity, planning supply run operations and providing security for them... and of course, training. For the primary QRT force, QRT Reserve, OP guards.

Lots and lots of training.

Other times they would take riding lessons or volunteer their time for various tasks for which the departments needed spare hands, or "Ables." It was a pretty good system that ensured work was distributed among as many hands as possible, while ensuring the Ranch had maximum defensive capability at any given moment.

QRT never went anywhere without their rifles. On duty, off duty... it didn't matter. QRT rifles sat against their beds, their chairs, strapped to chests on horseback, and even sat against the wall next to the toilets when operators were inside one of the latrines.

For QRT operators, arms were always within arm's reach.

Always.

So, when Johnson's helos first came, the QRTs were nowhere to be found.

Johnson knew nothing of them, not even of their very existence. All he observed were folks in the fields running to stations that provided the nearest cover. That would have changed rapidly had there been a combat engagement, of course, but the QRTs were not going to give away their positions and whatever element of surprise they could retain unnecessarily.

And that surprise would have come with three mortars, and a little something else. All aimed within seven minutes at the helo sitting in Pasture 3 as Johnson had watched from "safety" while Median talked to Ben and Jackson on horseback. Well, *probably* aimed.

Sort of.

Kind of hard to tell when you didn't have a chance to dial it in previously. But ammo for the mortars was severely limited, and they couldn't exactly have predicted a freaking helicopter landing in the middle of any given pasture in advance.

But the QRTs' three M82A1 Barrett .50 caliber rifles with high powered scopes were on Johnson the entire time.

Triangulated.

On his freaking skull.

The mortars may or may not have hit the helo or even come close enough to compromise its airworthiness. But there was no doubt that the asshole barking orders and, at one point in his first ninety seconds on the ground, towering over a subordinate, was The Man. His actions gave the ex-military QRT guys a very clear idea of who was in charge.

And he wasn't leaving without Bighouse approval.

Whether he knew it or not.

Sure, there would have been hell to pay, but all the QRT operators knew with the other available firepower on the circling gunships, any attack at all initiated by either side was virtual suicide for the QRTs anyway. Best survival chance they could hope for lay in a "shoot and scoot" tactic: Lay down an initial barrage of the heaviest fire that they could, then abandon the heavy weapons and scatter under cover of the woods while the helo's missiles destroyed their prior firing position.

Then they would have set all three of their M82A1 Barretts on the helos' turbine engines and prayed for the best.

On the first pass of the helos during Johnson's first visit, three groups of people set out virtually unnoticed. Half of the West QRT operators with a couple decoy Ranchers drove casually down the back lane from the Farmhouse and stopped near the tree line with shovels and pickaxes and began working.

On nothing.

They also surreptitiously offloaded a single mortar and a Barrett .50 caliber into the forest next to the old farm truck, timing it for when none of the helos were positioned correctly or close enough to see them clearly.

The other half of West QRT, stationed behind Ward, merely slipped away unnoticed into the woods twenty yards away. If they had been noticed, an observer above would have seen a couple of them carrying an oddly shaped cylinder and another bearing a small wooden cart before they disappeared into the tree line.

That was not one of the mortars.

But they would have recognized a second Barrett .50 caliber being deployed in West QRT's area of operation.

A squad of North QRT, six combat operators, slipped out of the old Kintis farmhouse between NorthGate and the solar farm, using the solar panels for cover. They carried one of the mortars but remained in their north sector. Four others slid down an old game trail with a Barrett picked up from the NorthGate sniper position as they passed by.

The last mortar and Barrett M82A1 .50 caliber were in possession of East QRT, stationed at the tree line at the easternmost position of the Ranch in a cluster of several old tow campers with thirty acres of wood separating them from the Outside. A couple more campers in the abandoned looking remote area were utilized by the East OP guard staff.

The East QRT mortar crew stayed back in a shallow clearing hidden from the helo's view, but the sniper crew with the Barrett snaked all the way up quickly and quietly to the edge of the woods directly opposite the Bighouse on GCR. Their only problem was going to be shooting *past* Ben and Jackson without hitting them.

But they could, if they had to.

Fortunately, they did not have to.

Each of the QRTs learned of a NorthGate or SouthGate "Command Ivan" situation at the same time through their own radio as Bighouse briefed Mike. However, East, West and South QRTs did not respond to a NorthGate situation.

Ever.

That was what North QRT was for.

Almost no matter what.

Each QRT was assigned to defend their cardinal directions. QRT Reserve and virtually the entire Ranch would have responded to a threat a NorthGate before East, West or South QRTs would leave their posts. This was by design.

Sort of.

It was, of course, a prior incursion and an unfortunate loss of life that had resulted in this directive to assign QRTs to protect their cardinal points on the compass, so that the operators knew where they were to defend.

It had only been a coincidence, Ben was pretty sure, but several months before the directive for QRTs to stay put in their respective sectors, an altercation at SouthGate had brought all the gundogs running from all over the Ranch.

A group of about 15 armed men were making demands and threats and the three outnumbered SouthGate checkpoint guards were seriously outgunned as well. The position was not well fortified at the time since it was exceedingly rare to see anyone approach from that direction and frankly, they were all pretty new to providing security in this whole 'end of the world' thing.

So, SouthGate guards did what they assumed was the smart thing when believing a shootout was imminent: They called frantically for all available backup to come to SouthGate.

STAT.

So, all the South QRT security guys and every nearby available Rancher with a rifle or sidearm and a pulse, which was all of them, made a beeline for SouthGate.

And so did all of the *other* QRTs, absent then of specific standing orders *not* to do that. They understandably just assumed protecting the Ranch from an imminent clear and present danger was their job.

But doing so left their sectors completely undefended. To the west, there had been a couple of permanently manned OPs to watch for approaches through the dense woods, but where the fields ended and the tree line began was a quarter mile long stretch with 100 acres of woods deep behind it. From those woods, a band of scavengers had snuck in and attempted to steal food. They had probably been living farther back there for days or even weeks undetected, just waiting for an opportunity.

When caught and confronted stealing food, seven of the dozen or so bandits were killed in a gunfight.

Some ranchers that happened to be repairing a cattle fence in nearby Pasture 5 came to the defense of some of the female ranchers tending the herb garden. The women had initially noticed and called out to the intruders. When the unknown men brandished weapons, the Ranch women called for help, and then the intruders started shooting.

And it basically all went downhill from there.

In the resulting melee, one of the Ranch's West OP guards in an old deer stand was killed and a fair amount of ripe produce stolen.

That was bad.

But the entire Ranch realized it could have been much worse.

What if, Ben had argued at the emergency senior staff meeting that evening, it had instead been an organized diversion planned by experienced combat veterans to get attention at NorthGate or SouthGate while a larger precision military assault was conducted elsewhere against them?

"We were lucky it was just some starving, pathetic scarecrows. They weren't trained, properly equipped and had no supporting fire. You folks had better start understanding how the world is now, and what can happen to us here," he had pleaded.

And yet, for "scarecrows" they had still done a lot of damage—had cost lives.

"Including one of *our* people," Ben persuasively argued. And *with* that, as Dex would say, the entire event had seriously demoralized the Ranch. If West QRT had remained on station, they could have handled the secondary situation immediately and effectively, perhaps even saving the West OP guard's life.

From then on, QRTs needed Bighouse approval prior to leaving their sectors. Bighouse didn't care if they swapped operators back and forth from time to time. Ben and Dex understood the need for change of pace, the need for cross-training of sectors by combat-tested personnel, as well as the inevitable personality conflicts that came with the high testosterone nature of the job.

The end of the world made for some unique management challenges.

But above all, QRTs must be where they were assigned, and at full strength.

At all times.

Hell, infiltrators didn't even have to have harmful *mens rea* to be a threat. They could merely be carrying the Covid-27 virus.

Or even something new.

After all, it wasn't like these days they could just consult the Center for Disease Control ("CDC") website for handy, dandy helpful guidelines and color-coded risk assessment charts.

Although they saw less and less evidence of illness now in the few stragglers that appeared occasionally at NorthGate or SouthGate, or even more rarely spotted wandering through the woods by an OP, infection was still a possibility.

There was no CDC anymore.

So, all newcomers admitted to the Ranch went through a two-week quarantine to ensure they were not infected, even though symptoms of Covid-27 had manifested within a week and usually killed within two. They were fed well and occasionally got to bathe while they rested in relative safety as compared to the Outside, which was more than almost any of them wanted. So, even under armed guard 24/7, most didn't complain.

But there was another reason.

It also gave the Ranch folks, especially the guards and the "Q Nurses" assigned to the Quarantine detail, time to observe and interact with them, listen to conversations, to gauge personalities and skill sets, vet their character and alleged histories, and evaluate and test the veracity of their assertions. People would say anything when they were desperate: They'd say they were doctors or engineers believing it increased their chances of admission or at least of a meal. They'd say it even if in reality they couldn't wipe their own backside or engineer themselves out of a paper bag.

Some survivors that found themselves at NorthGate or SouthGate, whether intentionally or having come across the Ranch checkpoints completely by surprise, would offer to trade sex or tiny amounts of scavenged drugs for food. These visitors were turned away with a warning not to come back or they would be shot.

One time, a few months back, a group had arrived at NorthGate and made an offer of three children for the Ranchers' "pleasure" in exchange for a meal. The two dirty men had made a teenage girl and two small boys stand in front of them so the NorthGate guards could evaluate their suitability for the proffered trade.

The NorthGate guards had immediately radioed Bighouse with a sitrep, and were given specific, though somewhat unexpected, instructions. But being professionals doing a difficult job, they unquestioningly obeyed and complied.

"NorthGate, standby for Command Ivan and his wife in three," came the return radio transmission to NorthGate.

The visitors were then told that the Ranch accepted their offer of sexualized children, and they were told this warmly with big smiles from the NorthGate guards.

CHAPTER 24

"Ninety-Two Days"

Of course, who the Ranch really needed to show up at NorthGate and SouthGate were machinists, midwives, blacksmiths, farmers, carpenters, plumbers, welders, mechanics, construction workers, engineers, dentists, doctors, veterinarians, beekeepers...

And a decent freaking farrier.

But more than anything, the Ranch longed for a power plant engineer. With experience.

To be fair, a power plant engineer *was* a little much to hope for, but it topped the invite list by far. Everyone at the Ranch knew if they drew guard duty at a checkpoint, OP or were on the Outside on a supply run—if they heard the words "power plant" from *anyone* they encountered, they were to immediately stop whatever else they were engaged in and immediately report that finding to Bighouse.

The Kintis solar farm sat on fifty acres on the northeast side of GCR, a football's throw from NorthGate and North QRT barracks on one side and, two hundred yards away, East QRT barracks on the other. It was composed of rows and rows of high efficiency solar panels to be tied into the Phase 3 grid and run its golden harvest of life-sustaining electrical power to a substation in Townsend. It was capable of providing somewhere between five Megawatts and 7.5 Megawatts of power. But until they found a power plant engineer, it would continue to just sit there.

Useless.

It could provide enough electricity to power 1,500 homes. Only fourteen actual homes were in use within the Ranch's sanctuary boundaries and a couple outside as abandoned looking OPs. Of those, only the Bighouse had power provided from its own roof-mounted solar array.

Yet, there sat the solar farm. Within the protection of the Ranch's boundaries. Still fully operational, too.

And everyone at the Ranch knew it.

The panels faced southward and swiveled daily in unison from east to west according to some automated algorithm designed to track the sun across the sky for maximum efficiency.

How?

Because they *provided* their own *power!*

Everyone had seen them swivel.

Ben's 22kW solar system on the roof of the Bighouse provided enough electricity to keep the Ranch functional but just barely now. It was getting dangerously overloaded because it was only designed to power the 2,200 square foot home, the 900 square foot barn and the 1,800 square foot stable. But within a few months of the Collapse, they'd had to add freezers, battery chargers for hundreds of power tools, chargers for 140 radios, chargers for dozens of 12-volt batteries that the Ward, the checkpoints and some other departments like Lifeskills and Kitchen relied upon. The two 10kW batteries that collected and stored the sun's power during peak production were already less efficient than they had been just a few months prior.

And there were 5 *Mega*watts of power...

Just sitting there.

Mocking their misery.

It was maddening.

Commandeering the Phase 3 existing power lines strung overhead had been discussed, but no one was too sure how to connect them to the array without risk of electrocution either now or if the grid ever came back online.

Delaware had lost power just over three months from the first state infection of Covid-27. That meant that either the automated safety shut down protocols had gone into effect in all the area's power plants connected to the grid, including the nuclear reactor located just across the Delaware river in New Jersey, or the plant operators had enough time to perform a managed shut down before the pandemic killed the majority of the world.

In the Before, power workers had been the unsung heroes of modern living. Doctors and Firemen got all the glory, but Linemen and Power Plant operators were among the most dedicated workers in the entire world. If those folks knew, really *knew* with certainty, that civilization was ending, they would consider it their personal duty to safely shut down operations for the survivors' and their future generations' protection.

With or without authorization.

These were the guys that climbed telephone polls in electrical storms and damn near hurricane force winds.

All so Dex could continue to stream gay midget porn uninterrupted.

Without proper system close-down procedures, the risks of equipment destruction, explosions, fires, and loss of life became a near certainty. But if properly taken offline by experienced plant operations personnel in advance, whenever recovery began it was merely a matter of firing the systems back up instead of replacing or repairing multiple damaged components, or even entire buildings full of necessary infrastructure, caused by allowing the systems to malfunction and self-destruct through neglect.

Power workers were unknown superheroes.

It was just too damned bad the Ranch didn't have any.

There wasn't even anyone left to ask if connecting the solar array *could* be done.

Ninety-two days after the first case of Covid-27 was announced in Delaware, the power shut off.

Lights out.

It was one of the hardest adjustments for everyone.

Still, the Kintis' solar panels swiveled.

Everyone hated the sight.

CHAPTER 25

"Penalty of Steph"

The guards at NorthGate had greeted their new guests welcomingly and offered to allow the men to join them inside the perimeter to celebrate their trade agreement with food and booze. Ranchers within earshot of radio traffic then received some very confusing and disturbing transmissions to all that overheard them.

The two visitors offering the children heard something about some head honcho coming up there personally, some commander guy named "Ivan" and evidently even his wife!

This must be some freaky place! They assumed, and then even more hopefully, *maybe we'll even be invited to stay!?*

Some other voice radioed that he was going to call all of the "whores" into work at "Brothel" to entertain their new guests, and instructed a place called "Kitchen" to break out "the good stuff" whatever that was. But it all sounded great. The guards at NorthGate told them they'd just have a few minutes to wait until a wagon came up from "Stable" to fetch the visitors.

All over the Ranch, people looked at each other in sheer confusion. What kind of place was this? Had this really been happening all along? All this time, right under their noses and without their knowledge? Then, they looked at each other considering a new horror... with the same thought.

Jesus, and where are the kids right now?

Steph wasn't fooled for a second, but then she was as quick as they came for delegation and anticipation. She had known Ben and Dex and their labor of love building the beef company in the Before as a like-minded, self-sufficient neighbor. As soon as she'd deciphered the strange radio calls, she immediately sent her husband and Monty outside of the Lifeskills building. She didn't want her kids upset or distracted while she and Carol were conducting lessons, so she told the men what she thought was happening, and to go meet and calm, *outside* of the children's presence, the expected imminent influx of enraged and terrified parents, stepparents and adoptive parents.

There were *lots* of that last category at the Ranch.

"Tell them to come to the windows one at a time to peek inside if they want to see their children in their studies, but they will *not* interrupt the lessons Carol and I are in the middle of, under 'Penalty of Steph'," she warned sternly, and sent the men off.

She'd have made another good candidate for the Bree-Sage "Bitch-off."

Especially if the topic for debate was Lifeskills' kids' welfare.

But the welcomed visitors at NorthGate were as happy as could be to be invited inside the Ranch perimeter. Once inside, the Ranch's NorthGate guards quickly took possession of the terrified, offered children and herded them away to one side, whispering softly to them. Ranch North QRT, suddenly on-hand, casual and non-threatening, subtly directed the visiting men away from a giant conglomeration of rotating solar panels nearby that had immediately captivated the newcomers' fascinated attention.

Did they actually have power here, too? The men wondered aloud to one another. *This was amazing! And man! If we get to stay...*

The Ranch folks pointed their guests to the other side of the road from the solar array, indicating they could wait there. They were shown where, at the back of an old car sitting on the side of GCR, a couple of folding chairs the guards used were shaded from the summer sun by the opened trunk lid and some umbrella-bearing deck tables.

The visitors were also allowed to retain their weapons.

After all, there was an amicable trade in the works.

In that trunk, the visitors were informed, was the answer to their power question; they would find a cooler with ice and cold water! There might even be a bottle of brandy underneath the water bottles if they looked carefully, they were told with a wink.

They could just help themselves and sit in the shade while they waited. The horses and wagon would come retrieve them and take them for a meal and then to the air-conditioned brothel next to the boss's house.

As the men fished around in the cooler for the brandy, they didn't notice as a short guy on horseback arrived and exchanged glances with the NorthGate guards, confirming the two men by the old car were the purveyors of the offered children.

They didn't notice how sweaty the horse was in the summer heat, as if the rider had pushed his mount as hard and as fast as possible without killing him.

They didn't notice that no one on the radio had actually ordered "Stable" to tack horses or hitch wagons.

They also missed the solemn nods of the NorthGate guards in confirmation of the rider's inquiry, and turned to just in time to see that the short horseback stranger wasted no time guiding the bay gelding he was on over to where they stood by the car's open trunk.

But they did happen to notice that he wasted even less time shooting them.

CHAPTER 26

· SUMMER 2027 ·

"Pimp Actual"

Ben had been called up to NorthGate under a "Command Ivan" and was luckily already nearby volunteering for weeding duty at the Farmhouse's giant tomato garden.

Thirty-seven different varieties of tomatoes grew in dozens of seventy-five-foot-long rows. Slice tomatoes, canning tomatoes, and fifteen rows of paste and sauce tomatoes.

Ben had a thing for good pizza.

And good sauce was the key to good pizza.

Buckshot was hitched nearby being watered in the shade at the Farmhouse trough after a hot afternoon ride checking the cattle fence in Pasture 7.

The term "Command" designated a request for leadership attention, and "'Ivan" was a code for "eyes on." In other words, NorthGate wanted someone from leadership to come take a look and advise. Ben had done a double-take at his radio when he'd heard the NorthGate "Command Ivan" message and what the visitors were offering but didn't ask them to repeat it.

He didn't need to.

He already knew he was definitely going to handle this personally.

Ben had issued carefully worded instructions to the guards. All Ranch gate guards already knew if "Ivan" was bringing his "wife," it meant to play it cool, keep the visitors calm and be accommodating and enthusiastic about their arrival. Buy time and don't raise any suspicions that might set off an unnecessary firefight.

The "wife" aspect was the code for the chill, smiling and receptive conduct because, after all, who was normally the more gracious, hospitable, and social in any given couple?

The husband?

Nope, he was always off looking for the bar.

It was almost always the wife.

Ben was hoping Dex would hear the truth of his plan in his voice and play along. They had no set protocol for this specific type of thing at the time, so they'd had to improvise on the spot. But the way this was handled became the *de facto* Ranch-sanctioned procedure should it ever transpire again.

Get the kids safe.

Kill the abusers.

No trial needed.

Treating children that way was *per se* sufficient evidence of guilt.

Not very "lawyerly" of the lawyer, was it?

Then again, Ben had spent nearly two decades in courtrooms nitpicking details. No way in hell was he going to let the Ranch put those kids through that.

Dex had picked up on Ben's unspoken intent immediately back at the Bighouse, judging by his impressively creative message about readying the fictional "Brothel" and "whores" the Ranch allegedly had on standby. *That was a nice touch, Dex. Guess you're the Ranch's "Pimp Actual" now,* Ben told him by radio when it was all over.

Of course, after that, everyone called Dex "Pimp Actual" for a couple of weeks. It was indeed very funny; but it just pissed Dex off only slightly less than having missed out on participating in the execution himself. But Ben and Dex could never confront a potential threat in an uncontrolled environment together in person at the same time.

One of them always had to remain alive to lead the Ranch.

Thus, Ben, being closer and able to get "Ivan" there the fastest, had the exclusive honor of executing those kiddy diddlers personally.

It was the single most horrible thing he had ever done that he never once ever regretted. Not even a little.

That blood had washed off very cleanly.

After the executions, Ben had then dismounted Buckshot and approached the kids, still holding the smoking Glock down at his side. As Ben didn't have children, and wasn't particularly good with them, he explained as kindly as he could, under the less than ideal circumstances of having just shot two people in cold blood in front of the now even *more* terrified children, "That is what people who would do this to you deserve," Ben said softly, pointing to the corpses with his free hand.

He had then, in a brilliant yet tardy moment of self-awareness, holstered his sidearm and dropped to one knee to meet them eye-to-eye, though staying several feet away.

Damned Irish temper.

"You have been through too much, so you *deserved* to see justice done. Understand? You *deserve* to see what happens to people like that for all you've suffered. Now they will never hurt you or anyone else ever again, and that will *never, ever happen* to you again. Not here. Not *ever*. You have my word."

Although at that moment quite unsure of the sincerity of Ben's promise, eventually, in time, they *did* understand. These Ranchers weren't like those others. They weren't the bad people.

But they definitely *were* people who would not hesitate to *do* bad things to bad people. They had seen that with their own eyes.

That day.

They didn't understand why at the time. But when they did, with that realization, came another realization.

They wanted to grow up to be just like these Ranchers.

CHAPTER 27

"Divide & Conquer"

W hat the fuck is that?" the SouthGate guard yelled to the others in the hut built to shade them from rain, wind, and sun. They heard an engine winding out as it grew louder.

Something big.

Something big was coming... and *fast*.

Reports from several South OPs of a large, armored vehicle heading directly for SouthGate squawked unnoticed by the SouthGate guards as they stared directly ahead at the rising sound.

At first light, a massive DelDot triaxle dump truck roared towards them at full speed, having had a solid quarter mile straightaway on a downhill slope to build it up. In the rear of the vehicle, the dump bed was full of armed people, their heads poking up over the ends of several mattresses piled upright against the forward bulkhead.

"What the... oh, shit!"

The enormous triaxle truck had to weigh at least twenty tons because when it slammed into the SouthGate barricade of huge fallen oak and maple trees, it pushed them out of the way like toothpicks in a heavy wind as they were only a couple tons each. A few logs were violently shoved several dozen feet backwards, right into the SouthGate guard post. Heavy metal plates had been welded to all four sides of the truck's dump bed, where the windshield had been, and against the passenger doors.

The SouthGate guards immediately opened fire, but to little effect. Their rounds ricocheted harmlessly off the armored truck. The invaders returned fire, initially not hitting any Ranchers but effectively scattering them and preventing an organized resistance as they all ran for cover.

Next from the truck bed came tossed Molotov cocktails, incendiary devices crafted from a glass bottle filled with flammable liquid, and a cloth "fuse" soaked in the same liquid. When the glass container struck something hard and shattered, the fluid was dispersed and ignited, setting anything it landed upon up in flames. Not hot like thermite but still definitely hot enough to get your attention if it landed nearby.

Or on you.

In the movies, these improvised explosive devices were reliable and effective, often resulting in the desired outcome for our desperate hero in his or her last-minute bid for justice. However, in real world combat, they were just a careless moment away in the chaotic and terrifying heat of battle from doing the user's enemy's job for them.

Which was what happened.

Sort of.

As several Molotov cocktails sailed out from the elevated truck bed, an enterprising and insanely accurate former Navy SEAL happened to be on watch at Southgate. After the truck's impact and Ranchers scattered, he had sought cover behind a standing oak tree 50 yards away.

He patiently waited for his shot.

He held his AR perfectly still, braced against its large trunk as bullets zinged past or exploded the bark of the tree that was his defilade. He ignored them and was only vaguely aware of the call-to-stations alarm bell ringing off in the distance. He focused his concentration, and his aim, just above the rim of the dump bed.

Waiting.

Patiently.

Finally, he saw an arm come up.

And he saw flame.

He made a minute adjustment and pulled the trigger.

The bottle exploded still inside the dump truck bed spreading fire and death to all within. Most of the occupants did not make it out.

But those who did exited stage left in a damned hurry.

The incendiaries that had been thrown against the SouthGate guards had started fires all around the Ranch defenders. The remaining Molotovs in the dump bed—and judging by the resulting fireball there had been *a lot* of them—all exploded virtually simultaneously.

The Ranchers picked off most of the attackers fleeing the raging inferno of the dump bed. Maybe six or eight remained by the SEAL's count. He moved to new cover as he lifted his radio to offer a sitrep but never transmitted.

He caught movement out of the corner of his eye and swung his rifle around, but saw it was just armed Ranchers running his way to assist. He recognized Saul and trotted towards him.

Behind him, in the heart of the Ranch, five huge explosions.

One after another.

Rapid succession.

They shook the very ground the SEAL stood upon. He turned back towards the approximate location of the explosions and involuntarily sucked in his breath.

A giant black cloud was seen just past the Bighouse. It looked from here like the entire Ranch had caught fire.

And that fire was rapidly spreading.

That was bad.

But what was much, much worse was a new, closer sound.

Approaching.

From above?

Mortar whistle!

"Incoming!" He yelled, diving to the ground. It exploded three hundred yards away, on nearly the other side of the Ranch, somewhere just beyond the Bighouse.

Wait, was that ours or… didn't sound like ours?

The SEAL processed the scene so fast he didn't even know where the thoughts came from. He was aware only that his training conditioned him not to question what his senses knew.

And there was one thing that was absolutely certain.

He flashed back to a BUD/S lesson in basic strategy. Specifically, a 2,000-year-old work by Master Sun in his definitive collection on strategy, tactics and leadership, *The Art of War*.

Now, gunfire.

Lots of it.

Back and forth.

ARs pinging and the heavier thumping of AKs.

Then...

After a substantial passage of time, seconds, minutes... a heavy weapon, a machine gun.

American. An M240.

But is it OUR M240? Sound proximates are consistent with...

More mortar whistles, outgoing, landing now.

Farther away.

Those were definitely our M224s.

The SEAL automatically categorized and registered the small arms fire by sound as he briefed Saul on what little he knew and left him in charge of SouthGate.

"Much confusion."

"Little that's certain."

Except for what Master Sun taught two thousand years ago. Not "Divide and Conquer," as popularly expressed.

> *"Divide, then Conquer."*
> *—The Art of War 1:23*

The Ranch was under attack from the opposite side.

CHAPTER 28

"Hit"

Ben and Dex, and indeed the rest of the Ranch, heard the impact of the collision at SouthGate followed by a barrage of sustained gunfire. At that moment, dozens of vehicles rapidly approaching the tree line were reported by every East OP guard.

The invaders came streaming out of a nearby development at top speed, down the road leading out of town, and then left, straight across the field bordering the Ranch's eastern perimeter, passing within a football's throw of a now defunct cell phone tower standing its lonely watch.

The collision at SouthGate sounded like a bomb going off, with echoes repeating until drowned out by the Ranch's defensive fire. The M240 gifted to the Ranch by Median in their beef trade that was placed at SouthGate was rendered useless, buried under the rubble of the SouthGate checkpoint command post by the logs pushed into it by the invading triaxle truck. The Ranch put up a valiant fight, though two South QRT operators were killed.

Saul took charge organizing the handful of Ranchers available at his disposal after the SEAL's departure. When no additional attacks were forthcoming, and it became very clear that the real fighting was taking place at the other end of the Ranch, he sent all his reinforcements there to assist.

East QRT heard the radio traffic from the East OPs and immediately descended *en masse* toward the vehicles approaching from the east. The tree line there was the thinnest of all the woods surrounding the Ranch proper and therefore availed itself to a "blitzkrieg" type attack where speed and proximity to the objective were paramount.

Nothing was heard from Bighouse since an interrupted transmission right before the mortars exploded, but Saul was well known as senior staff and frankly...

Fuck it.

Close enough.

In the fog of war, anything could have happened.

Maybe Bighouse was knocked out entirely already?

West and South QRT split the difference. They sent the majority of their operators to the fight while keeping two of each squad at their posts.

He crept slowly, cautiously towards the lone figure keeping watch where their triaxle had breached the southernmost perimeter. The guy near what was left of the checkpoint guard station was not paying attention to the south. He was looking to the north and speaking into a radio where the Creeper's compatriots were executing a full force attack.

The Creeper was crouched in excruciating pain. First and second-degree burns covered his back where the gasoline from the exploded Molotov cocktails in the dump truck bed had singed him. His clothes had caught fire, and he'd jumped over the armored side when the bottle his brother had been throwing exploded in his hand. His brother, and everyone else in the truck bed, was dead. Several more of his people lay near the rear of the truck, shot dead by these assholes, as they tried to jump to safety.

He paused where he was, trying to ignore the pain of a thousand hot coals that felt as if they were laying all across his back, and looked around the place they were attacking.

There was *so much* here!

Too much for any one single group to possess. They were commanded to share by the laws of nature. And if they wouldn't share...

Well then, his crew would just have to take everything from them.

He continued forward, even slower, got down on his belly and crawled the last hundred feet.

Then, slowly.

More slowly.

He only had one round remaining in his Smith & Wesson
.22 revolver, and it was not a particularly accurate weapon. He
would need a nearly point-blank headshot to succeed, but then
this side of paradise, this oasis from pain and suffering of the
masses, or at least of his crew, would be completely open for their
triumphant occupation.

His target was a big guy, wearing a ballistic vest but it looked to
have already been compromised. A tear and a crack were visible even
at this range, about twenty feet, where the Creeper hid behind the
ruins of the SouthGate command post. Flames licked up between him
and his victim, and just seeing them made his pain worse.

The Creeper drew a ten-inch combat knife from its sheath and
clamped it between his teeth before silently sliding forward once more.

Dex immediately ordered Ranch's call-to-stations bell to begin
broadcasting the alarm and Ben radioed South QRT to respond to an
active threat at SouthGate.

NorthGate's M240 machine gun remained viable but was rendered
ineffective to defend the Ranch as the invaders skirted the road
to NorthGate and placed the solar array between NorthGate and
its machine gun and guards and their point of infiltration to the
northeast, assuming that the defenders would not shoot *through* the
solar array with it, nor back toward the Ranch tenements once they
passed the array.

And they assumed correctly.

Smart.

The invaders streamed across the open expanse of cut field
corn like locusts. Several individual squads could be identified in
formation, though spread out sufficiently that concentrating fire on
any one group was pointless.

Christ, there has to be at least a hundred of them! Ben thought as
he observed from the Bighouse's northern facing picture window.

"SouthGate, Bighouse, sitrep stat!"

No response.

More gunfire.

"QRT, QRT, Bighouse! Priority! All QRTs report…" but Ben never finished the order because a couple hundred yards away the quarantine tent exploded.

Five times.

"Out! Now!" Ben commanded, before the second round had even struck. Everyone scrambled out the rear door and into the chaos.

By this time, the lead invaders had crossed the field and were approaching GCR from the Kintis' side. They were still several hundred yards away from the Bighouse, and NorthGate sat helpless, as to fire on the invaders would effectively mean firing upon the solar array or the Bighouse and its occupants too.

The invaders approached the Ranch's only true road when an M224 mortar shell landed directly in front of them, blowing two into nothingness and leveling a dozen more. Most did not get up. But many did.

Those who did recovered with amazing speed.

And they kept coming.

Now with reinforcements gaining rapidly behind them.

Dex stood at the corner of the Bighouse facing the invaders approaching GCR and swarming towards where he stood. He braced his rifle against the corner of the building and began picking off individual combatants with the speed and precision of a competition level shooter.

Which he had been, a decade before.

The attackers quickly identified his position and returned fire from standing and kneeling positions.

Dex merely disappeared behind the house.

"Barn!" Ben yelled and they hot footed it fifty yards to the Bighouse Barn. Jackson and two of his guys came flying out of his home and started to meet them halfway, but Ben waved them off and pointed to the Bighouse Barn.

"Breach! Fall back!" He screamed over the deafening gunfire chasing them.

Another mortar shell landed in the Kintis' field across the road and then several more. At least one of the QRTs had gotten their shit together. But the mortars were only effective at removing a handful of intruders at a time.

Not enough.

When they reached the Barn, Ben stood outside and waved everyone through the rear door issuing commands and popping off suppressing fire to keep their pursuers at bay. Once everyone was inside, he knelt just inside the doorway, cognizant of the limited cover around him and unloaded half of a thirty-round magazine at the half dozen invaders that had reached and rounded the corner of the Bighouse from where Dex had just been firing just moments ago.

Three went down.

Three kept coming, now firing back.

And a dozen more rounded the corner in pursuit.

They all opened fire on the Barn.

One Rancher hit.

CHAPTER 29

"Twenty-Four Feet of Death"

By now, NorthGate and North QRT were done being helpless. They had fended off the few squads of invaders that had come their way around the North QRT barracks in the old Kintis farmhouse. Turns out passing an apparently abandoned two story single home that actually contained a houseful of highly trained US military killing machines on your way to harm their allies was not a particularly wise career move.

Sufficiently defended for now, North QRT left four operators to guard the machine gun and the Northgate position. The remaining six QRT gundogs wove silently through the solar array and set up an ambush where yet more of the invaders were attempting to cross the Kintis field.

They only managed to pick off a few before they were pushed back to Northgate.

There were just too many.

NorthGate, for its part, elected to fire straight down GCR past the Bighouse and directly into the dump truck at the far end of the road.

They just hoped no Ranchers were in the way. Ranchers were *everywhere* now, streaming out of the Farmhouse, Brig, and Ag buildings, Machining, even from Custodial. And they were flowing north like a wave from the homes on the south side of the Ranch, from Kitchen, from Ward.

All had rifles.

All knew the stakes.

All knew this was a "winner-take-all" fight.

But they quickly were being overrun, pushed back with concentrated fire at every skirmish at which they attempted to confront and halt the attackers. Ranchers had few options for cover and no internal defensive positions for a situation like this.

Given the devastation to the general population as a whole, no one had thought they could be invaded by more than just a few individuals. The Ranch had failed to consider what an invasion by an army the size of its own population could do.

And just *how quickly* that it could be done.

So, NorthGate made a dangerous call firing into the interior of the Ranch. But a small rise in the road just north of the Bighouse meant if they fired low, their chances of inflicting a "friendly fire" scenario and creating casualties among the Ranchers was minimized. They had to *do something* before it was too late.

Dex ran past Ben straight through the Bighouse Barn and out the opposite side through the vehicle bay door. He turned back towards the Bighouse, ran alongside the chicken coop past the bonfire pit and settled behind a six-foot-high thick stack of mature cherry wood tree trunks cut from around the head row along the pastures. Dex threw himself against the wood pile and began picking off targets starting with those closest.

And damn, they were close.

Three more down.

Less than thirty yards now separated these Ranchers from the leading edge of the invading forces, but the Ranchers had some cover here and home field advantage. They knew the terrain, buildings.

And the wood pile.

Tanner and Sage crouched beside Dex with Jackson and his two guys. All together, the six of them laid down a withering firestorm upon the invaders now caught crossing open ground with no available cover. The dozen or so invaders dove prone, rolled and returned what fire they could before succumbing to the ranchers' onslaught.

"They're down, we're clear here," Dex shouted. He turned to look for Ben, but he was still inside at the doorway covering their rear.

"North, South, and West OPs report no targets. Mike says it's a single front incursion from the northeast," Tanner repeated from incoming radio traffic. "He wants to…"

"Get Ben," Dex yelled to Sage, and she popped up with her rifle and ran to the barn. They heard the rapid, heavy thumping of the M240 as it opened up and, amazingly, saw tracer rounds streaming *down* GCR right in front of the Bighouse a hundred yards away. The continuous fire was deafening to those already deafened by the rifle fire of their own weapons.

Was that our M240 shooting into the Ranch? Had NorthGate been overrun? Has it been commandeered by the invaders?

Jesus…

But despite the cacophony of thunderous gunfire and explosions around them and the equally distracting internal explosions of thoughts and uncertainties, they still noticed when Sage stopped suddenly at the Barn's vehicle bay door.

And they all heard her scream.

A typical roadway lane was approximately twelve feet wide in a given direction of travel. Several dozen invaders were now approaching in preparation to cross both lanes of GCR, the main bulk of the offensive force moving from the Kintis side to the Bighouse side of the road.

NorthGate defenders had waited for this moment.

While the invaders appeared fanned out laterally from the perspective of the Bighouse as they approached it, when shooting straight down the roadway perpendicular to the invader's direction of travel, as from NorthGate, the invaders appeared on the road itself as a hundred-foot-long clump, filling both lanes. Or, as NorthGate's M240 machine gun saw it…

Twenty-four feet of death.

A kill zone.

In the moment, facing certain overrun by unknown, unanticipated, and overwhelming invaders, the NorthGate operator of the as-of-yet unnamed machine gun swiveled it 180 degrees around from facing towards the Outside to pointing within the Ranch itself. The remainder of the NorthGate forces with some North QRT assistance covered him from the occasional invaders still attempting to approach their position.

The NorthGate machine gunner aimed into the interior of the Ranch, straight down GCR, slid back the charging handle and unhesitatingly pulled the trigger just as the bulk of the marauders were crossing the road between the solar array and the Bighouse.

That specific M240 was later christened "Fat Lady."

And oh, how the Fat Lady sang, hitting every note with perfect pitch.

Until it was all over.

CHAPTER 30

"A Safe Space & a Therapy Animal"

Dex rushed over to where Ben lay on the barn's concrete floor. A large pool of blood was forming around the chest wound. Remembering his training from the Before—his pre-pandemic ranch basic life support classes that Ben had sponsored to prepare his staff to deal with immediate-response medical emergencies such as being gored by a bull or trampled by a spooked horse—Dex fell into well-rehearsed action.

"Sage, call Mike now!" He ordered. "Jackson, Tanner, secure our perimeter!"

"Bighouse to Medic One, report Bighouse Barn fucking stat!" Sage practically screamed into her radio while groping with her other hand for the pressure bandage in her IFAK.

The volume of machine gun fire screaming down GCR from NorthGate prevented any of them from comprehending the response heavily laden with static, but it sounded like Mike's voice. The phrase "Medic One" denoted to Mike that he was being called as a medic for an acute combat or trauma scenario and not tactically as QRT Actual.

Ben whispered something Dex couldn't make out. He leaned closer, but Ben had stopped speaking and closed his eyes.

Fuck THAT!

He immediately shook Ben violently.

"What'd you say, bro? Come on, man."

Dex initiated a sternum rub to return Ben to consciousness.

No response.

"Ben! Hey! Wake the fuck up, asshole! There's work to be done, and you're being a bitch!"

They were all panicked now.

"We need you to tell us what to do," Dex continued desperately, appealing to anything he thought would result in a response. He was scared, shaking Ben again as he began applying the pressure bandage. Dex knew that keeping Ben awake and alert was going to be the difference between him living and...

He could not even acknowledge the alternative.

None of them could.

"Bighouse, NorthGate & North QRT reporting invasion retreating! Repeat, invaders in full retreat!"

Dex ignored the radio call, so Tanner copied for him that Bighouse acknowledged. Ben still didn't respond, so Dex shook him again even more aggressively then backhanded him across the face. Ben flinched and half opened one eye. He slowly, painfully whispered another sentence.

"I can't hear you," Dex said, panicked, leaning closer.

Ben spoke slightly louder, using effort he did not know he had but this time, Dex caught the words. He rocked back and forth while he broke out laughing partly at the absurdity of the statement but mostly from relief.

"You fucking asshole, you scared the shit out of us!"

"Whaaaat?" from Sage.

"What'd he say?" Tanner inquired, followed by similar questions from the other combatants.

Dex just smiled and shook his head as he adjusted the pressure bandage tighter. "This cocksucker says he's filing a complaint with HR for the slap... and demands a safe space and a therapy animal."

CHAPTER 31

"Four Legs with Fangs"

Ben's eyes fluttered open, and he gazed around uncertainly. A frantic day of recovery and tending wounded had elapsed since the assault, but the Ranchers had beaten their enemy.

Sort of.

Many of the marauders had escaped, and bodies had littered the overrun East OPs and SouthGate command posts.

The Ranch was near certain they'd be back.

Dex and Jackson were there when he woke. Jackson called for Bliss to advise Ben was awake, and she came in moments later with another nurse bearing a food tray and two doctors.

"Sir, how are you feeling?" a doctor asked him.

Bliss roughly brushed him out of the way and clamped a hand down on Ben's head while sticking a thermometer in his mouth.

Actions, not words.

"Well, Doc, I... *guck!*" Ben started to respond but was cut off by the thermometer. She then immodestly pulled his robe up and checked for spread of the infection. Several ink marks surrounded the stitched wound, each color coded and dated.

Bliss and her freaking color coding.

If the redness spread beyond the ink marks, particularly redness of spider webbing veins, that would indicate severe and spreading infection. Fortunately, the infection did not appear to be advancing.

"Yull cul av ju puld it dow," Ben said around the thermometer. "Ith a thowder woon!"

"No talking," she admonished in a sing-song tone. "Besides, I couldn't accurately gauge your pain level without embarrassing you and then testing your reaction to humor. We *have* met before, you know."

"Uhm nah embalust."

She gave him a stern look as a warning against speaking further, then her voice took on a clinical tone as she turned to the male doctors.

"You see, gentleman, with patients like this, and this particular patient for sure, asking him to rate his pain on the typical pain scale of one to ten is useless. Patients like this will just lie to you all day long about their pain level to seem more 'manly' not understanding that as medical professionals, we *rely* upon the accuracy of such data to assist us in properly judging things like immune-response to infection, recovery status, internal bleeding and such. So, with a patient like this, we have to employ other means."

She looked down at Ben's exposed body, then turned to Dex.

"I mean, I guess you could call that a penis?"

"Uck u ah-hol," Ben said, trying not to laugh because it really, really hurt to laugh.

"How's that again?" Dex asked, smiling. It was good to see Ben laugh.

He didn't know if he'd ever see it again.

"I told you, no talking," Bliss said, suppressing her own laughter as she pulled the robe back down. "I'd put his pain level at about a five, which would probably be a nine for anyone else, but as you know, cowboys are tougher than the rest of us," she added sarcastically with an eye roll. "At least until they get the flu."

"What about the dick?" Dex asked, playing along so as not to interfere. He hoped to God it was the right call because Bliss obviously didn't know yet.

He would have to tell her later.

But he was going to have to tell Ben now.

"The dick? I'd say a solid six there," she removed the thermometer and read his temperature. "Absolutely the only time I will ever say this about you, Ben... you're 'normal.'"

"Hey, *you* try getting shot, Nurse Ratchet,"

"No thanks, I'm smarter than that," she paused.

Then she got in his face.

"And if you ever do it again, I'm going to help whoever did it to finish the job next time," he said sternly, trying to be menacing but her eyes welled up with tears, and she leaned down and hugged his head tightly, causing his injured shoulder to shift.

"You fucking asshole."

"Ow, ten! Okay, Jesus, it's a ten! Okay?"

"Shit, I'm sorry!"

"Well, it was actually only a two where your boobs were smashed against my cheek, though, but on the bright side, the other hit a new record of seven and a half," he added with a wink.

They all laughed, and the doctors asked him a couple questions and made him show them his range of motion of the injured arm with and without pain. Satisfied, they offered some treatment suggestions to Bliss as she excused them. The other nurse, now profusely blushing, set a tray of food next to his bed, and Bliss excused her as well. She scurried out of the room giggling hysterically.

Dex and Jackson recounted the events after Ben was shot, including his comments about filing a complaint with Human Resources and his demands.

"So, I'm assuming Mike arrived in time?"

"Actually, no. He's a couple rooms down with a broken leg," Jackson responded. "He was heading to SouthGate from Kitchen but then redirected when he got the call to come to us."

"Seems a stray bullet caught the front tire of his ATV near the corral. Sent him into the wood fence and flipped him," Dex added.

"He okay?" Ben inquired.

"Aside from pissing off my nurses after Doc set his leg," Bliss responded with mild disdain.

"I'm going to leave you guys to talk," she made some notes on Ben's chart. "I'll check on you in a couple hours. Try not to be an asshole while I'm gone."

"No promises."

"Yeah," Dex continued as she left. "Evidently as soon as Doc was done, Mike tried to *leave* before the cast had even set, and it took six nurses cornering him and a concession to get him back in bed."

"Concession?"

"He insisted on meeting with the QRT squad leaders immediately in his room here. Said it couldn't wait and either they came here now, or he was leaving. When the squad leaders arrived, he made them reinforce defenses," Dex answered. "Named Danny as his, now get this, 'QRT Acting Actual.' He was still under anesthesia when he did it, so go easy on him about the title. He's a bit sensitive about it now. But it's a good thing he named a second, we hadn't thought to do it."

"Half the QRT guys wanted to go out after our attackers, but Mike said no and sent Danny to make sure they repaired and shored up the perimeter defenses instead," Jackson said.

"Mike also ordered Machining to convert the NorthGate M240 and the recovered, and miraculously still operational, SouthGate M240s into 'Technicals' as used in Somalia and other countries as mobile point of fire weapons systems," Dex continued. "Tripods and hardware are being fabricated to mount them in two pickup truck beds. Anyway, Danny doubled the observation posts and ordered QRT to run three-mile spiral patrols by two-man operator teams from each unit in tandem on horseback. They didn't find anything except... a lot of dead bodies."

The last words hung in the air with foreboding.

Ben closed his eyes. He knew this conversation was coming.

"How bad?"

No one spoke.

Dex wasn't ready just yet, so he said, "I mean, it was mostly them... oh, but Craig lost three of his attack dogs, and two more had to be put down."

"Not surprising," Ben commented. "In war, two legs with guns are not nearly as terrifying as four legs with fangs. How many people did we lose?"

"No doubt. But Craig has got his hands full now getting the taste of blood out of the rest of their mouths. They want to attack everything in sight and killed one of the heifers."

"Dammit, Dexter! *How many?* How many did *we* lose?"

"Eleven," Dex responded heavily, dreading this conversation. He knew what was coming next.

Ben exhaled slowly, "Who?"

"Well, they must have thought the quarantine tent was some kind of forward command post because it took five direct mortar hits. Luckily, they were the only ones too, and they were some kind of homemade job, not like our M224s," Jackson jumped in diplomatically, glancing over at Dex to give him a moment to collect his thoughts.

"They probably hit it because they can see it from the woods beyond the checkpoint, and there's so much daily activity there," Ben reasoned.

"Mike said we should make note of that as an intentional diversion tactic going forward, except obviously with no one actually in it," Dex added, nodding his appreciation to Jackson. "He and I agree that they avoided damaging any buildings because either they wanted to move in after killing us all, or they correctly figured there might be food, weapons or supplies they wanted *in* those buildings. But they got that family of four that came in last week, the young couple that had already been quarantined for a week and a half. And four of our people, QRT guys."

Dex named them.

Jackson shifted uncomfortably.

"That's ten," Ben said.

Dex just looked at him silently.

Ben read the energy from his best friend easily.

"What aren't you telling me?"

"Rachele," Dex barely whispered. "I'm so sorry, man. She was on herd watch at the old corral SouthGate when they came, near where Mike's ATV flipped rushing to us after you got hit. She must have been terrified when the attack came, but she was still at her post when they found her. It was quick, brother. A shot to the head, probably stray. I mean, she never..." Dex trailed off.

Ben closed his eyes again, struggling to keep his focus, "What else?"

"The rest are casualties, most expected to fully recover," Jackson blurted out.

"We did have three amputations. I don't think you'd recognize the names," Dex said, relieved the terrible news was out. "There were three individuals, two arms and a leg. None of them look to survive the procedure and infection, and our first antibiotic manufacturing attempt failed as you know. So, the count will probably be fifteen total after they pass. Oh, but you'll like this," Dex continued, attempting to remove some of the sting of his previous news. "Your cousin Saul is in the next room over with Mike. He took two rounds to the chest."

CHAPTER 32

"Clean Up in Aisle Three"

Ben's eyes flew open. "Why the fuck would I like that?" he demanded angrily.

"Because he's expected to make a full recovery, probably be released tomorrow," Dex explained. "Only one of the rounds penetrated his vest. The ceramic plate must have been weakened or corrupted by the first round, and the second hit close enough to punch through. Or maybe it was a ricochet that bypassed the armor altogether. But whatever happened, it only resulted in about a two-inch penetration from the second bullet, just a .22LR. First one was probably a 7.62mm, so he was lucky. Doc got all the fragments out, and Saul's only still at Ward to watch for infection. Sherrie and their girls are with him now. Like I said, Doc thinks he'll make a full recovery. Hell, he might even come back stronger."

"Not sure that's even possible, that is one strong bastard," Jackson commented about his father-in-law.

"Well, that's good, I guess?" Ben responded uncertainly to Dex's revelation.

"That's not the part you'll like," Dex said with a smile. "The part you'll like is where your cousin, after being shot twice, then ripped the damaged plate carrier off himself and beat his attacker to death with it."

"Wait... *with the vest?*" Ben said incredulously. He started smiling, too, now.

"Yup. The guy approached him with only a knife but there was a giant pile of rubble between them, and he was burnt really badly. Saul said he was out of ammo, and the other guy must have been too. Didn't think to use his rifle as a club. He'd pulled the plate carrier off to see how damaged it was when the dude jumped him. So, he used the only weapon he had, the one in his hands. Said he didn't even know he'd actually been shot until reinforcements arrived. South QRT guys spotted the wound when they repositioned to SouthGate after the battle was over. Gave him basic first aid and took him up to the Ward, eventually."

"Eventually?" Ben inquired, cocking an eyebrow.

"Yeah. Well, I don't know if you know this about your Irish Taurus McKnight cousin, but Saul can be a bit... bullheaded. He even wanted to fight QRT for trying to make him leave his post," Dex laughed. "Actually punched one of the QRT guys when he put his hands on him to make him go to the Ward for medical attention. That big ex-Navy SEAL in your cousin Danny's squad. Know who I mean?"

"Simmons?"

"Yeah, that's him," Dex confirmed. "Evidently his shooting skills are why the south invaders weren't as big a problem, though their force was only a small fraction of what came out of the east."

Like the Huns. Ben thought silently, then said, "No, the SouthGate attack was the diversion, to get everyone here responding to that while the larger force came from the other side. Classic *Sun Tzu* strategy."

"That's what QRT said, too," Dex said, surprised. "And also..."

"That if they had split their invasion force equally and applied a 'pincer' move instead, attacking with equal strength at both points, they would have been successful and overrun the Ranch?"

Dex nodded silently.

"Maybe even the Fat Lady," Jackson acknowledged. Noticing Ben's confusion, he then explained how the NorthGate guard had saved the Ranch and that the M240's moniker derived from the classic phrase, "It's not over until the fat lady sings."

"Fucking Median," Ben mused. "If not for getting that machine gun in that trade deal, we would all be dead right now."

"No doubt," Dex concurred, as Jackson nodded in agreement.

"I want to meet him," Ben said.

"Not a problem, we can arrange that." Dex offered.

"And Simmons..." Ben tasted the name thoughtfully. "He's been here damn near since the beginning. One of our first arrivals at NorthGate. Has a wife and a little girl, the one that plays with Westin?"

"That's him," Jackson said, acknowledging his son's favorite playmate. "I don't think he and Kim are married, and the kid isn't either of theirs. She's been adopted by another Ranch family, so she has same-age siblings now. Kim rescued her after the Collapse and met him on the road. They just arrived here together."

"Is he okay?" Ben inquired.

"Well, he's got one less tooth to chew his steak with. Took it well, though. He and Danny visited Saul yesterday to clear the air and make sure he knew they weren't holding a grudge."

Jackson added, "I was there when they came by. Simmons told Saul he'd have probably done the same thing under that much adrenaline, except he wouldn't have 'hit like a bitch.' Saul damn near busted his stitches laughing. They're all buddies now."

Everyone in the room smiled and laughed despite themselves. The story was one of the bright spots of news and heroism that had come from the attack. Though Ben was just hearing it, the tale had already spread across the Ranch like wildfire.

Cornered alone as the last defender standing at the destroyed SouthGate and out of ammo, Saul had still managed to best the remnants of the attackers' diversionary assault force. He exchanged shots with one attacker, killing him with his last round, and was then jumped after removing his body armor by a second with a knife. After dispatching that one, he helped via radio to identify the actual main battlefield where the real assault force was amassing.

Bighouse was thus able to effectively reposition the brunt of the QRT forces and guide Ranch supporting fire to where they were actually needed to fend off the larger contingent of attackers. Without Saul's intel, all the QRTs would have instead been impotently led astray to SouthGate where no other attacks were forthcoming.
Or split between there and the real threat from to the northeast. Saul's dominance of his situation and level head had been a critical component to preventing the marauders' main force from completely overrunning the Ranch.

"Bet that plate carrier isn't in very good condition," Ben joked wryly.

"Either is the guy that shot him," Jackson added. "We found what was left of him in the SouthGate command post. Pretty much needed a mop to..."

"I get it," Ben said, holding up his hand. "'Cleanup in aisle three.' Why don't you go tell my cousin to wheel his crippled ass over here when he's done laying there being a bitch?"

"On it," Jackson said and bounded out of the room.

"Fucking love that kid," Ben muttered with satisfaction, watching him go.

"On an unhappier note, we have several pending civil commitment petitions with some urgency," Dex said. "I know you're not up to it, but... well, some are pretty severe."

"Let me guess, PTSD from the battle?"

"Hell, we *all* have that. No, well, maybe. I don't know. Could be trauma induced by it. Bree thinks a couple are full blown schizo and a handful of others won't eat or work or, well, even move or respond to attempts to communicate."

Ben dropped his head to his chest and shook it slowly, "Okay, convene a hearing panel at Ward the day after tomorrow. I assume they are all in The Brig?"

"Yessir," Dex responded.

"Okay, let's go over them."

CHAPTER 33

"She's Just Crazy"

In the Before, Civil Commitment hearings, and indeed all such trials, were routinely held by a Judge. But at the Ranch after the Collapse, they had to make do with what they had. Though the Ranch had acquired a couple of attorneys through post-collapse migration, they did not have a designated judge and no one, Ben or Dex included, had wanted the position.

The compromise Ben had offered was that the community itself would share in the responsibility and the public opinion liability inherent in deciding the fate of others.

They would empanel a jury.

The Hearing Board acted as a jury in deciding the actual outcome and included folks from all over the Ranch. The only criteria for Hearing Board composition were it had to include one member of the Ranch's medical community, one family member or friend of the victim, two unassociated members of the general population, and one senior staff. In practice, it was normally composed of senior staff for all but the victim's positions.

Everyone still hated jury duty.

Ben and Dex were excluded from jury participation since they served the Ranch in the most critical executive function, but one of them presided over the hearings as Chairman, lending legitimacy to the proceedings and keeping the event formal and court-like.

The proceedings, held at first just outside Kitchen, were conducted after dinner and unfolded in a trial type format. They were open to the public and followed a meal, so no one was "hangry" during the proceeding. In a world where the convenience of machines and electronics had been replaced by backbreaking physical labor and mental taxation far exceeding that routinely experienced in pre-collapse life, this was a very real concern.

The petitioner, the individual who brought the case to have the accused "civilly committed" by the Board, presented their case first. The petitioner's job was to outline for the Hearing Board participants and the observing public why commitment was necessary. They could call witnesses and present physical evidence if any were available. Sometimes there was video surveillance from the cameras but usually a few pieces of broken furniture or equipment were presented.

Destruction of Ranch property, particularly its crop production and manufacturing equipment, was particularly frowned upon as the Ranch counted on such for its very survival. Hard to spread fertilizer to grow food if someone in a rage had taken a sledgehammer to the manure spreader.

If commitment was warranted, the defendant was required to report to the Ward every day for medication, therapy or whatever else was warranted to reduce their dangerousness, including taking medication in front of Ward staff. Failure to do so would lead to banishment. There had been several banishments for medication noncompliance and dangerousness to self, others, or property.

It was the same thing society did before the Second Pandemic, only with reversal of locations. In the Before, those civilly committed were sent to the state "nut hut" for treatment. They were removed from the outside and put *inside*.

Now it was the opposite.

Now they were taken from inside the Ranch and placed on the Outside.

To fend for themselves.

Either way, the principle was the same: Remove them from harming members of the community by removing them from the community.

While they tried to take care of people that wanted and were able to help themselves, those that could be worked with, the end of the world had been the breaking point that most people hadn't known or even considered that they'd had. The survival instinct was strong in many species, but humans also are self-aware.

Sometimes, merely living isn't enough.

When all waking hours are filled with emotional torment and pain of the lost, suicides among the remaining population were quite common after the Collapse.

Sometimes even after they had reached the relative safety of the Ranch.

So, whether it was full blown schizophrenia, schizo-affective disorder, major depressive disorder, bipolar, post-traumatic stress disorder, or any other name, sometimes people for whatever reason had just had *enough*.

Criminal trials were conducted the same way but with much more serious consequences and the Hearing Board made up of only senior staff and unaffiliated persons. They had only held a handful of such events and only ever in the earliest days of the pandemic when the Ranch had accepted almost anyone seeking refuge. They had since learned to be significantly more selective of those appearing at either the NorthGate or SouthGate begging admission. Those selected for admission must bring a needed skill set and thus were generally very well behaved.

Perhaps also because the rules were very clear.

The Ranch had no police force or constabulary to conduct arrests. QRT handled what few "enforcement" matters required it. Complaints were handled via "petitions" as in the civil context. An aggrieved person would file a single page with the allegation and naming the transgressor, situation and any witnesses or victims. Bighouse reviewed the petitions and then charged the individual accordingly. The defendant was informed that he was to report to Brig, and trial would occur two days after. QRT only had to go find a defendant once; all others followed the rules.

Modern folks are so amazed that it takes only the word of one person accusing another resulting in a criminal charge. It seems they expect some sort of safeguard, a gatekeeper of sorts to prevent the innocent from being accused. But historically, this is how criminal law was always practiced. The American system largely derived from English Common law, dating back a thousand years to the Norman Conquest of 1066.

So, no "proof" to file a petition was required in the form of computer records, video evidence, or even eyewitnesses. Truth be told, some corroborating evidence was usually needed at trial unless the accuser was so well known and respected that his or her word alone was sufficient to establish guilt beyond a reasonable doubt of the accused. Since the Ranch population was not large, and true privacy was scarce, it was not hard to figure out most times who did what to whom.

Relatively minor infractions, harassment, disorderly conduct, refusing to work, and the like earned the offender a few days or weeks in Brig, smaller rations of food, followed by some of the less desirable jobs that had to be done such as weeding the gardens in the summer, digging out rocks from the fields and splitting firewood. If found guilty of misdemeanors such as theft, hoarding or unjustified assault, the punishment could include banishment of the accused... and everyone with whom they had arrived.

Leaving sympathizers behind to rot the morale of other Ranchers was a very serious risk.

Such stringent punishment alone was enough to keep most people in line and for friends and family units to police their own and solve their own problems. If they couldn't, they knew they would be risking banishment from the Ranch to the Outside where they would be on their own.

For more serious offenses, robbery, rape and murder, the accused was executed at the close of trial.

At the Ranch, there was no luxury of appeal.

Of the three doctors the Ranch began with in its first few months, one doctor, the only OB/GYN they had, was accused of raping a patient during a Ward visit for pregnancy test. There had already been one execution for a rape conviction, so everyone knew the rules. There had not yet been a robbery or a murder.

But as with all things human, it was only a matter of time.

However, the community instinctively assumed that because Ben's girlfriend Rachele was pregnant, he would commute the death sentence to ensure a healthy delivery of his first and only child.

They were wrong.

The trial concluded and the defendant was found guilty based on the testimony of the victim and her mother. The victim's boyfriend, a man she had met after the Collapse who had been fleeing the same neighborhood, sat on the Hearing Board.

The vote had been 5-0 Guilty: The required vote to sustain an execution upon verdict. The logic being if everyone agreed to the sufficiency of the evidence, execution was warranted for justice to be served.

During the trial, the victim's mother admitted being out of her daughter's room during the alleged assault but insisted her daughter would not make such a thing up. The Board pronounced the death sentence even as the defendant desperately continued to maintain his innocence. Ben had his sidearm to the defendant's head and was about to execute a sentence when a nurse from Ward came flying up in one of the Ranch's electric golf carts, nearly hitting several onlookers. Dex's longtime girlfriend jumped out waving her arms and screaming for Ben to stop.

Ben hesitated just long enough to lose his nerve. Truth was he didn't want to execute their only OB/GYN, for any one of a dozen reasons, not the least of which being what he knew from personal experience.

That blood *never* washed off.

Well, almost never.

But the law had to be followed; the community had to have faith that justice would be served, and that there would not be exceptions for personal reasons.

No one was above the law.

The very integrity of the Ranch community depended on the fair administration of justice. Thus, Ben had elected to carry out the sentence himself.

Personally.

"She's crazy!" Bliss screamed, jumping out of the golf cart and rushing toward the scene. "Stop! She's just crazy!"

During a particularly brutal influx of sick Ranchers resulting in a thirty-six-hour straight shift, Bliss' radio had lost its charge, an event which would never repeat itself again among senior staff. She went on to detail to the stunned crowd how the woman had been under psychological evaluation and treatment with the Ranch's limited psychiatric medication supplies for some time. But she had stopped taking them.

She had an illness called Pseudocyesis, a rare condition where individuals experience such a strong belief that they are pregnant that they actually manifest objective physical symptoms of pregnancy, like distended abdomen and breast changes. She had been privately treated in an otherwise unused area of Ward by Jackson's wife Bree, a clinical psychologist and mental health counselor now turned *de facto* Psychiatric Nurse Practitioner at the Ranch. The accused's condition was kept quiet so as not to embarrass her and publicize her condition.

The Ranch medical personnel had such HIPAA mandates so ingrained in them from their positions in the Before so as to be virtually incapable of realizing such a condition was a public safety threat in their new reality. Thus, it had been one of many details that had escaped attention of the Bighouse and senior staff in meetings, given their primary mission to keep everyone alive, fed, and secure from outside threats.

Not a small task.

With no shortage of details.

Because Ward's medical staff was frequently and habitually on duty serving the Ranch community, they had no idea the Hearing Board had been convened nor even that the Doc had been accused until Rachele had come in for her appointed maternity checkup and her doctor could not be located. An off duty injured Rancher with a twisted ankle had just so happened to mention during Ward's intake and triage procedure that he was on his way to attend the Hearing for the Doc when he had slipped on a cow pie and injured himself. Intake had notified Bliss because Rachele was waiting for that doctor.

Bliss had flipped the fuck out.

After this event, any time a Hearing Board was convened for either a civil or criminal matter, senior staff always made a general announcement during the evening meal at Kitchen and allowed a full day to pass for word to get around before a trial was conducted.

A mistrial was declared by Ben, as Chairman of the Hearing Board and a re-trial was held with Dex as Chairman, and Bliss and Bree testifying. The doctor, much to his relief, was found not guilty and resumed his duties. It was a mere formality and only conducted so they could identify and eradicate the kinks that allowed such a scenario to occur in the first place. After that, known close associates of the victim were precluded from serving on the Hearing Board.

That slot was now filled by a known close associate of the *accused.* Hindsight, and all of that...

A criminal trial for the mother and daughter was subsequently held on the charges of Perjury to the Board, Attempted Murder (on the doctor via the death sentence), and Disorderly Conduct, and the verdict was banishment from the Ranch. The Hearing Board recognized that the Ranch was ill-equipped to deal with such disruptive and demoralizing issues with no redeeming skills possessed by the woman nor her mother to benefit the Ranch community itself.

It was "cold" and "heartless," some grumbled in the aftermath, but most Ranchers understood they simply did not have the resources to accommodate the complex psychological trauma of the woman. And all of the Ranch men were keenly aware that they could be the one next accused. The women were all aware that their men, brothers or sons could be next accused, too.

The boyfriend testified at the second trial as to what he knew about her being pregnant. It was all she ever talked about, bordering on obsession. Whether he was telling the truth or merely attempting to avoid the fate of banishment with the victim and her mother was unknown, but the Board deemed him credible.

Dex also presided over the second Hearing as Chairman, and upon his motion for clemency for the boyfriend, the Board voted unanimously to spare him from banishment. He was a skilled mechanic, a hard worker and by all vicarious accounts was completely ignorant of the alleged victim's mental condition. She seemed normal to him, truly to them all, in every other way.

But it also came out during questioning by the second Board that the mother knew of her daughter's condition and thus had lied to the entire community to protect her daughter's reputation.

That choice had cost both of them dearly, but had very nearly cost the doctor his life.

Ranch civil commitment hearings were born that day.

CHAPTER 34

"The Community v. Laura Light"

et's begin," Dex said from his seated position in the center of the plastic folding table. "First is the matter of The Community v. Laura Light. A civil commitment hearing."

To his left were three members of the Hearing Board, and to his right the other two. A seventh unofficial member of the board sat alone at a smaller table nearby with an old laptop computer taking notes to create a record of the proceeding. There were about thirty Ranchers in attendance, all off duty from their responsibilities.

"The Board members will identify themselves for the record."

"Saul McKnight, Construction & Maintenance Actual."

"Danny Powers, Brig Actual, South QRT squad leader."

After several tours in Iraq, Ben's cousin Danny was a natural to lead one of the Quick Response Teams. A mountain of a man with an incongruously pleasant personality and quick to smile, he had excelled in his role as a military police sergeant and also served the Ranch as Brig Actual, an "Actual" being the person in charge of whatever came immediately prior. In this case, Danny was the individual in charge of the Brig: the Brig Actual. As such, he and all other Actuals answered only to Ben and Dex.

Danny's wife Christy and their two early teen children had been surprisingly late arrivals to the Ranch. Danny had confided in Ben after the family's arrival and during their quarantine that he had wanted to leave their Middletown home sooner, but Christy was adamant about not exposing the children to potential pandemic infection and insisted they stay where they had been safe so far. It made sense, and Ben couldn't fault them for their prudence even though he would have personally preferred that they arrived much sooner.

So, the family had waited it out, barricaded inside their house until the last scrap of food was gone. Only then did they make the potentially perilous, but ultimately uneventful, fifteen-mile trip through a dead world to the Ranch. Ben was overjoyed when NorthGate had reported their unexpected arrival.

"John Light, Ag worker, husband of the accused."

"Kim Nguyen, East OP night shift."

Kim was a former Army recruit who had assisted in determining the placement of the original observation posts in the northern sector of the Ranch. Saul and his construction team had erected them at the strategic points she and QRT had determined to monitor potential threats approaching or near the Ranch. From the North OP, a sentry in a camouflaged tree stand could see up to a mile away along Caldwell Corner Road which intersected GCR in an X-type crossing to the north.

"Bliss Weaver, Ward Actual."

"Wait," the accused, Laura, blurted out. "The Ward is run by a *nurse?* Why not one of the doctors?"

"Because we prefer to actually get things done here," Dex responded briskly. "Nurses know more about a patient's personality, idiosyncrasies, acute symptoms and the specifics of their general condition and spirits than any doctor ever will. And frankly, having doctors answer to a nurse has created an *entirely* different standard in patient care, one that we are damned proud of. Doctors actually have to think about what they do now that it isn't all about proper procedure for billing Medicare. And there will not be any more interruptions during the Hearing. You will have your opportunity to address the Board at the proper time."

Dex hated this. Meetings, ritual, rules... he silently longed for some grease and an engineering challenge. He wished Ben were around to break something so he could fix it instead of doing this crap.

Ben and his Irish temper were always good for that.

But this had to be done, and Ben was still at Ward currently fighting a possible opportunistic infection incurred during an ill-advised hiatus from his recovery room. But Dex couldn't blame him for that. He understood Ben's need to get eyes on the Ranch, to see firsthand how its people, livestock and current operations were fairing, especially immediately after the attack.

Frankly, Dex knew he would likely have done the same thing. Managing the Ranch was more than a full-time job. It was a daily imperative requiring multiple competent people to execute its various operations effectively.

There was no time for personal problems.

The infection wasn't serious... yet. But Dex was still legitimately concerned and not in the mood for interruptions. Additionally, Sage had reported her mare was sick and the Ranch's only vet was with her now. Dex intended to spend the remainder of the day after the hearing helping the vet and his daughter support the mare's recovery.

If nothing else happens... he thought.

"Who brings this Petition?" Dex asked.

"I do," responded Laura's mother.

"Let the record reflect that the petition is brought by the respondent's mother, Janice Lowe. Call your first witness, Ms. Lowe."

"Petitioner calls Dr. McKnight."

"Doctor, please take the witness stand and raise your right hand," Dex instructed. Bree took her seat in the witness box constructed of pallets and finished with an attractive plywood veneer. She raised her right hand.

"State your name for the record."

"Dr. Bree McKnight."

"Dr. McKnight, would you prefer to swear or affirm?"

"I go to church," Bree answered flatly. While no one was sure who would win a "bitch-off" between her and Sage, *everyone* knew they would have been there to see it.

"Okay. Do you solemnly swear to tell the truth, the whole truth, and nothing but the truth, so help you God?"

"I do."

"Petitioner, Respondent, and members of the Hearing Board: This witness is known to this tribunal as an expert in the field of psychology so we shall forgo the formality of qualifying her as an expert witness. As such, she is permitted under the rules of evidence to form opinions and testify as to her conclusions based on what would otherwise be hearsay evidence. Let the record reflect the same," Dex intoned, reading from a prepared memo. "Petitioner, you may proceed."

Laura's mother walked the psychologist through her daughter's treatment, diagnoses, and recent behavior. Although carrying a pre-pandemic diagnosis of bipolar, she had nonetheless been a highly valuable member of the Ranch as a trained phlebotomist. She, of course, assisted nurses with patient care duties, but her real contribution was her efficient collection of blood samples for the limited testing capabilities of the Ranch's medical staff.

She also had diabetes and was surviving only on the rapidly dwindling supply of available insulin. Additionally, the remainder of the insulin supply had exceeded its expiration date. The medical staff was fairly unified in confidence that eventual spoilage was a greater threat than immediate contamination, but it was just one more question mark in the daily lives of those already struggling every day for their very survival.

To be fair, Laura's mother, the petitioner, stressed that she had brought this petition out of love and an abundance of caution because her daughter's bipolar illness coupled with her diabetes being treated with marginally effective insulin was destined to result in either a manic episode or keto-acidosis, which was a "drunk-like" condition caused by mismanaged diabetes.

Or both.

Simultaneously.

Since the attack, she had become averse to the very sight of blood after assisting with the three necessary amputations and could no longer perform her job. A civil commitment, the petitioner argued, was therefore necessary to protect her daughter from herself in the event of rapid decompensation.

It was an emotional plea for help from a loving, concerned mother for her daughter's well-being, but Dex and the Board were despairingly aware there was no real help they could offer. Sure, they could incarcerate her, or search for her bipolar meds and insulin on the next supply run, but those were short term solutions. The long-term problem was that sooner or later, Laura was going to have a meltdown. And because of her position at Ward, she could possibly harm innocent patients or staff there as well.

Shit, what are we going to do about this? Dex wondered.

All senior staff carried radios, always on, day and night. Even in their charging cradles. NorthGate and SouthGate always had at least two radios operational as did Ward, Stable and other critical operation centers that may depend on immediate communications.

So, when the radio call from NorthGate came over the airwaves, it was received by each senior staffs' radios… simultaneously.

"Bighouse, NorthGate."

Dex stiffened.

Fucking now what?

"Bighouse here, what's up?"

As Dex spoke, every nearby radio repeated the feedback and almost unconsciously all the senior staff members reached to turn down the volume on their radios.

"Did not copy, Bighouse. Say again."

"You're interrupting a Board Hearing. Advise priority?"

"Apologies, sir. But request Command Ivan, but *not* stat, repeat *not* stat. We have visitors."

Thank God. When Ben's better, he can deal with this shit.

"Copy, standby for Ivan. He'll be there in ten."

CHAPTER 35

"Nurse Trainee Harper Quigley Reporting"

It was with the memory of seeing those three ragged, malnourished and terrified children rescued by Ben and the NorthGate guards as they had passed the Bighouse in the horse-drawn wagon last summer on their way to Ward, that the first thing Dex did was alert QRT on their channel; two steps down from their normal radio traffic.

The second thing he did was send Jackson to NorthGate to see why the Command Ivan had been issued. Since it was not a priority situation, it made more sense for Jackson to go. While not technically "Bighouse Command," and really not even senior staff, but "still pretty damned smart for being just a dumb kid," as Ben would say, Jackson held the confidence of Ben and Dex to assess the current situation at NorthGate as a surrogate "Ivan" and make a logical recommendation to Dex on how to proceed. With Ben still down on injury reserve at Ward, Dex couldn't risk going personally, so he sent someone he trusted to do it for him. The fact that anyone overhearing the radio traffic would think some head honcho named "Ivan" would be personally appearing was just a bonus.

All war was deceit.

Dex left the Civil Commitment hearing rapidly. He jogged over and mounted Reno on his way to yet another Command Ivan situation at NorthGate, but he would handle this one from the Farmhouse. From there, he could get eyes on the situation through binoculars without jeopardizing his immediate safety. Between that and Jackson's firsthand report, he could figure out what was going on.

He pointed Reno down the Ward driveway past Kitchen and approaching the Lifeskills building on his way to GCR, the most direct route to the Farmhouse.

Even though it had been several months prior, he was still somewhat bitter about Ben's hasty decision to just so impatiently execute both of those pedophiles on the spot.

That asshole could have saved one for me to shoot… he thought with a good-natured smirk. But he knew there was no need for them both to have blood on their hands.

Ben just handled it.

Oddly enough, Dex noticed he just so happened to be passing one of those kids from that day at that very moment. She was a pretty natural blonde, and yes, it was easy to tell these days. Most folks had their natural hair color since the Collapse, but hair coloring was recently making a comeback. A couple enterprising ranchers on a supply run had cleaned out the hair dye aisle, banking they could sell their product at Market.

Ah, free enterprise!

Her hair shone against the brilliant fall sun. Small frame, with a look of innocence that belied what Dex knew she had endured. She was wearing color mismatched scrubs two sizes too big for her; yet somehow, they still seemed merely an extension of her personality, as if the trademark clothing of medical professionals everywhere had themselves chosen *her*, rather than vice versa.

She waved to Dex with a big smile as she made her way on foot up the drive from Lifeskills to Ward, probably reporting for her shift as a nurse trainee, judging by her attire and age. She couldn't have been more than fourteen or fifteen years old; but children grew up so quickly now, burdened with the responsibility, pain, and loss of being among the living in this world.

Dex couldn't remember her name, not because he didn't care about that situation, but because, like Ben, he hadn't wanted to know too much about what had happened to them. As a result, Bighouse had always been too busy to take the time to get to know any of those three kids.

Dex decided right then and there that he and Ben were going to remedy that.

"Shouldn't you be at Lifeskills?" Dex called to her as he waved back with a smile. She stopped and her smile widened, honored that someone from Bighouse was speaking directly to her.

Dex made a mental note. *Yup, we are definitely going to get to know these kids, fucking stat,* he thought to himself, halting Reno to engage her.

"No sir, my classroom work ends at noon, and then I'm off to practicals at Ward. I am a nurse trainee there!" she said proudly and gestured behind him, as if Dex didn't know where the freaking Ward was. He'd helped a dozen Ranchers in the earliest days convert it from Neighbor Mike's two story home to the miracle of modern medicine that it was today.

Sort of.

Or at least by today's standards.

Still, he couldn't help but grin at her nervousness and enthusiasm.

And that got him inspired.

"Young lady, I have a very special assignment for you, will you accept?"

Her face registered complete shock, and she literally dropped her satchel of... whatever it was she was carrying... to the ground in surprise. She recovered quickly and bounded over to the horse and rider... and proceeded to actually freaking *salute* Dex.

"Yes, sir! Nurse Trainee Harper Quigley, reporting for duty, sir!"

Dex just couldn't help it, he burst out laughing at her military style formality. She was surprised at his reaction, but she still retained her poise.

Hell of a fighter, this one. Not easily shaken, he noted.

So, Dex decided to play along and give her what she clearly expected. She had obviously overheard radio traffic and had been paying attention to their quasi-military, concise and efficient communication style, and was attempting to make a good impression.

And oh, had she ever!

"Nurse Trainee Quigley," Dex began as seriously as he could muster and as fast as he could think. "Bighouse needs you to gather the two individuals you arrived with and meet me at Ward immediately following evening chow. We're going to pay a visit to Mr. Ben and check on his recovery, and I think it would be very good for him to see how well you have adjusted here. The Ranch is proud of you, and Bighouse is *damned* proud of you! Do you copy all that, Nurse Trainee?"

Her face virtually exploded with pride and amazement. She struggled to get words out, stammering, "Y-y-yes, yes, sir! We will be there, sir!"

"Knock off the 'sir' crap, Ms. Harper. You're a *nurse*, even if a trainee, but more than that: You are a *Ranch* Nurse Trainee, so you will call me 'Mr. Dex.' Nurses around here have a special place in everyone's hearts, but especially in mine, if you hadn't noticed," he added with a wink. "Copy that?"

"Copy that, si—uh... Mr. Dex," she beamed, just overwhelmed at her sudden good fortune. "I know Ward Actual Weaver, and..."

"That will be all, Ms. Harper."

"Yes, um, Mr. Dex," she blushed, immediately thankful he had prevented her from gushing nervously and embarrassing herself.

And probably him, too.

They parted and Dex cantered south, feeling good for the first time in a while, down Ward's driveway leading to GCR, then trotted across the asphalt until he came to a place he could ride in the field adjacent and cued Reno back to a canter.

Reno hit the soft dirt and took off like a Ferrari with a dropped clutch. Dex reined him back a tad to keep him from wearing himself out unnecessarily on the half mile run to Farmhouse.

Nah, fuck it, Dex thought after a few moments. *You wanna run? Let's RUN.*

"Let's go, Reno, git sum!" he yelled, digging his spurs in hard. Reno the Rocket did not disappoint. It felt *good* to run.

And Reno *wanted* to run.

So did Dex.

CHAPTER 36

"Bent My Hat"

Dex returned disappointed from supervising the NorthGate "Command Ivan" situation from Farmhouse having not been able to execute any pedophiles but with some extremely exciting news. Seeing all was humming along nicely, he headed to Kitchen for evening chow. He sat with Mike and talked QRT matters over their meal since Bliss was still on duty at Ward.

He caught Quigley's eye standing by Kitchen's exit. She nodded and pointed outside as she was talking to another girl about her age. No doubt they were comparing notes on how to be kick-ass females in a world that desperately needed more of them. Two younger boys about ages six or eight stood next to her.

Dex and Mike both noticed how protectively she unconsciously shielded the boys with her body from those walking by even though she was in animated conversation and laughing with her peer.

"Tough kids these days," Mike commented.

"The toughest," Dex agreed. "Wish they didn't have to be, though." He excused himself to collect the kids and make their way to Ward.

The boys were very quiet, and Harper was clearly very nervous, too, as Dex led them through Ward's reception, up the stairs to patient rooms on the second floor. It had been restructured to accommodate six large double rooms and four private rooms. Ben, of course, was in one of the private recovery rooms. Dex knocked and entered.

The NorthGate guard that had saved the Ranch with his daring use of the Fat Lady was there. Dex had mentioned to Mike in passing that when the operator was off duty, Ben wished him to stop by to meet him.

He had evidently done so nearly immediately.

"Dex, meet Tim Rawlings. He's the 'Savior of NorthGate,' as it were. Fifty-eight confirmed kills in under seven seconds," Ben said proudly.

"The M240 operator during the attack," Dex acknowledged with a smile, shaking Tim's hand. "The Ranch owes its continued existence to your quick thinking and action."

"I mean, I really just... I wasn't sure at the time it was the right move," Rawlings looked sheepish at the praise. He saw the kids standing in the doorway, though Ben did not.

"Mike, me, or Dex would have made the same call if any of us had been there, don't think any more about that. Though Dex probably would have wrapped the barrel in something pink and fuzzy first."

"The QRT guys kept trying to convince me, but when I offered Fat Lady to them, they declined responsibility. But kept telling me it was the only way..."

"Because QRT had other things on their mind, such as reputation and status. You only had doing the right thing for the Ranch on your mind," Dex countered. "And I would not have, Ben."

"Unicorn horn?"

Dex tossed his head back indicating behind him, then said, "Sir, may I present Nurse Trainee Harper Quigley, 'Ms. Harper' to us, and Ryan and Neil from Lifeskills. They are the kids that came in... um, before." He looked at Ben self-consciously, hoping he'd get his meaning without more detail.

He did.

Evidently, so did Rawlings because he excused himself, nodding to the kids on his way out.

"Hey guys, come on in! Sorry I can't meet you under better circumstances, but I seem to have fallen off my horse and bent my hat."

The boys giggled, and Harper smiled at his lame attempt at deflection from his condition.

But every single person on the Ranch already knew that a member of Bighouse command that had brought all of them this far through the pandemic and the end of the world had been shot during the incursion.

"Nice to meet you Ms. Harper. Tell me about yourself?" Ben asked pleasantly.

She froze in place, like a deer caught in a spotlight. But despite her outward timidness, Ben sensed something much deeper in her.

Strength.

Resilience.

With a paralyzing fear of strange men.

He had asked the wrong question of her.

She stared at her feet holding her hands together before her.

"I'm… I'm nobody, sir. I'm just a girl that was fortunate enough to… I mean, that was brought here to you, um… to the *Ranch* I mean…"

"I understand from Mr. Dex that you have made quite an impression here as a nurse trainee," he interrupted her. "And Ward Actual Weaver tells me no one has contributed more or worked harder of all of the Ward staff than you. Is this all true?"

She smiled and looked up at him, relaxing slightly. "I don't know if it's true, but I know it's my intent to prove my value here, sir."

Yup. The "right" question came from a place of security, not obscurity.

"Ms. Harper, I'm gonna assume Mr. Dex has addressed the 'sir' thing with you already?" Ben said with a smile.

She smiled back, "Yes, Mr. Ben."

They talked for a while about what the boys had learned in Lifeskills, what topics and activities they enjoyed the most. Harper warmed up rapidly and assisted in coaxing responses from the uncertain boys. Ryan, age six, really liked animals, especially the horses. Neil, a bit older, confessed bluntly that his favorite was anything that had to do with Ms. Dee and Ms. Sage at the stable.

I don't know why, Neil thought. *But Mr. Ben and Mr. Dex seem to find that very, very funny.*

Harper mostly stayed quiet herself but watched the exchanges with glistening intelligence in her eyes, Ben noted. He glanced at Dex, who nodded.

"Okay, guys, we've bothered Mr. Ben enough for one day," Dex said, barely able to suppress his own laughter at Neil's admission.

"They seem to be bouncing back nicely," Ben observed, clearly energized at having enjoyed their visit. "Good call, Dex. We should have done that sooner."

"Well, we would have, but no one had shot you yet," Dex quipped, after asking Ms. Harper to wait outside with the boys. When she'd taken them into the hallway, Dex closed the door and turned to face Ben.

"You're not gonna shoot me again, are you?" Ben asked with mock trepidation.

"No, and I didn't shoot you in the first place. But I'm also not gonna tell you I haven't thought about it from time to time, especially in the Before. Seriously though, I have something more interesting to discuss."

He detailed his encounter with Harper outside the Ward earlier, then told him how it inspired him.

"Call Bliss in here, that's a great idea!"

"Already did, when you were cracking dumb ass jokes,"

"Moi?"

"Which one of you two needs his ass kicked today?" Bliss demanded as she slammed open the door and entered in a pretend huff. "Some of us actually work around here," she said with mock contempt, then rolled her eyes as Ben and Dex both raised their hands.

She kissed Dex then came over to Ben, kissed his forehead, and held up a thermometer.

"No kiss for me, thanks, I'm on the wagon. And as to the thermo-thingy..."

"Boy..." Bliss started to warn him.

"Ahhhh," Ben said cooperatively, opening wide.

"I got something you can kiss, and if you keep mouthing off, I'm going to show you where."

"Don't threaten me with a good time," he responded, briefly removing the thermometer.

"Why did you call me away? I've got..." Bliss began.

"A new assignment," Dex cut her off.

She wheeled around to face him. "Boy, you can shove that 'Bighouse command' shit right back where it goes when it comes to my patients. You get to tell me what to do in exactly *one* room, and this isn't it. So don't push it!"

Ben removed the thermometer again. "Is it the bedroom? Because, I mean, if so, technically there's a bed in here…" he pointed out helpfully, then gestured to the hallway. "I can just go…"

She picked up a large bore catheter and waved it at him.

"I'm sorry, did you say something?" she inquired sweetly.

"No ma'am," he responded tactfully, replacing the thermometer in his mouth.

It was always the same when the three of them got together out of the public eye, or "unsupervised" as they always joked. Just like in the Before at the beef company. It hadn't been work, exactly. They just did whatever needed to be done, usually laughing and making fun of each other the whole time they did it, regardless of how strenuous the tasks were. It gave them all a sense of normalcy to spend a few moments together as their old, pre-pandemic selves.

So, fun was had by all, right up until Dex told Bliss her new assignment.

It did not involve the bedroom.

"And more news," Dex continued. "We just had a few new arrivals while you were getting your beauty sleep the last couple days."

He gave Ben the good news. And then gave him even better news.

"You had better not be fucking with me, Dex," Ben said as he struggled to sit up, but only managed to induce a bolt of pain through his wound. "Tell me you're not screwing around, man? You know they got me on these painkillers."

"I wouldn't joke about that, brother. If I wanted to screw around, I'd just tell you you're a sexy bitch in that hospital robe."

"Screw you."

End of the world, and we still have these dumb ass hospital gowns.

CHAPTER 37

"Gotta Love Rednecks"

Think that's got it," Dex said, wrenching the clamp tightly into place around the rubber fitting on the small engine tri-fuel generator.

"Alright, let's fire it up," Tanner said to Jackson. Jackson grabbed the pull start and yanked twice in rapid succession on the handle. Nothing.

"Again," Dex said, sniffing the connection. "No leaks."

On the third pull, the engine roared to life and Dex fiddled with the air intake adjustment until the motor smoothed out. Ben walked into the barn with a sling around his right arm and gauze peeking out from under his shirt. He paused and took in the scene.

Three guys, tools everywhere and the most heinous looking contraption ever witnessed just slowly vibrating its way across the concrete floor. He stood there silently observing while the guys made various adjustments and loudly traded suggestions, observations and, as only men can, lowbrow compliments over the roar of the generator.

After a few minutes of ensuring the generator was functioning properly, they put it under load for a few more minutes, then shut the engine down looking mighty proud of themselves. Then they noticed Ben watching behind them and turned around.

"Do I even want to know?" Ben asked cautiously.

"Pet project," Jackson volunteered.

"Got it running," Dex said proudly.

"I see that. On?" Ben inquired.

The guys all grinned at this.

"Shit," Tanner laughed.

"Technically, methane," Dex corrected. "Remember a couple months ago we built that compressed gas transfer tank with a regulator?" he pointed to a thirty-gallon propane tank. "We took the whole thing out to a latrine where we had also installed a port in place of the open septic vent. Gave it about sixty days to build up pressure in the septic tank and boom, instant methane. Then we used the solar electric to charge it to pressure with the air compressor. Just had to get the air mix right."

"A hundred people make a lot of shit," Jackson offered.

"Even more if some of them are lawyers," Ben agreed. "What did you make that fugly regulator out of? It looks like Mrs. Frankenstein's emergency vibrator."

"Let's just say one of the unused cars around here won't be starting any time soon," Tanner responded with a mischievous grin. "We sort of borrowed some of its vacuum tubing, and Dex modified some other parts at the machine shop."

You just gotta love rednecks, Ben thought, proud of his guys. *They could do anything.*

"How are you feeling?" Jackson asked.

"Like I went twelve rounds with Mike Tyson, then got shot," Ben answered. He pointed to the sling on his right arm below the bullet wound on his shoulder. "Doc says I gotta wear this bullshit for a month."

"Must really cut back your social life,'" Jackson said, pointing at Ben's hand sticking out of the sling, then immediately mentally chastising himself for not thinking of Rachele and...

Jackson was a father.

"Nah, I use my left for that," Ben joked it away.

"Not like you ever do anything around here anyway," Dex added to keep the mood light, and they all laughed.

Then Ben got serious.

"Listen, you guys did a great job running everything while I was down. Thank you."

"We know how much your ugly ass needed some beauty sleep," Tanner smiled.

"Looks like you need some more," Dex noted, actually assessing Ben's countenance. "You don't look too good."

"No doubt but listen… we need to talk about this… this *prisoner* Dex told me we have. Has anyone interrogated him?"

"We got him under twenty-four-hour guard on a two to one," Dex answered, meaning two Brig guards were present for the one prisoner at all times. It was an exorbitant use of manpower but necessary under the circumstances.

"Mike and some of the QRT guys made a couple passes. They, um… they weren't gentle," Dex admitted.

"Pretty sure Mike hit him with his crutch, too," Tanner added.

"Get anything out of him?"

"No."

"Okay, well I want to meet with all senior staff at dinner tonight," Ben said. "We need a plan."

Dex grabbed his radio. "All senior staff, Bighouse. Sound off and listen up."

"Go for QRT Actual," Mike responded from his bed at the Ward.

"Go for C&M Actual," came Saul's reply.

"Go for Ward Actual," Bliss said.

"Go for Ag," a voice from Farmhouse Barn.

"Go for Lifeskills," Steph called.

The acknowledgments continued to pour in in a predetermined order.

"Dex," Ben said suddenly. "Have we changed frequencies since the attack?"

"Fuck!" Dex immediately keyed his microphone. "Terminate sound off, repeat, immediately terminate sound off."

He paused to make sure the channel was clear, then said, "Tango, tango tango. Repeat, tango, tango, tango."

Tango was the codeword for everyone to go to a different predetermined channel. Dex waited a moment for everyone to switch their radios over, then changed his.

"All stars, Ivan eats. All stars, Ivan eats. Pass offline. Tango dark."

"Ivan" was code for "eyes on" meaning to physically gather at the Bighouse for dinner, which was the next scheduled meal. "Stars" referred to senior staff. "Tango dark" meant radio silence on the new channel.

The radio wordlessly clicked and chirped as each senior staff member acknowledged the message. When the correct number of responses was heard, meaning all departments had checked in that they had received the message, the radios fell silent.

"Fuck, I fucked up," Dex admitted.

"A lot to remember, isn't it?" Ben teased good naturedly. "Look, it's done now, but I think we need to rework all radio protocols."

"I'm on it," Jackson said, grabbing a nearby legal pad and pen. He sat and began writing furiously.

"What are we discussing, besides comms?" Tanner asked.

"I just came from Ward," Ben said slowly. "Three of our people are missing."

CHAPTER 38

"Come Here"

In the chaos of the days immediately following the attack on the Ranch, no one had thought to get a community-wide head count. Though the succession plan had always been for Dex to take over in the event of Ben's death or incapacity, the raw terror and adrenaline of their first major gunfight and battle for everyone's survival at the Ranch had resulted in small family units, close friends and immediate neighbors checking on one another. Since no true headcount of the entire Ranch tribe had been calculated, it was not until Ben awoke from surgery and began thinking clearly a few days later that he had thought to gather all of the department headcounts and total them.

That total had come up three short.

Ben immediately tossed the legal pad he had been doing the dreaded "lawyer math" on and checked himself out of Ward against multiple protests. He had placated their valid medical concerns by promising to return in the evening and made them promise not to tell the Ward Actual until he had a ten-minute head start. He needed to see the recovery efforts and damage to the Ranch's resources firsthand, he had explained. But he also needed to find out why the census was short three bodies without creating a panic.

A couple nurses he'd discreetly interviewed on the subject on his way out had told him that there was an eyewitness that claimed the girls had been abducted as the marauders withdrew. Unfortunately, everyone had heard it from someone, but no one seemed to know the original source.

He walked from Ward towards what was formerly his farm property heading for his home, the Bighouse. Ben stopped suddenly and stared at the route ahead. Going this way, although the shortest route, meant he would have to take the woods road along the other side of the head row past a fenced pasture that led past the old corral SouthGate.

Where Rachele had given her life during her shift on cattle watch. No.

Given *their* lives, he reminded himself.

If he stayed on this side of the head row, it would block his view of where they had died. After a moment of reflection, he made his decision.

He passed the woods road entrance and continued down the driveway from the home that served at the Ward. Although lacking solar power and far from high tech, the few medical machines Ward now possessed—O2 generators, portable X-ray and ultrasound machines and other medical devices that had been "liberated" from the nearby Middletown urgent care clinic after it was abandoned—now ran on 12-volt batteries charged in rotation as needed by the Bighouse's solar array and transported by horse-drawn cart to Ward.

The Ranch rednecks, and there were more than a few, had rigged AC inverters to convert the batteries' DC charge to allow the AC machines to run off them. This allowed several smaller machines or one of the larger machines to run at a time.

Medicines requiring refrigeration were also protected by several large refrigerators. A plan was in the works for the next supply run to obtain more 12-volt deep cycle batteries, materials to manufacture them, and a second solar array to be mounted on Ward's roof.

Another advantage to using Neighbor Mike's home as Ward, and the real reason it had been volunteered by him and his amazing family, was the presence of an outdoor wood furnace. Mike's entire home was heated via an outdoor wood burning boiler that utilized a circulator powered by a 12-volt DC battery and AC inverter to warm the entire structure. As a result, Ward was always warm even in the dead of winter, leading to no shortage of Ward volunteers, at least during the colder months.

Plans were underway to add a steam engine to his furnace thereby ensuring a secondary source to constantly supply electricity to Ward. So far, the complex nature of the project and discerning the necessary safety precautions to operate it without catastrophic explosion had relegated it to the proverbial "back burner." The same had happened with the Kintis solar array.

Nobody had any idea how to make it work safely.

Neighbor Mike also had raised sheep in the Before and still had a sizable herd providing sustenance and wool to the Ranch's population along with flocks of several hundred chickens raised mostly for meat but also for eggs.

Kitchen used *a lot* of eggs every day.

Ben instead wandered past the sheep pens towards Brett and Steph's home where the school had been set up in their garage. It was referred to as "Lifeskills" at the Ranch since most kids had a pretty negative association with the "schools" of the past.

And "Lifeskills" was indeed a more apt moniker for the lessons taught there. Ben's cousin Carol had, in the Before, run a daycare for decades out of her home along with her husband Monty, a jovial maintenance technician. The two of them had come to the Ranch almost immediately when services began breaking down having heeded Ben's pre-pandemic words he'd uttered for nearly two decades:

If the shit ever hits the fan, come here.

It was the same reason so many of his friends and family survived Covid-27. The ones who had waited, who ignored, who forgot… did not survive.

When Ben arrived at the Lifeskills building, Carol was in the garage/large classroom with about twenty children aged four to seventeen. The world may have ended, but education did not. It was arguably more important now than ever.

Although the lessons were considerably different than in the Before.

CHAPTER 39

"Favorite Libs"

Ben had frequently joked for years that Monty and Carol were his "favorite libs" and that their only redeeming qualities were being hardcore Philadelphia Eagles fans like him. Though related to Carol by blood on his father's side, being on polar opposite sides of the political spectrum would cause many families to stop speaking altogether. But for Ben and his fave libs, it turned out instead that their intellectual and philosophical differences fostered more than a few deep conversations, resulting in an even deeper mutual respect.

Now, Ben wasn't going blue any time soon, and Carol and Monty certainly wouldn't be pulling the voting handle in favor of the orange guy, either.

But none of them cared.

They had actually turned their political rivalry into a source of fun and amusement by having bets where the loser had to stand in front of their football tribe on game day and find nice things to say about their chosen political candidate's *opponent*... in public. This resulted in near endless laughter when Carol had to "Make America Great Again."

But it was even funnier when Ben lost, and Carol made him "Rock the Slut Vote." The costume alone that Ben had come up with to make his speech had resulted in unabated laughter of their entire football tribe. Unfortunately, that was followed by several nights of severe nightmares witnesses had endured of being chased by a horny, rabid chupacabra in a miniskirt.

With really hairy legs.

But when the Collapse came, and Bighouse had to pick someone to care for and educate the kids at the Ranch, Ben could think of no one better suited to entrust the Ranch's future generations than Carol.

Steph was there right by the entrance door at a changing table with her own young children. Ben said hi and answered the standard questions about his injury and recovery. No, Steph didn't need to take his temperature; and yes, he knew he looked like shit.

He was getting that a lot lately.

Carol was helping some of the younger children solve math problems on a chalkboard, while Steph was caring for the infants and assisting Monty and her husband Brett, a chemical engineer, who were conducting what looked like a scientific experiment of an indecipherable nature.

"You guys do know that alchemy doesn't work, right?" Ben said by way of greeting. "You can't just make gold out of aluminum and then print yourselves endless Market credits."

The men looked up from their racks of beakers and chemicals and smiled at seeing him.

"Not even close," Brett responded, coming over to shake Ben's hand.

"Meth lab?"

"Nope."

"Good, cuz they're still a little young," Ben gestured to the students.

Monty, tall and fit, broke out in his trademark grin within his graying goatee and gripped Ben up in a giant bear hug.

Yes, it hurt his shoulder, but Monty was one of those guys blessed with a personality and charisma that insisted you just had to love the guy.

No, really, you *had* to.

You didn't even get a choice.

"They're learning how to make a battery from scratch," Monty explained. "We only have a little bit of the extra chemicals needed to mix the sulfuric acid, but we're putting it to good use. The wire, cathode, and anode metals we have plenty of."

"They're attempting to charge it now," Brett pointed to a nearby bicycle with a belt attached to the rear wheel which ran to an improvised matching pulley on what appeared to be a car alternator. Wires ran from the alternator geared to the rear wheel to the experimental battery on a workbench surrounded by the observing class, captivated by the possibilities.

The wheels of the ten-speed bicycle had been removed, and Monty had constructed a platform and anchors to keep it stationary. He had cut the seat stem and refitted it lower with an elongated adjustment range, so it was suited for riders of all sizes. Nearby removable blocks with straps affixed to them were stacked to attach to the peddles, if needed. A child of about nine was sitting on the bike and pedaling furiously.

"After they see how it works, we're going to manufacture and install these at all the houses' well pumps, including the Bighouse in case your solar goes down. All homes can then be fitted with a pressure tank to at least get all of the toilets working," Monty added. "People hate going all the way out to those latrines."

"That's ten minutes!" Steph called, changing one of the infants. Much to her chagrin, washable cloth diapers were most definitely back in style. She had made them herself from old pillowcases and bed sheets, although she did request on every supply run that the Ranchers please "clean out" the disposable diaper section wherever they went. So far, her pleas had fallen on deaf ears, or at least on selective male hearing. The truth was that supply runs had higher priorities than convenience. They were focused on necessities; luxuries came in on the list of items to be scavenged somewhere around six hundred and forty-fifth place.

But everyone knew Steph's real talent was baking bread and keeping the men's language in line around the Lifeskills pupils which she and Carol both referred to as "their kids."

The child bounced off the bike, with energy only a child can have, and another youngster of similar age immediately took her place and began pedaling.

"Getting a workout of mind and body, I see," Ben commented. "I like it."

"Took a bit of trial and error to get the gearing and charge potential correct," Brett admitted. "But Monty wouldn't quit on it until he got it just right. Steph and Carol wanted the kids to be able to go ten minutes at a time, so the math would be easy to calculate.

You need six per hour. It takes *a lot* of energy to fully charge a battery this way."

"Definitely takes more energy than I have," Ben agreed. "Bet it cuts down on the ADHD diagnoses around here too."

CHAPTER 40

"S-h-e-l-t-e-r"

None of them have reported any difficulty sleeping since we started this last week," Brett said, missing the joke about lack of exercise in the Before translating to skyrocketing ADHD diagnoses among children and the inevitable pill prescription fortunes they had generated. "The immediate trauma from the attack really had them all shook. But we sheltered in the basement for the whole thing. The youngest ones have completely forgotten about it since they didn't actually witness much."

"Smart move, but we really should have had a protocol in place for that."

"We do now," Steph stage-whispered from across the room. "Carol and I are drilling the kids once a week with the word 'S-h-e-l-t-e-r.'" She caught Carol's eye.

Carol nodded.

Do it.

"Lifeskills, Shelter! Now! Go! Shelter! Shelter!" Steph suddenly yelled out of the blue, clapping her hands in the middle of Carol's lesson. Every one of the kids immediately jumped up from their seats, off the bike-charger thingy, and one even came charging inside a moment later from out of the makeshift latrine in the yard.

Lifeskills' staff made a point of looking at Ben to see if he noticed a boy of about eight grab a confused four year old girl by the hand and gently lead her with him saying, "C'mon, we're going to all play a game!"

He did.

The kids all lined up at the door to the inside of the home and the leader, a girl that couldn't even be seven years old, opened the door to the basement.

"Drill! Drill! Drill!" Steph and Carol called out together.

Ben couldn't help but be impressed.

His own parents couldn't even get him to take out the damned trash as a kid.

The students all returned to their seats and resumed their studies with Carol, while Steph continued explaining, "Brett and Monty have an arsenal locked up down there with enough canned goods and water to last us all three days in case it happens again," she explained. "Even buckets and sawdust for..."

Ben held up his hand to stop the explanation, pulling the radio from his belt with his good arm. "I get it, Steph. I can guess what that's for."

"Kitchen, Bighouse."

"Go for Kitchen Actual," Sherrie immediately responded.

"I'm here at Lifeskills with a group of the smartest damned kids and instructors on the freaking planet," Ben began, earning a warning look from Steph. She held up one finger.

That's one. She mouthed sternly.

Ben couldn't help but smile as he nodded his understanding.

"Kitchen, what are the odds we have sufficient homemade ice cream on hand for dessert tonight as a reward for some very impressive students?"

A collective gasp of excitement from the kids.

"Standby." A pause. Sherrie was checking with her staff. "Odds are zero percent we have sufficient available, Bighouse. But they are also 100 percent that with some help, we can make it happen by evening chow. Need five ables. Advise?"

"Standby, Kitchen," he glanced inquiringly at Carol.

"Okay, kids, are there any volunt—okay..." Carol began but didn't even get the word out before twenty juveniles had their hands stretched as high as they possibly could with, "oh, oh, me, me," in their eyes.

And one adult.

"Ben, put your hand down," Steph laughed.

"Aw, man!" Ben complained. "I never get picked."

The kids found this just hysterically funny.

Steph selected five boys and girls and sent them up to Kitchen for the twenty minutes it would take to prep their homemade ice-cream maker for the staff to complete.

"So how does this work here?" Ben asked. "I never really got to check in on how you guys operate, though I know Dex has been here regularly."

"We spend about half the day on practical education, experimenting, learning by doing, and the rest on traditional book learning," Steph answered.

"Make sure you teach them proper history, Steph. You know, how the democrats caused this whole pandemic thing that ended the world. That's why there's no more Xboxes for the kids to play with and why they should all grow up to be conservatives," Ben joked, rarely missing an opportunity to needle his favorite libs. Monty grinned again. Ben glanced over at Carol to see if she had heard him. She had, but just shook her head, rolled her eyes and smiled—never for a second interrupting her math instruction.

"Brett is still working on a procedure to make insulin from sheep and cattle pancreas," Steph continued, walking over from across the garage. "Hasn't given up on the antibiotic thing either, though God knows I wish he could. There's a whole room of mold growing on different mediums in sealed jars that used to be my walk-in closet."

"She had too many clothes anyway. And yes, insulin's definitely doable," Brett confirmed. "But it will take more equipment than we currently have. For example, we need a more robust centrifuge. We've got more than a few diabetics, as you know, still surviving off the stockpiled insulin we got from the pharmacies around on supply runs. But that's not going to last forever. Any chance of another supply run any time soon? And maybe a Spectrophotometer and a gas chromatograph?" he smiled.

"Not a chance in hell. At least, not until we assess whatever threat that group that attacked us still presents," Ben said firmly. "Besides, I thought Ward had a centrifuge? We used to make thermite with it. Don't they use a centrifuge to determine blood types for transfusions and such?"

"They do, but they need it for that purpose, and it really isn't large enough for what we need to do to make insulin. We have the shakers and incubators from my home lab, and we built a bioreactor out of an empty one-hundred-gallon propane tank."

"Well, you could try Amazon?" Ben said ruefully. They all missed the days when anything you could want or need was only a couple mouse clicks away. Today, leaving the Ranch was akin to risking one's life, but staying stagnant was a certain death. Thus, correct risk/reward analysis was critical to survival.

So was Lady Luck.

"I was thinking more like the labs at one of the colleges," Brett said.

"That's a really good idea. Okay, well, make a list and…"

Brett smiled and picked up a folder sitting on a table near their freak science experiment. He removed a three-page stapled document.

"Here ya go, just waiting for you to ask. That's your copy."

Ben just smiled and asked Brett to fold it for him. Then Ben carefully slid it into his pocket with his good arm.

"Kids still doing daily Stable visits? Cattle chores and livestock education?"

"Yup, and they can all ride, too," Brett said proudly.

"Probably better than you," Steph added sardonically. Ben started to give her the finger, then remembered he was in a schoolroom with kids, and that *that* would be two… and that he definitely wasn't well enough to suffer Steph's wrath. They even had a special term for what followed if one made Steph mad.

Penalty of Steph.

"Sage has them all brushing and picking hooves," Brett continued. "And even the five-year-olds can ride without a handler. Obviously, they can't tack yet, and most need a stool to brush."

"Next week Carol's going to start some of the reading-age kids on cursive writing," Monty offered. "They may come across documents one day written in cursive with important information. Need to be able to read it."

Ben held up his hands in mock defeat. "I'm not here to micro-manage. You guys are doing a kick ass job. The Ranch's only requirement is that you keep it up. And yes, I agree. Probably a good idea that the generation that's going to be tasked with rebuilding society be able to read things like the Constitution and the Declaration of Independence," Ben confirmed. "Matter of fact, we should have those documents hanging in here, too," he gestured at the large American flag hanging from one wall. Monty and Brett looked at each other and smiled. Ben took that to mean "Mission Accomplished."

"So, what's next for the kids on the practical side?" Ben asked.

"They're going up to the Farmhouse after lunch to see the butcher shop. Tanner and Akim are going to assist them in cutting up some meat. We had planned to do it with the next steer, but Tanner shot a deer this morning. It's in the walk-in cooler up at the Farmhouse now, which reminds me I hope someone is keeping an eye on those 12-volt batteries. Anyway, he had to field dress it to get it back, but they'll learn everything else by *doing*."

"Maybe take that bike charger thing and a couple rambunctious kids up there after class?" Ben suggested. "Can't wait to see what Kitchen does with the venison this time. Remember when they made 'Sloppy Does' from that deer meat? They were slamming, too! Wait, at these ages, though, to cut up meat? Some are pretty young. Any blow back from the parents?" Ben asked with concern.

"Nobody bitches about stuff like that anymore, Ben, okay?" Carol said, walking up having completed her lesson. She carefully gave him a hug and said, "No grocery stores plus the need to eat to stay alive is a very simple equation, even for your intelligence-challenged conservative ass. I can give you a refresher in basic addition if needed. I have time right now before the next lesson begins, okay?" she smiled.

"No, ma'am, I do not. And you are absolutely correct," Ben laughed, properly subdued.

CHAPTER 41

"The Courthouse Floor"

Ben's next stop was the temporary Quarantine. With the original quarantine tent destroyed in the attack, and not as much need for the rare occasions when smaller numbers of drifters arrived and were admitted as potential new Ranch members, Bighouse instructed Saul and his crack construction crew to convert the top level of the barn at the Farmhouse. There were some questions at the staff meeting if this was a good idea since the bottom floor of the Farmhouse Barn housed the Ranch's ever growing arsenal, known as the Armory. That earlier senior staff meeting had been held at the Ward in Ben's room the same day Ben awoke from his surgery and learned of Rachele's fate along with that of their unborn child.

"Might not be the best idea to put strangers together with all of our guns," Jackson had pointed out.

"That's true," Ben responded from his Ward bed. "But remember these folks arriving here now are weaker and weaker; some can barely walk. I get your concern, and it's a valid one. But if we have them two to one under twenty-four hour guard and located on a second floor with only a single point of egress—the staircase—it's easier to keep an eye on them and discourage any unauthorized moonlight walks. Saul, can you construct an entrance from that unused door of the west side over to the stairs? Maybe a hallway eight or ten feet high with zero outward visibility? That way they won't even know the Armory is right under them."

"Does a bear shit in the woods?"

"I don't know cuz; we don't have any bears around here. But if we did, it's just as likely these days they'd shit on the courthouse floor. So, is that a 'yes?'"

"Yes, sir. Take maybe three days, assuming we have the lumber."

Ben considered this, then looked out the Ward's window at the tree line where one-hundred acres of hardwood grew. "Better make it five days."

"We used a lot rebuilding after the attack, and we're not doing a supply run till we find out if those assholes that attacked us are still around," Dex reminded them.

"We'll get to that in a minute," Ben said. Then, turning back to Saul, "Do it. Mill the lumber if you have to: Harry has an Alaskan Mill over at his chicken farm; you'll just need a couple more chainsaws."

Harry Nussick was another like-minded neighbor to the Ranch, although his farm was about a mile and a half past SouthGate on the Outside. Harry had elected to stay at his place rather than seek refuge at the Ranch because Harry was a *real* chicken farmer.

No, really.

Now, many people in the Before had dozens or even hundreds of chickens in their "backyard" flocks. The move toward farm-based, non-processed foods free of hormones and antibiotics raised like the beef company's delicious Dexter cattle was already catching on after Covid-19. Many younger couples just starting families had elected to forgo the uncertainty of "Big Egg" corporations and instead produce their own fresh eggs. Others added processing their chickens for meat and some even had milk or beef cows. But Harry just had chickens.

250,000 of them.

See, Harry grew chicken commercially for a well-known, and rather religious, chicken fast food place that had become enormously popular. His six grow houses, each one a thousand feet long, were largely self-automated, so long as there was power. Harry had thought ahead and purchased several diesel generators but even that had only lasted so long. These days the chickens were mostly outside foraging in giant fenced pens the Ranchers had assisted in helping him to build once it was clear fuel would run out for the generators. The grain tanks the chickens relied on for food were also running dry, even after having been supplemented by grain harvested that fall at the Ranch.

So, after having commandeered a large walk-in freezer and set it up next to the Bighouse to make use of its solar power, thousands and thousands of chickens had been "processed" for "freezer camp."

Harry remained on his farm with the surviving flocks from the "Great Chicken Massacre of 2027" to tend his birds and tinker with what he could get working. He and his family were fairly safe from threats as the place was set back well away from the road and looked like just another abandoned property to anyone passing by.

Besides, Harry was a pretty big guy.

With an attitude to match.

At least 6'4" and topping 300 pounds, he was nonetheless as friendly and helpful as they came, and he had all manner of helpful tools, machines, and knowledge to share. One of those was an "Alaskan Mill" which used bracketed ordinary chainsaws along a track of scaffolding framed around a large or medium log to plane horizontally into what was known as "rough hewn" lumber. That lumber could be used for construction and was as good or better than going to the lumber store, if one happened to have 100+ acres of woods nearby.

Which the Ranch did.

So, a symbiotic relationship was established between Harry and the Ranch with no real score kept of favors swapped. If something was needed, they just worked together and got it done.

"And tear the siding off of one of those old campers if you run out of plywood," Ben was saying to Saul at the Ward staff meeting "But don't wait. Jackson, take a detail and clear out just an area large enough on the second level for them to be comfortable; tell Danny and the Q nurses to blindfold them *twice* before they take them anywhere near that building. And drive them around in the wagon to disorient them first. Keep two guards on at all times plus the usual nurses. Tell our guests that if they so much as stick their heads down that staircase, we will blow them off."

"Copy that."

"Matter of fact, see if Danny can spare a couple Brig guards. Those guys are bad ass; most are just a hypothetical flat foot from making QRT anyway. And where is he?"

"We're still waiting on After Action reports from several departments, including Brig," Dex had responded.

So, Ben thought, somewhat bemused outside Lifeskills as he silently stared across the field across the Ranch to the distant

Farmhouse barn. *Maybe we actually should have picked some place closer.*

He looked across the quarter mile separating his current location from his destination: The Farmhouse's barn housing the new Quarantine Saul was busily constructing was literally on the other side of the Ranch from his present location. He could hear the battery-operated power tools clear across the fields and pastures.

He took a deep breath and put one foot in front of the other.

CHAPTER 42

"Good to Be the King"

He hadn't gotten far when Sage came riding up on Teeter. Her mare had made a nice recovery from what their vet Doc Gruber had diagnosed as just a mild bout with colic. Ben was relieved to see she had Buckshot tacked and ponied. Mounting the smaller Buckshot was a lot easier than pulling himself up on the much larger Reno.

"I'm pretty sure you're supposed to be back at the Ward, Boss," she said, bearing her patented resting bitchface countenance and using the moniker she'd settled on back when she was the beef company's Livestock Coordinator.

"Don't you ever get tired of lecturing me, LC?" Ben grumbled. He only called her that in private anymore, and usually only then when talking about life in the Before. Ben accepted the horse and made a show of checking the cinch and backstrap, then testing the snugness of the saddle.

He knew he needn't have bothered. He knew Buckshot had been properly tacked by his former LC and current Stable Actual.

He also knew it would piss her off.

Which was exactly why he did it.

"Don't *you* ever get tired of needing to be?" she shot back, not fooled for a second at his act, but still irritated nonetheless.

Touché. He thought to himself. They were always good for pushing each other's buttons. Even better at stomping on them, at times. So instead, he asked, "How did you know?"

"Ms. Bliss radioed me when you left Ward. Told Dad, too. Don't worry," she added quickly. "She used a private channel. No one knows you're out here being a dumb ass."

"Okay, that'll do, fockette," Ben said, glancing up sternly at her insolence, but using his pet name for her when she was still a child. "Got a ranch to run, you know… people to keep alive. Besides, it's good for folks to see me up and about after what happened."

She sighed, "I know, I'm sorry. Just, Jesus! That whole thing scared the shit out of us. We all know the world has gone to hell, and people are evil and everyone still alive has lost most of the people they've ever known in their entire lives. But to be *attacked!* Shot at… and then you were…" She collected herself quickly.

"Yes, I recall that part," Ben said gently, pointing to his sling and ending the unpleasant thought.

"And, well frankly, you don't look *that* good."

Ben noticed she said the last part after she got that "clinical" gaze in her eyes, as if she were evaluating whether to amputate an injured duck's leg or induce labor during difficult calving.

Damn LCs, even more annoying than lawyers, if that were possible.

But she was probably right, too.

He felt like shit.

"If it matters, I feel much worse than I look. Listen, seriously, I'm just going to the Farmhouse to check a couple things. Then I promise it's straight back to bed for me. You can come with, if you want. Make sure I obey Stable Actual's orders."

Sage rolled her eyes but grinned a little.

"Okay," she agreed.

She radioed back to Dee at Stable that she'd be at the Farmhouse but would return in less than an hour. The last part she said looking sideways at Ben to see if he got the hint. He did but pretended not to notice. After she delegated a few housekeeping tasks to her second, they began a leisurely, slow horseback walk up to Farmhouse.

"What do you know about our guest?"

"I only overheard a little when I took the cart up to NorthGate to transfer them. They were nearly too weak to walk. Kitchen sent up some food; I transported it. Did you know they actually have an 'Arrival Special' meal specifically for people coming in from Outside? It's got fruit preserves and bread, apples, and vegetables, plus a ton of chicken protein. Even bottles of Gatorade."

"You under the impression Sherrie doesn't know her job?" Ben laughed, then grimaced from the twinge of pain it sent through his chest. "Why would that surprise you?"

"It doesn't, really. I just think it's so cool that someone even thinks of stuff like that nowadays," she responded.

"Nobody here goes hungry with Sherrie on the job at Kitchen," Ben confirmed. Saul's wife Sherrie had decades of experience planning and coordinating large family events, feeding dozens of people, as well as canning and preserving food from Saul's family garden.

Still, it was a completely different set of challenges to ramp that experience up to feeding over a hundred people twice a day, especially with limited resources in ingredients, selection and even cooking facilities and fuel sources. But Sherrie and her Kitchen girls made it look easy; they were nothing short of miracle workers. Ben joked they made, "Survival food that you could sell in a restaurant."

They rode in silence for a while, then Ben asked, "How about the prisoner?"

Her mood visibly darkened at the mention of the surviving marauder that had been part of the assault on the Ranch.

He had been captured by North QRT who had the presence of mind to just wing him during his retreat. Shot in the leg but with a through and through wound, he had been held in the Brig for over a week now. No one who had tried interrogating him got so much as his name. They'd even sent in a "honeypot"—an age-old spy craft tactic of using an attractive, desperate sounding female to emotionally connect with the target and woo information from him or gain his compliance.

He'd seen right through it. Or at least, it had so far been a complete failure.

They rode in silence for the remainder of the trip to Farmhouse. On arrival, Sage took the horses to a nearby trough, several of which were located throughout the Ranch, for a water break. Ben proceeded the short distance to the Farmhouse Barn on foot where Saul's crew was banging out the construction, quite literally.

"Shouldn't you be working?" Ben asked, entering the barn and seeing Saul dripping in sweat as he lugged several large split timbers over his shoulder through the west door at the opposite end. Construction of the hallway and visual barrier was apparently proceeding nicely.

"Why don't you stop fingering your vag and give us a hand?" he responded. His visual assessment of Ben indicated that was not even close to what he was actually thinking. "You look like shit, cuz. Doc released you?" Saul asked with concern.

"No, not exactly. But I couldn't talk him into it, and I don't have your reputation for a right hook. So, let's just say 'It's good to be the King,'" Ben said, quoting Mel Brooks' *History of The World*.

"Maybe, but it's probably better to listen to the doc and stay alive."

"Probably."

"And for your information, yes, I *was* cleared to leave. No sign of infection."

"Good, well take it easy," Ben advised, watching him toss down the heavy timbers like toothpicks. "That all you could carry?" he asked with mock derision.

"Nah, I can go get one more to shove up your ass," Saul grumbled.

"Okay, just take it easy, man. No one wants you overdoing it. So, how's the build coming? Looks good!"

"Slower than I'd like. We had some delays milling the lumber, but now that those kinks have been worked out and the crew down at the tree line has some idea what the fuck they're actually doing, we're rocking right along. One more full day at most."

"Git 'er dun, cuz," Ben said. "I'm going to see our new visitors."

"You need to take your ass back to bed."

"Yes, dear."

CHAPTER 43

"Something Against Solar"

Ben left the new quarantine project and walked to the temporary quarantine area. It was a couple dozen yards away in a drafty lean-to on one of the Farmhouse's outbuildings. All that the seven quarantined newcomers could see from inside their temporary housing was old farm equipment next to them and, if they squinted through the hundred-year-old wooden slats, a peek at NorthGate several hundred yards away, where they had arrived.

Ben entered the outbuilding and made a right turn to the lean-to's internal entrance. He approached and spoke to one of the guards who pointed to another that sat at a card table set up ten feet away from the Dutch door leading to where the quarantined were. They had just been served a meal, he was told by the first guard on duty, and were currently eating.

"Ask the guy that knows power plants if he'd like to talk to the person in charge here," Ben told the seated guard.

Four point seven seconds later, a man appeared at the edge of the Dutch door separating him from the guard station. The topside of the Dutch door was swung open while the bottom remained latched. There was a chair on the quarantine side, and Ben waved to it as he turned a chair at the guard's card table towards the quarantined man and took a seat. Ben gave him a quick once over.

He was in his mid-sixties, shaggy white hair around the temples and a bald pate. He had been chubby in the Before, judging by the loose skin on his face. His demeanor was apprehensive, but his eyes were clear and bright.

Rare for newcomers.

"Have a seat, sir. My name is Ben, and I want to thank you for meeting with me. I'm sorry to interrupt your meal. What's for lunch?"

"I dunno what you call it, but it's the best meal we've had in months, sir. I can't tell you how much we appreciate…" Ben held up a hand to stop the gushing of appreciation. It always led to a story of what they had endured on the Outside since That Day, how thankful they were to be at the Ranch, followed by a near certain breakdown as they traced their experiences with Covid-27 back to the loss of loved ones. Ben didn't mean to be rude, he just didn't have much time.

"What's your name?"

"Eddington, sir. John Eddington."

"And who's in your group, Mr. Eddington?"

"Well, there's my daughter and son-in-law; he worked with me. My wife didn't make it. We were getting div-… We were separated. There's also two couples; well, I guess they are couples now, anyway. A man and woman who met after everything collapsed. He worked commercial construction as a carpenter, she was an accountant but dabbled in beekeeping and gardening. They'd had a run in with one of those gangs, and we came across them trapped in an obviously unworking walk-in freezer in a Middletown restaurant. They'd been looking for food when the gang showed up and they'd hid in there and got trapped. This was in the early days, but we've been together scavenging ever since. I can vouch for them. And… um. Well, two others."

Ben suppressed a smile.

He knew what that meant.

He waited to see if John wanted to elaborate but when he didn't, Ben tossed him a lifeline.

"The last couple, male or female?"

Eddington looked more than uncomfortable now, he was scared.

"Mr. Eddington, do you speak for your group?"

"I do."

"Then tell them this: We don't react very well to that flaming, flamboyant fag shit around here. You use those exact words, so they get the point. That attention seeking behavior will not be received well by the community. Do you understand?"

John nodded slowly, looking less uncomfortable, and more hopeful.

"Having said that," Ben continued, "Whether now or in the Before, none of us really give a rat's ass who someone loves or who they go to bed with, so long as it doesn't cause *them* drama, personally. We have a few homosexual couples here; and even a... what do you call it, when three people are all knowingly involved in a relationship?"

"Throuple!" came an unseen voice from the back of the quarantine area. Ben knew their conversation could be overheard through the ancient, broken wooden slats, but still had to smile at the audacity.

Whoever that guy was, Ben liked him and his moxy already.

"Thank you," Ben called back to the unknown speaker. "Yeah, we got one of those, too. Or one that I know of, anyway. Like I said, no one cares as long as people do their jobs, obey the rules and keep any drama private. We have children here. Those children all know their traditional pronouns and will *not* be introduced to any new ones. They are not confused about which bathroom to use, and they will not become confused as a result of new arrivals. Are we clear? You understand?"

John was nodding, the relief evident on his face.

Ben turned to one of the guards.

"Who has the next shift?"

The guard consulted a clipboard and named the two replacement guards.

"Okay, let them know there will be two visitors coming and staying for the evening meal to chat with our guests. All counter-infection protocols remain in place, of course."

"Rita and Annie?" the guard asked. Ben nodded affirmatively.

The guard made a notation on the clipboard and went back to his book as Ben lifted his radio.

"Kitchen, Bighouse."

"Go for Kitchen," a voice responded.

"Are Rita and Annie on duty there tonight?"

"Negative, Bighouse. I believe they volunteered this evening to do some weeding at Greenhouse."

"Copy Kitchen, Bighouse out."

"Greenhouse, Bighouse."

"Greenhouse Actual," came Neighbor Mike's reply. "Heard from your message to Kitchen you're looking for our two favorite girls? Hope you're not planning to steal them tonight?"

"Bad news, Greenhouse, you are going to lose them, but only for a couple hours to chat with our new guests during the evening meal. Copy?"

"Copy and will relay. Anything more?"

Ben thought about telling him they had started a pool, a "betting square" on when Neighbor Mike and his wife would announce their next child. Ben was pretty sure the current crotch goblin count was somewhere between six and forty-seven. He had purchased two squares himself. He decided now wasn't the right time to tease them. Not about having children, anyway.

"Negative. Bighouse out."

"Greenhouse out."

"Who are Rita and Annie?" John inquired.

"Our favorite resident lesbian couple," Ben responded. "Though don't tell the other ones that. And really, it's only because we knew them in the Before and were close friends then. But I think talking with them will set your minds at ease and explain what life is like here, how things work. We don't have a ton of rules, but we're damned serious about the ones we have. And we've found that those two have been the most successful of all the folks we've had give orientations to new arrivals. You'll love them, it's hard not to."

And very unwise not to, Ben added silently via his gaze.

He tried very hard not to play favorites between his friends and family in the Before and the newcomers that had been added to the Ranch family since the pandemic. But it was hard not to, even if unconsciously. Like Rita and Annie, Dex, Saul, Danny and his other pre-pandemic friends and family that were known individuals.

In short, they were *trusted.*

New arrivals much less so, at least until they had been here long enough to establish their own value. It was a constant challenge. But if he were being honest, Ben would have to admit it even today it was much harder to come down on people like Jackson, Carol, or Bree than it was on, say, Jack Simmons, Laura Light, and Kim Nguyen.

"Tell me about yourself, Mr. Eddington."

"Call me 'John.'"

"Not yet, Mr. Eddington. So... ?"

"Well, I grew up here in Delaware, got married and worked as an electrical engineer, first in traditional fossil fuel powered electrical grids, but eventually designing and installing substations at solar farms..."

Ben completely failed to contain his excitement, as he had planned to, when hearing the words out loud.

Instead, he practically fell out of his chair.

He had been told by Dex back at Ward there was a man among the newly quarantined that worked in solar power, and that knowledge was one of the drivers that took him from his Ward bed against all medical advice. He just couldn't lay there anymore wondering and hoping and thinking.

He'd just *had to know*.

"Are you fucking kidding me?!" he shouted with delight, literally jumping out of his seat and barely noticing he'd busted a stitch doing it.

The startled guard seated next to him immediately dropped his book and his hand reflexively drew his sidearm in the same moment as he jumped to his feet.

"Shit, stand down, stand down!" Ben said, trying not to laugh in spite of himself. But he was still unable to control his joy. He was also damned proud of Danny's Brig guard. Danny was clearly doing active threat drills with them on the regular.

This dude was *on it*.

After the impressive display at Lifeskills, and now this, Ben made a mental note to make a Kitchen mealtime announcement that Market credits for spot inspections would be issued for all outstanding performances like Lifeskills and this one—for the staff *and* for the Actual in charge. It would encourage innovation and compliance with otherwise routine stuff that could be easily overlooked in the hustle and bustle of modern survival at the Ranch.

But poor John Eddington looked like he needed to change his shorts, not understanding what was happening. The color had drained from his face, and he was terrified by the unexpected reaction of Ben jumping up and the guard drawing his weapon.

"That is fan-*fucking*-tastic!" Ben nearly screamed in delight, as the guard sat down and picked up his book to resume reading. Ben turned back to Eddington.

"We have been looking for someone like you. We have an array… well, you'll see. You want a job, John?"

Though Eddington had been blindfolded on the wagon ride from NorthGate, he couldn't help but to see the acres of solar panels from the outside of the NorthGate checkpoint when they had first approached it, arms splayed in supplication. It was only a gigantic set of mirrors reflecting the sun. Who could miss it?

"Oh, thank God," Eddington said after a moment, some color returning to his face along with a slight smile.

"For a second, I thought maybe you guys had something against solar."

Ben busted two more stitches laughing with him.

Bliss was going to be pissed.

CHAPTER 44

"A Good Dentist"

Ben's final stop before honoring his promise to return to Ward was The Brig. The Brig Actual, Danny, was on duty with South QRT, so he wasn't there. Ben checked in with the duty guards then stood at a hole-in-the-wall type viewport installed in the room next to the prisoner's cell and silently observed him. Then, he observed the back of Kim's head where she was being held in an adjacent cell.

When he was first captured, Bighouse had asked the Ranchers quietly for volunteers for the honeypot assignment, and Kim Nguyen had been first in line.

Kim was tough, the type of woman who spent her Army career doing everything twice as good as her male counterparts only to be thought of as merely competent, and not recognized as the extraordinary human being that she actually was. But Kim wasn't just tough, she was a lethal adversary: smart, determined, and resourceful.

Kinda cute, too.

The honeypot plan called for her to be "thrown" into Brig in the cell adjacent to the prisoner's, with the guards screaming about her being an "intruder" in a "secure area" and threatening her with hanging for stealing food.

They might let her go if she had information on any food storage areas on the Outside that hadn't already been pilfered dry. The goal was to plant a seed in the prisoner's head, without directly saying it, that information was the only currency worthy of release. It turned out that Kim's second calling was acting.

Her first was whatever the hell she put her mind to.

Kim was aware of the rumor that three of her new family, her new Ranch sisters, had been kidnaped by those marauding bastards. After an exhaustive search and inventory of the bodies left in the wake of the assault on the Ranch, the three girls could still not be located.

Nor could the source of the rumor.

Their loved ones had pleaded with QRT Mike who brought the issue to the attention of Ben and Dex. When the "honeypot" scheme was hatched in an attempt to find them, Kim was tapped for the lead role.

Kim didn't think about the humiliations the kidnaped girls must now be suffering. She didn't need to think about it.

Kim already knew.

And there was *no way* she was going to let those assholes get away with it.

Not satisfied with the honeypot plan as designed, Kim asked her boyfriend, Jack Simmons, the QRT operator that had been punched by Saul after the attack at the SouthGate checkpoint and lost a tooth as a result, to hit her.

She needed to be roughed up a bit to look the part she was playing, she'd explained. After all, the prisoner had been *shot*. How would it look if she got tossed in the cell next to him accused of *stealing food* but without a scratch on her?

After he finished laughing, it was obvious that her boyfriend wasn't going to help her. So, she approached some of the other QRT guys only to receive the same bullshit response.

Men don't hit women, they had mansplained to the stupid female.

Now, more disgusted than ever with men's weak egos and self-serving moral codes, Kim did what Kim had always done.

Kim took matters into her own hands.

Armed with the knowledge that the marauders had taken three young females as captives and the only way to find them was to make prisoner-boy talk, Kim was convinced that legitimacy was the key to success in selling her role as a beat up, abused woman caught stealing from the Ranch.

She had immediately stopped eating and bathing for three days, figuring prisoner-boy hung out with the type of "men" that looked for desperate, helpless women. Not to assist, but in order to further victimize with the least amount of effort possible. Not just bastards...

Lazy bastards.

She knew the type.

She'd been married to one in the Before.

Thank God he was dead now.

Growing ever more angry no one would help her to help her Ranch sisters, she went to the Bighouse Barn and rigged a short piece of 2x4 on a spring held down with tension by a clamp, kind of like a giant mousetrap. When she released the clamp, the spring launched the board forward… straight into her skull.

The first one was the worst; she had stood too close to it and managed to fracture her orbital socket. But her eye had darkened nicely. Once the nausea had passed, she examined it in a mirror the way a glamorous Hollywood actress might evaluate her makeup. After that, she took another, more controlled, hit directly in the mouth, effectively splitting her upper and lower lips.

She spat blood for a few minutes and checked the mirror again, very pleased with the results so far. She had a contusion and now a couple lacerations but decided that she needed an abrasion on her cheek to complete the look. She glanced around the Barn for a suitable implement. Her gaze fell upon the perfect tool.

Hello, belt sander.

When Kim came to Kitchen that evening for dinner, an off-duty Simmons had just so happened to see her entering and had a conniption. He followed her inside loudly demanding to know who had the balls to honor her request to beat her up? He was going to kill the son of a bitch. He stood there a giant of a man yelling at her tiny 5'2" frame while the whole Kitchen area from the folks waiting in the chow line, to the twenty picnic tables filled to capacity where families were eating, to the entire Kitchen staff… all watched.

But all Kim saw was her dead douchebag husband…

Version 2.0.

Everyone stopped and gawked at the unexpected outburst. No one knew, or could even understand, who would do such a thing or why Kim had been beaten up. But someone had definitely worked her over.

Her face was a mess.

She let her boyfriend rant another couple of moments, looking around without an ounce of shame to make sure everyone was watching him embarrass himself.

And they all were, every pair of eyes were upon them.

All watching.

And that's why they all saw the exact moment when that tiny, little beaten-up girl stood up on her tiptoes... and punched her massive combat operator boyfriend as hard as she could squarely in the mouth.

It had been a bad week for poor Jack Simmons.

He really needed a good dentist now.

CHAPTER 45

· WINTER 2027 ·

"Consigliere"

When Ben was released from Ward a few days later with no sign of infection and a Ranch to run, he had found out all that had transpired at Kitchen between Jack and Kim.

And he went through the proverbial roof. He had wanted to have Simmons thrown in the Brig. But Dex talked him out of it.

Sort of.

It was entirely possible word had traveled about the Kitchen blowup between Simmons and Nguyen to the Brig guards who may have unintentionally allowed the prisoner to overhear just enough to thwart their honeypot plan.

Ben made a mental note to ask Danny about it.

A fundamental part of any covert operation is it had to be a freaking *secret*. And now the whole Ranch knew. That monkey had jeopardized the entire operation, and God only knew what else by extension.

The guy had been publicly humiliated, Dex argued, and by now everyone knew the real reason Kim had looked like she'd been hit by a truck at Kitchen that day.

"Whatever, Dex. Just get Mike's ass up here, right now!"

Dex radioed for Mike to come to the Bighouse stat. QRT was Mike's responsibility, and one of his boys was seriously out of line.

When Mike arrived and was briefed on the situation, he took it well. He agreed that something had to be done.

"It's not about honor, not like *this*. This is... just chest thumping. It's 'badge of honor' bullshit. Completely unnecessary. It's just 'Look at me protecting my woman.' And at least part of it directly stems from not taking her and the Ranch's needs fucking seriously in the first damned place. Look at what she did to *herself*, for *our people!* She was not just willing to endure it but took it upon herself to make sure this mission succeeded because *she* fucking gets it! Just look what she did to try to help them... the three of *our people* that are *out there!*" Ben had ranted loudly to no one in particular, pointing out one of the Bighouse's picture windows as he did so.

Dex and Mike both already knew Simmons caused the problem one way or another. And Kim...

No one in their right mind would fuck with Kim after half the Ranch watched her deck her behemoth boyfriend.

"I'll handle it," Mike said.

"How, Mike?" Ben challenged. "You can't Brig him with the prisoner. Christ, we can't even bust him down a rank because we don't have fucking ranks."

"I will kick him off QRT," Mike responded bluntly.

Ben stopped pacing and stared at him. "No, *fuck that!* He may be a giant stupid asshole, but he's a giant stupid asshole that could hit a fly with iron sights at thirty yards... *in flight*. No, that's not an option, Mike. For the Ranch's safety, we need his rifle on the battlefield if... *when* those assholes that attacked us come back! What else?"

"Let it go," Dex advised.

Ben stared at his long-time closest friend in a combination of frustration and amazement. Dex didn't pick many battles, especially with Ben and where the Ranch's best interests were concerned. The two were nearly always in lockstep on such issues anyway, or at least talked it out until they came to a mutually acceptable resolution.

But when Dex did pick a battle, he was rarely wrong.

Asshole.

Still.

"Okay, *consigliere*. You're suggesting that this guy makes a huge public scene, jeopardizes a critical mission whose goal was saving three of our own, and in response, Bighouse does... nothing?"

"Yes."

"Hmmm. You make a strong case," Ben said sarcastically. "Now what happens the next time he does it, or someone else does, and twenty people die as a result?"

No response.

"Are you gonna put Kim on trial for punching him?" Mike queried. "X-ray said she didn't just knock out a tooth, but actually hairline-fractured his jaw. Broke it."

"As far as I'm concerned, Jack deserved the punch. We're here to talk about if he deserves *more*. Besides, no one has even breathed a word about trying her, as far as I know. Any petitions been submitted?"

"Of course not. That offense requires an assault to be unjustified," Mike said. "Fifty people, including kids, witnessed him screaming at her and half the men eating at the time were about to beat his ass. As it turned out, that wasn't necessary. Kim did it first." He couldn't help but smile out of respect.

Ben exhaled heavily, shaking his head and walked to the picture window to gaze out over the Ranch. Dusk was setting, and a beautiful sunset was forming against the clouds behind the tree line. Ben stared across the quarter mile of pasture and gardens to the tree line and watched the sun sink. Back in his attorney days, the view had always helped him to clear his head.

But not anymore.

Now all he saw was the fragility of the entire Ranch operation; how easily everything his people, his new extended family—and the *only* family any of them had left—could be instantly and irrevocably destroyed. Their very lives depended on Bighouse making the right decisions.

Every.

Single.

Time.

It was nothing short of exhausting.

He turned back to Dex and Mike, and looked at each of them in turn, "Tell me why you want to let it go."

"We risk making it worse by publicly punishing him. No one wants him or Kim tried. The Ranch just wants it to go away. But even more than that... Look, I talked to him that night. You didn't know anything about it and had already gone back to Ward. Jack was mad as hell with a bruised ego and another missing tooth. But I'm telling you, he was mostly mad at *himself*. If Bighouse comes down on him additionally, and officially, *publicly*... there's no telling what could happen. Everyone's under enough stress as it is, especially after the attack."

Tell me about it. Ben thought, as his shoulder throbbed; but considered the words briefly.

He paced back to the window and stared out, "You guys know better than most how precarious our situation here is," Ben began slowly, still facing the window. "Is it your collective opinion to sit this one out?"

"I'm for a consequence, brother," Mike said without hesitation. "But Dex has a point. Jack's paid two severe ones already. Publicly humiliated and lost another tooth."

"You wanna go tell those girls' loved ones that's the reason their girls won't be coming back? Because Jack's ego got in the way and ruined our best chance of gaining actionable intel to find and save them? But fuck it; Bighouse's position is we're not going to do anything about it? What kind of message does that send to the Ranch? To all those people depending on us?" Ben just couldn't let it go even though he saw Dex's logic.

"Ben, you told me once that criticism carries no sway with you," Dex reminded him. "Because no one is harder on you than *you*. What if Simmons is like that, too?"

"And what if he's *not*, Dex? So basically, we can't have discipline here because people might not like it? Or even go postal? The guy's a fucking Navy SEAL, for Christ's sake, a QRT combat operator! He's not some pussy snowflake."

Silence ensued and Ben returned to the window. He stared out for several minutes. Dex was just about to break the silence when Ben suddenly turned and spoke quietly.

"Here's what we're going to do."

CHAPTER 46

"Honeypot"

The next evening, Ben and Dex met with Simmons privately. Ben asked few questions and mostly only then to keep the conversation on track. Jack's answers were honest and convincing. Ben admonished Simmons severely but backed off when he saw the big SEAL hanging his head in shame.

Dex was right.

Asshole. Ben thought with mild amusement, but he was actually very glad for Dex's counsel and of the decision he'd made to talk to Jack first before deciding how to proceed. Ben softened his tone and spoke kinder words. Simmons looked up after a while and nodded. After a few minutes, he actually looked hopeful. When Ben announced that the meeting was over, Jack sounded surprised.

"So... wait. So, that's it?"

"Ben can yell at you some more, if you'd like?" Dex inquired with a grin from his seat at the bar, away from their conversation.

"Man, he can yell at me all fucking night! Hell, I know I fucked up. I should have taken her more seriously and thought about what those poor girls needed from me. I was just focused on my ego and seeing Kim looking like that... Man, it just set me off! But Jesus, that's really it? I thought sure you were going to banish me."

Ben started to tell Jack the truth, that he wouldn't even permit him to be kicked off QRT, let alone banished, but then thought better of it.

It was what parents called "a teachable moment."

"Jack, we're family here. We *have* to be."

"It's the only way the Ranch has any real chance," Dex added. "Our real strength is in our people. Our community. You didn't actually hurt anyone, and you didn't try to. Plus, you're a hell of a protector. That's worth a lot."

"Well, pretty good at protecting against everything except right crosses," Ben observed wryly, with a smile. "Not too effective at protecting himself against those."

"Think the first one was technically a right hook," Dex corrected with amusement.

Simmons's response to their quips would be a good indicator in determining if they'd made the right choice in how to handle him.

Jack smiled.

Sort of.

But without a dentist, it qualified as a smile for him these days.

Unfortunately, the prisoner wasn't as cooperative. Kim had reported to Brig for her honeypot assignment the same night she punched Jack Simmons. She spent the following week in that cell playing the role the best she could.

And she was damned convincing. Even the Brig guards were impressed with her acting but treated her according to her role every second.

Either the prisoner had made her ruse, or he was a professional spy or soldier, she thought. Bighouse pulled the plug at the end of the seventh day.

Kim wanted to be angry at Bighouse's decision to pull her out, but the truth was she couldn't honestly say she had even made any progress.

The prisoner had never spoken once.

Barely even looked at her.

She had cried, ranted, and cursed at the Ranch guards. Even threw a meal at them. She had been vulnerable. Been aggressive. Even been suggestive. She had done everything she could think of.

Nothing worked.

The prisoner never spoke.

In appreciation of her volunteer efforts, self-sacrifice and bravery, Bighouse awarded her a generous helping of credits that she could redeem at Market for luxury or convenience items brought back from the supply runs. Credits gave folks a sense of normalcy and inspired volunteers for the uglier jobs at the Ranch that needed to be done.

Kim accepted them, but she didn't use them. She placed them under her pillow before she cried herself to sleep that night, and for several nights thereafter, for her failure to accomplish her mission and help the girls.

At least she could save them to give to her Ranch sisters when they finally came home.

CHAPTER 47

"Jaw Breaker"

When the Brig guards released her after her "honeypot" week, Kim was told she was expected at the Bighouse. The meeting with Kim went much more quickly and smoothly than it had with Jack. There was less to discuss, and the meeting was really more of a debriefing about the little she had been able to learn. It was late in the day by then even though that meeting was over in less than a half hour; it was long past dark o'clock when it concluded. She had made a couple interesting observations about the prisoner.

She began with a physical description: medium build, no visible scars, or tattoos. He was from a Middle Eastern or Mediterranean descent, judging by his hair color, texture, and complexion. He was obviously still in pain from his gunshot wound but rarely so much as grimaced unless standing.

He was on near constant alert. He never slept more than twenty minutes at a time, and she could never tell if he was really asleep or just faking it. His eyes took in everything around him with a sheen of intelligent glaze about them. He listened to the Brig guards' conversations and what little radio traffic they could overhear from their cells.

He watched Kim intently when she was performing her role, acting out to him or the Brig guards about her unfair treatment. But he would not respond when she attempted to engage him, only stared at her unblinking, like he was reading a book. Then, after a few moments, he would close his eyes and ignore her.

His proxemics were aversive but then so were most peoples' during the Second Pandemic. "Social distancing" as a concept was introduced by Covid-19 and perfected by Covid-27. No noted self-soothing behaviors despite the high stress environment he was in.

Kim was no longer angry with Simmons and even confided to Ben and Dex that she may have let some personal history interfere with her judgment at particular moments. Ben didn't ask her to explain; he just wanted her to know that they had addressed Jack's behavior and the consequences to their missing people and their families and friends. They didn't expect any future problems from Simmons.

Kim's face was healing nicely by then, so she smiled beautifully when she said, "He'd better hope not. He may be in a dark place now, but he's only got so many teeth left before he'll be drinking his meals through a straw if he messes with me again."

"Seems you really lit a fire under his ass," Dex agreed. "He's not just really sorry for what happened to you, and for risking the "honeypot" plan; Mike says he's actually been a different man since. Hey, that gives me an idea! Do you want to punch Ben for me, too?" Kim laughed pleasantly and looked over to Ben and smiled again.

But Ben was looking at Dex strangely, then at Kim. He jumped up and strode quickly to the window. It was pitch black out and cold, but he just stared into the dark void. The meeting broke up, but Ben was oblivious, lost in thought, barely aware Kim was leaving. He said a perfunctory goodbye to her when prompted and then walked to the built in bookcases taking up the majority of two walls in the nine hundred square foot Bighouse's Greatroom.

Dex congratulated her on her new adventure as he said goodbye.

During the meeting and after she less-than-enthusiastically was awarded, and accepted, the Market credits for her "honeypot" effort, Kim much more animatedly mentioned that Mike had offered her a QRT Reserve position. There were a dozen or so Ranchers who volunteered and qualified for QRT duty as reserve forces. Those part-timers, known as QRT Reserve, provided substitute QRT members when one of the active operators was needed elsewhere, sick, injured or had been killed.

Kim would be training under Mike with the active QRT operators on all four cardinal direction teams in order to learn their tactics, signals, and other tools of the trade. Though meant as a "consolation prize" in recognition of her efforts to help the missing Ranchers,

Mike acutely and astutely recognized Kim was definitely tough enough and had what it took to qualify for QRT duty if she so chose.

Kim was absolutely elated.

Within two weeks, she had demonstrated exceptional skill, battlefield prowess and an intuitive understanding of strategy and tactics. She'd also earned a boatload of respect from her larger, all-male peer combat operators by accomplishing jobs that even men nearly twice her size had struggled to complete. This diminutive, fragile looking female hoisted logs into defensive positions, learned to build booby traps, and critically analyzed strategic and tactical situations correctly. She devised impromptu levers out of whatever was around to move objects too heavy for her to lift. And never once had she had so much as a mere look of frustration on her face.

Kim Nguyen was 100 percent pure, uncut determination.

A couple of well-meaning operators had tried to give her the "little sister" treatment, offering to assist her if she had any problems accomplishing anything or had questions about their very manly vocation.

Kim responded by challenging them to hand-to-hand combat if they ever spoke to her like that again, even inquiring ever so sweetly of one slightly pushy operator if he enjoyed being able to chew his food.

After that, she was accepted wholesale by the entire QRT group as a one of them, a legit QRT operator, comprised by then of some of the best combat specialists left on the entire planet.

And little Kim Nguyen was now their equal.

But she didn't stop there.

Truth was, Kim had found a new calling. She'd needed this outlet. With these new skills, she felt she was actually going to be able to help get her Ranch sisters back when Bighouse figured out where they were. She was actually *doing* something about their situation, not failing miserably again like the "honeypot" fiasco.

With that realization, her motivation doubled.

By the end of the month, she was so in control of the reserves that Mike petitioned Bighouse to create a new senior staff position: QRT Reserve Actual. Mike did so in recognition of her overall badassery and contribution to the now independent and cohesive QRT Reserve squad.

They weren't just a bunch of individual Ranchers helping out with manpower issues with QRT anymore, they had started behaving like their own unit. QRT Reserve didn't just rally around Kim…

They wanted to *be* Kim.

She became a full-blown Ranch celebrity, a role model, and an inspiration. Young women and little girls all around the Ranch threw their fists up and jumped into a playful fighting stance with gigantic smiles whenever they spotted her. To them, it was like coming across an A-list Hollywood actress in your neighborhood convenience store and imitating her latest movie character.

Except Kim wasn't acting.

Kim really *was* that badass.

And Kim was building her own army.

When she saw the kids, she would immediately stop whatever she'd been doing, or wherever she'd been going, to playfully engage her admirers, correct their technique, then ask their names and ages and if they wanted her to show them a few moves.

"No," was a response she'd never once received.

They giggled as they watched the comparatively huge male QRT operators all step out of her way.

Move, bitch. Little, tiny Kim coming through!

And *all* the teenage boys at the Ranch just gawked at her in unabashed adoration.

Around that time, Kim had unintentionally held up a senior staff meeting at the Bighouse for fifteen minutes, to which she had been invited as a test run for her possible advancement to senior staff. When she'd finally arrived, Bighouse politely inquired as to what had delayed her?

"I stopped to demonstrate a jujitsu throw at Lifeskills. The kids had been after me to do it for a couple days and I said I would, so I did. I borrowed an off duty QRT guy and went over there first. It took longer than expected, though."

"Well, Kim, that's admirable and all, but…"

"Oh, and Lifeskills said to mention that they need a new changing table, and your QRT guy has a dislocated shoulder."

"Um… is he okay?"

"I don't know, but Ward probably will," she said casually, moving gracefully as a panther across the room to an open seat. "But either way, Reserve will cover for him 'til he's fit for duty. The kids loved it though, and Steph said it was an old table they had been meaning to replace. Anyway, sorry. I thought he was heavier than that."

Senior staff at the meeting all exchanged surprised glances.

So, wait... she threw him into the freaking table?

Jujitsu was known for the philosophy of using an opponent's strength, weight, and force against him, thereby allowing the practitioner to turn offensively intended kinetic energy into *defensive* kinetic energy against the aggressor, resulting in a smaller person dominating a much larger opponent.

"And sorry for holding y'all up," she'd shrugged, taking her seat.

Bighouse, quite wisely, did not have any follow up questions.

Ben and Dex had declined, however, to form a peer position equal to Mike's QRT Actual, reasoning that QRT as a whole needed to have only a single captain to keep the hierarchy clear. Instead, Bighouse agreed that she most certainly had earned and *would* be asked to lead QRT Reserve. She would continue Reserve training under Mike but with a dedicated operational callsign of her own choosing, in place of the "Actual" senior staff title, in recognition of her ascension to senior staff, but still under the command of the QRT Actual, similar to an Asset Manager.

So, just a little under five weeks after publicly punching her boyfriend in the face and completing her subsequent performance debut in Brig as a novice honeypot spy, the public announcement portion of the evening meal at Kitchen one Friday night contained a very special message: Kim's advancement to QRT Reserve Director.

QRT Reserve now had its own leader.

Five-foot two heartbreaker, Ms. Kimberly Nguyen.

Kim came forward in front of two-thirds of her entire Ranch family with a gigantic smile. She stood next to Ben and Mike as she accepted the position. She was beaming at the assignment, but somehow simultaneously managed to exude a feminine poise and grace so out of character with her "kick ass" reputation.

She took the offered microphone to the battery powered sound system and expressed her appreciation of the praise and accolades

that Ben and Mike had heaped upon her during their announcement
with a humility and charisma no one knew she possessed.

She spoke humble words to her captivated audience about the
oasis from the misery of the Outside that was their Ranch, briefly
about her struggle to get there, and then more expansively about
the opportunity the Ranch had provided her not just to survive, but
to actually *thrive*. To create something resembling a real life in an
otherwise dead world.

The crowd hung on every word.

She then went on to admit she'd had trouble coming up with
an appropriate callsign, but that the well-meant compliment
"heartbreaker" mentioned at her introduction had inspired her in
that very moment to decide on one. Even though, she laughed, she
hardly saw herself that way.

Nevertheless, she intended to adopt the compliment completely in
spirit, but with one little modification.

She announced her official radio callsign.

There was an outburst of much needed, tension-relieving laughter,
followed by the entire room erupting in applause and cheering that
quickly escalated into an all-out standing ovation.

And that was how the Ranch met "Jaw Breaker."

CHAPTER 48

"Blood on Your Glock"

What about the prisoner? I'm starting to think it's time to get..."
Dex began, after Kim had left the Bighouse debriefing on the
"Honeypot" assignment.

"9 p.m.," Ben answered absently without looking up. He was nose
deep in a thick book on psychology he'd pulled from the bookshelf.

"Huh?"

"Tell Danny to have three of his guys bring him to the Bighouse
Barn tonight. And make sure the cameras are rolling."

"Want to fill me in?"

"No."

Dex waited a few moments to see if Ben would say anything else.
When he didn't, Dex got his rifle and strapped his IFAK to his plate
carrier and said, "Okay, man. Unless you want a drink before dinner,
I'm going to head out? Got dinner with Bliss."

When Ben appeared not to hear and continued studying whatever
that fat book was telling him, Dex turned and opened the back door.

"I won't be having either tonight, and I'm not telling you because
I don't want you thinking about it over dinner, Dex. Frankly, *I* don't
even want to think about it. And I know how rare it is that our
schedules and Bliss's sync closely enough for y'all to eat together. Go
enjoy it, bro. And tell her I said 'hey.'"

He put down the book and went to the bookcase to pull another.
He found whatever he was looking for, opened it to a particular page,
and compared it to the one he had just been reading.

Dex watched Ben for several more moments, thinking about the
loss Ben had suffered recently with the death of Rachele and their
unborn child. He obviously wasn't dealing with it well.

In fact, he probably wasn't dealing with it *at all*.

He should want revenge more than anyone at the Ranch.

Ben put the book down and again walked back to the bookcase, seemingly unaware of Dex's continued presence. He scanned the shelves and then retrieved a large, rolled scroll. He turned towards the adjacent pool table, unrolled it with his good arm, and spread a topographical map of the area over its hard cover using the psychology books to hold down the ends.

"Oh, and tell Tanner and Jackson to be there, too," he added, without even looking up.

"Copy."

Dex was about to close the door behind him when Ben inhaled sharply, then abruptly called out, "And Dexter?"

"Sir?" Dex poked his head back through the doorway.

Ben looked up from his study of the map so fiercely Dex was momentarily taken aback, not sure if Ben was mad at him or at something else.

No. Not mad.

Enraged.

Literally shaking.

Normally fun-loving and mild-mannered, Ben never got pissed about anything more serious than a broken pasture fence line or a temperamental tractor. He'd throw a wrench and spew some creative string of expletives, most of which were frequently quite humorous.

But in fifteen years, Dex had never seen the way Ben looked at him at that moment.

His eyes held nothing short of murder.

"Warn them all there will be nothing pleasant about this evening, starting with the prisoner's removal from Brig at 8:40 p.m. sharp. He is in no way to enjoy it. Clear? I want his head fucked up. And 'no evening meal, he won't be needing it.' Use those exact words on that last part, and make sure a Brig guard is standing somewhere near his cell with his radio on when you transmit that message. Copy all?"

"Yes, sir. Copy all."

After Dex left, Ben went to the picture window and watched him walk past the pond towards the former beef company's barn and stable, then out of sight down the wood's road towards Kitchen.

Once he was out of sight of the stable, Ben tore the sling off his right arm and tested his range of motion. It wasn't good.

But it was going to have to do.

He gingerly picked up his rifle and press checked it. Then clumsily removed and press checked his holstered sidearm.

That was pointless.

He wished he'd taken Mike's advice in the Before when the firearms instructor had warned him he had better learn to aim, reload, and shoot left-handed, too. At night. With grease on the grip to simulate the slickness of blood in combat.

You've got to be ready for the day there's blood on your Glock, Mike had taught, looking at Ben with intensity. *And it would probably be YOUR blood.*

Too late now, Ben thought as he replaced the nearly useless Glock in its holster with his nearly useless right arm. He could move it and use it, sort of, it just hurt like Hell's blazes to do so.

Turned out that Ben was right after all, though, so Mike could just suck it.

Because before the night was over, Ben wouldn't ever need to simulate blood on the grip of his sidearm.

He'd know the real thing.

CHAPTER 49

"Humming Wagner"

Ben grabbed extra magazines of ammo for both weapons out of a drawer in the Bighouse's bar and moved to where his body armor hung on a wooden valet he had crafted from cedar.

He slowly and carefully lifted the heavy plate carrier off the valet. He swung it painfully over his injured arm down onto his chest and tightened the Velcro straps as much as he could, wincing repeatedly at the pain, trying not to tear his stitches loose.

Not that it was going to matter.

He looked at his radio sitting on the bar counter and started to turn and leave it behind. On second thought, he picked it up, tuned it to an unused channel, then turned it off and secured it with the clip onto his body armor.

If he were killed or captured, at least it wouldn't be of any use to whoever found his corpse.

He left the safety of the Bighouse and walked towards Stable. He stopped at the nearby bonfire pit next to the Bighouse Barn and lit a medium sized bonfire. He basked in its warmth for a moment and rubbed his hands together gently so as not to aggravate his injury against the cold December night air.

Ben didn't normally lie to Dex. And he didn't suspect Dex normally lied to him either by commission or omission.

And really, it wasn't even a "lie"... technically, Ben tried to console himself, ineffectively. He had meant it when he said it and had no inkling at the time he'd end up doing anything different. But dammit, this was life and death.

And fucking death was just what he felt like already.

Ben positively detested going back on something he had said he would or would not do; but if he were going to survive this evening, and maybe even, God willing, save the Ranch...

He was going to have to break his word to Dex.

Shit, I'm sorry, brother. I told you I wouldn't but... it's a damned cold night, and it is far, far from over. Hope you'll forgive me, man.

He reached in his back pocket and pulled out a flask. He opened it with his good hand then swapped the cap with his other, less functional hand and took a long pull.

Ahhhhhh. The warmth spread through him as the whiskey worked its ancient magic, and he took another small sip.

Told you I wasn't having a drink or dinner tonight. But somehow, I think you'd understand, bro, he thought with a smile.

Tonight, this is both.

He stared at the bonfire flames and imagined to himself how the evening was going to play out; visualized himself successfully completing the things that needed to be done. Then he drained the remainder, recapped the flask, and slipped it on the inside of his plate carrier.

He turned and continued the dozen or so yards to the stable and entered.

Sage's second, Dee, was there feeding the horses. She turned, obviously surprised to see him there this late. She greeted Ben with a big Dee smile and asked what he needed.

He told her nothing and to go get herself some chow. She looked puzzled but didn't question the guy that had thought so far ahead as to have provided for all their safety and security in this crazy, new, and "unexpected" reality. She left saying she'd only be gone twenty minutes and would bring them both back a food plate. Ben absently thanked her and went to Reno's stall.

Reno came over to greet him, and Ben haltered and brought him out for a quick brushing and hoof picking. Then he tacked Reno up, tossing several bottles of cold water from the adjacent vet tech area's refrigerator into the saddle bags while Reno drank from a bucket fortified with Gatorade powdered mix. Then he refilled the flask with a mix of whiskey and powdered Gatorade for himself.

Ben called his special cowboy concoction…

Whiskey-Ade?

Really?

Yeah, Ben wasn't very creative.

He thoroughly checked the saddlebag's contents, verified the med kit was in there along with a few other items he might need, then rechecked and tightened down the saddle tack. He moved to stand directly in front of Reno and gripped the horse's face gently with both hands and took several slow, deep breaths, syncing his energy with Reno.

They synergized into One.

Ben spoke softly to his equal while stroking Reno's nose and scratching behind his ears, looking into his eyes the entire time.

Reno was the first horse Ben had brought to the Ranch, and although he loved riding Buckshot and adored Moonshine, Reno remained as Ben's very first horse. And he was the fastest, most bomb-proof mount they had.

And now Reno understood their mission.

They could not possibly fail because Reno was crucial to their goal.

Ben led him outside and mounted up. He rode north through the fallow field parallel to GCR at a steady trot. Not fast, but not slowing for anything, including those he passed walking and riding bicycles headed to Kitchen for their evening meal.

They waved and shouted greetings, but Ben ignored them. He had no time for pleasantries or distractions; he had to hurry.

He only had a few hours left.

As he approached the NorthGate checkpoint, he cued Reno to a canter, then at the last hundred feet, into a full-blown gallop.

Straight at the NorthGate guards.

They leapt out of the way as, together, Reno and Ben blew through the NorthGate checkpoint and into the Outside. Reno jumped each of the fallen tree barriers without even breaking stride. Ben hung on for dear life with a look none of the NorthGate guards had ever seen on him before.

He was angry, which they had seen.

And elated, which they had also seen.

But it was extremely unsettling to see anyone express
both simultaneously.

The NorthGate guards didn't like it at all.

They'd liked it even less when Dex called a quiet emergency
meeting of the witnesses and select senior staff, mostly Ben's family,
at the Bighouse ten minutes later to discuss what to do. Dr. McKnight
told them that psychologically there is no condition that equates to
merely the two facial expressions of anger and elation in a single
moment, according to the DSM-V, but there is a common term for
that look. When she said it, they realized they all already knew it.

And it fit.

Madness.

But before that occurred, when NorthGate was still on the radio
with Dex less than four seconds after Ben and Reno disappeared
into the Great Wide Open of the Outside, they had to admit, it *was* a
glorious sight.

Reno was a damned good horse.

The guards were waving their arms, shouting questions, concerns
and even commands as Reno and Ben blew past them, but Reno
ignored them. He was getting to run balls out.

Ben didn't respond for a different reason: He didn't even
hear them.

He was humming Wagner.

ACKNOWLEDGMENTS

Thank you to the lovely ladies and staff of Synergy Publishing Group who walked a clueless dinosaur-lawyer/cowboy turned author through the required technology to make this series possible.

Special thanks to George Madison for technical advice on all things solar; to combat and firearms trainer and consultant Mike Hughes; and to the entire past and present TBC Crew for their near endless antics that have helped to inspire this novel.

This book is intended to be fun and satirical. And yet, a fair amount of this book is true; not in the sense that the world has ended, of course. At least not yet.

But it *is* coming.

It is true in the sense that most of the characters are based on real people, all the science and technology described is accurate and can actually be done, and most of the places exist as described. The quarter horses are Author's actual working ranch horses, the draft horses are fictional. Author engages in the careers and general pursuits as described...

Well, sort of.

Except for the more violent aspects of this novel because the story is, of course, just a story. It is merely Author's imaginative interpretation of what might occur in a "Covid-27" type scenario.

Some names are minutely changed, but the characters' personalities remain intact to the best of this Author's limited ability to accurately describe these wonderful people. Those written about should certainly know who they are in the story. Many of the Ranch's senior staff characters, and those mentioned specifically by name, are true to life; and truthfully, even more amazing in person.

Other characters are an amalgamation of several individuals known to Author.

And Y-E-S!! Dexter beef really *is* that delicious! That's why we raise them here!

So, to all the real-world based characters, the best parts of you are described at length to the best of Author's ability, and therefore any negative interpretations are *per incuriam. Wrong, by definition,* as to Author's intent.

As to any other "less than perfect" parts of you that may, or may not, exist...

Those are simply unknown to this Author.

So, thank you for being you.

Except for Ben.

Because that guy really is an asshole.

READ ON FOR A PREVIEW

The Ranch: Delaware

Volume Two

SPRING 2026

CHAPTER 50

"Single Rider"

The prisoner arrived bound and gagged, per Ben's directive to Dex, at exactly 8:57 p.m. by Dex's old-fashioned wind-up watch. The prisoner was escorted by Danny and two of his Brig guards in the horse drawn wagon driven by Sage.

Dex immediately sent her to the Bighouse upon their arrival.

He didn't know what Ben had planned, but he was pretty sure he didn't want his young daughter seeing it.

Tanner had hitched a ride in the wagon down from his residence at the Farmhouse since the Brig was located in one of the Farmhouse's multitude of outbuildings. Jackson had merely walked from his neighboring house.

A fire, untended for hours, was dying in the bonfire pit, casting a glow of just enough light for the ranchers to see one another as they conversed. The prisoner was still seated in the wagon and everyone summoned was present.

Except Ben.

"He *what?*" Jackson demanded, when Dex told them about the message he'd received on a private channel from the NorthGate guards leading to a quiet meeting of Ben's family a few hours before. The decision was made not to disseminate the news just yet, so not even Jackson's wife, Dr. Bree McKnight, had breathed a word.

Ben had run the checkpoint without explanation. Just disappeared into the Outside. Radio traffic with those on the Outside was normally done by citizen's band radio, like truck drivers used in the Before, but radio calls to reach him had not been fruitful. They had been very careful what was said over the Ranch radio, which was monitored by many, including the OPs.

"Look, knowing Ben, whatever he's doing, he's doing it for us. For the Ranch," Dex said sternly to quell any uncertainty. "I have no idea what he's thinking, but I do know he wouldn't just abandon us without a damned good reason."

"No doubt, but what happens if he doesn't come back?" Tanner asked realistically.

"NorthGate reported quietly to me that he returned fifteen minutes ago. He's meeting with Mike and the North QRT guys in their barracks at the old Kintis farmhouse. Simmons got called in too, even though he's leading West QRT now."

"What the fuck?" Jackson muttered. "So, what are we doing then? We got this asshole out of his cell..." He gestured toward the prisoner who eyed him back defiantly. Danny noticed and instantly cracked the prisoner sharply on the side of his head with the butt of his M4 rifle.

As he did, a rhythmic sound floated softly from behind him in the darkness, like a ghostly echo. The others heard it too and strained to see into the black.

They knew that sound well by now:

Hooves.

Single rider.

Ben appeared suddenly, abruptly out of the darkness astride Reno. The horse was covered in sweat, clearly and overwhelmingly exhausted. Illuminated by light of the bonfire, steam rose off Reno in shimmering waves from his head, neck, sides, and rear. His nostrils flared rapidly and repeatedly, breath crystalizing in the cold December air and his eyes were wide and wild with strain.

Ben didn't look a damn bit better.

Forever a study in contradictions, that man in that moment physically manifested that particular dichotomy. He looked both completely worn out while still ready to take on the world. Pale, drawn and ill-looking, he remained straight in the saddle, somehow still full of energy.

Very, very *negative* energy.

"Where's Sage?" he barked as he rode up, eyes ablaze.

"I sent her home. I didn't think she should..." Dex began.

"Call her back. Now! Stat! Tanner, take Reno to Stable until she gets here. Water only, measured. And no hay until he cools off."

Tanner came forward and took Reno's reins as Ben dismounted. As Ben leaned forward and threw a leg over the saddle, gravity peeled his body armor away from against his chest, creating a gap between it and his shirt. Tanner gawked in surprise as he noticed that behind Ben's plate carrier, the front and side of his shirt were completely soaked in blood.

CHAPTER 51

"253 & Some Strap"

Y ou're bleeding. You hit?" Tanner asked quietly, so the prisoner wouldn't overhear. The prisoner was faced the opposite way from Ben's direction of approach still seated in the wagon.

"No, just a hard ride," was Ben's terse response.

He neglected to mention every one of his stitches had torn loose in the earliest minutes of his hiatus. The gunshot wound had ruptured as he pushed Reno past all semblance of common sense. His outbound trip had been fast and hard, but the return trip back to the Ranch was nearly supersonic by comparison.

As a result of the wound's initial dehiscence a couple hours ago, he was lightheaded from blood loss. Or the exertion.

Or both.

He stumbled slightly after dismounting, gripping the saddle to keep from falling over. Dex didn't hear or see the exchange as he had turned away with his radio to call his daughter back. It was too dark for anyone else to see Ben's bloody shirt under the plate carrier. Tanner just shook his head and walked the exhausted horse slowly and carefully towards the stable.

Ben regained his balance and looked positively irate as he stomped over to the prisoner seated in the horse-drawn wagon.

"Pull him out, Danny."

Danny glanced at his Brig guards who immediately hefted the bound prisoner over the side of the wagon backwards, one on each side, then literally threw him to the ground.

He lay there, heaving painfully from the impact with the frozen soil.

Tanner returned, having tied Reno off with a small bucket of water at his disposal.

"On me," Ben said to his crew, walking away. Dex, Jackson, and Tanner walked several paces away from the wagon and bonfire around the side of a huge chicken coop next to the Barn to meet him.

While normally Danny would have been included in that directive, he was a professional soldier in the Before, and thus correctly intuited that in the present context, it was his more important job to remain securing the prisoner.

Despite his curiosity.

"What the fuck is... " Jackson started, when they were all gathered. "Jesus, are you bleeding?"

"Later!" Ben spat viciously.

He looked each of them briefly in the eye as he spoke in a low tone. They stared wide-eyed at him as he revealed what would happen in the next few minutes. He gave specific instructions to everyone. When he was finished fifteen seconds later, they were all silent.

"We get exactly one chance at this, so follow my lead. My energy is your energy. Copy?"

They all nodded.

Without another word, Ben turned and stomped back over to the prisoner exuding sheer malevolence. The others followed, scowling, allowing Ben's radiant negative energy to fill them.

"Stand his ass up!" Ben commanded. The Brig guards jumped to haul the prisoner to his feet and stood on either side holding his arms.

Ben got right up in the tall prisoner's face.

Well... sort of.

As best he could anyway, while looking up at him. The Brig guards tensed even more at the close proximity.

"Oh, you *are* going to talk today, asshole! I just met with your crew across the Maryland line over in Warwick. Guess what? They want you back. You must be an important man."

The Ranchers all looked at each other, completely stunned at this revelation.

Ben had said nothing about that.

That's where he'd gone?

How did he even find them?

The prisoner said nothing, but they all noticed his eyes flare involuntarily at the mention of the marauders' base of operations. However he had found out...

Ben obviously was right.

Still, the prisoner remained silent.

"Have it your way then and *thank you!* It would have just pissed me off to have to give you back," Ben said venomously, drawing his Glock with his blood-soaked right hand and ignoring the pain.

He gripped the back of the prisoner's head with the hand of his uninjured arm and slammed the Glock's steel barrel as hard as he could into the prisoner's mouth, busting several front teeth in the process. They both grunted in pain and the prisoner attempted to recoil, but the Brig guards held him fast.

Ben's face momentarily registered the pain to himself from performing this maneuver using his weakened arm on his injured side. He pulled the gun back, desperately attempting to maintain the slippery grip on his sidearm as well as some semblance of trigger discipline at the same time with his barely functional hand.

The prisoner spat several mouthfuls of blood, and a couple broken off teeth, but otherwise never made another sound.

"No, wait! I've got an even better idea," Ben cried, sounding completely unhinged. He holstered the bloody Glock as he walked over to the bonfire pit. He spent a few moments coaxing live flames from the dying embers while everyone watched.

Sage arrived.

She stood away from them, confused at the scene but didn't speak, and not daring to approach the bound prisoner. Ben saw her and walked rapidly over to her with purpose. He spoke briefly and quietly. She looked terrified as her gaze left his face and traveled to his blood-soaked arm.

Although no one could hear the words, everyone couldn't help but watch her reaction as her eyes grew wide and her face even more afraid. She glanced quickly and now in complete horror at the prisoner, then stared even more horrified at Ben as he finished speaking and turned away from her. Then she uttered a brief sobbing sound as she turned and scampered into the stable, sliding the heavy farm door closed behind her.

The quiet of the night magnified the sound of the eight-foot-wide sliding door's solid lock mechanism being engaged.

It seemed unnaturally loud.

And very, very final.

The fire had flamed up rapidly under Ben's prior counsel, and he returned to toss more split wood on it with his good arm from a nearby stockpile until it became a raging inferno. He stared at it for a long moment then returned to where the prisoner stood.

Ben was positively oozing malignity now. He glared at the bound man who attempted to return his gaze defiantly, but in his painful state could only manage to do so a little less confidently than before.

To all the observers, an eternity passed.

"Dexter?" Ben said softly, his visual combat with the prisoner unwavering.

Dex already knew that whenever Ben used his full Christian name that something quite unpleasant was likely to follow. Before the Collapse, it usually entailed disciplining a staff member or some other less-than-fun task that had to be done, but had to be done correctly, and was thus thrust upon Ben's most trusted compatriot.

"Sir?"

But this time, Dex noticed that, for the first time ever, Ben said his full first name with a most unsettling smile. Ben continued speaking, still locking eyes with the prisoner's now uncertain stare.

"Go get the 253 and some strap."

* 9 7 8 1 9 6 0 8 9 2 5 5 3 *